HER HEART'S PROMISE

CAROLYNE AARSEN

FOREWORD

Her Hearts Promise was previously published as A Bride at Last by Harlequin Love Inspired.

It has been rewritten and updated to make it part of the Sweethearts of Sweet Creek Series.

Enjoy Nadine and Clint's story!

Carolyne Aarsen

CHAPTER 1

adine folded the letter she had just read and carefully slipped it into the envelope, as if any quick movement might jar and scramble the disturbing words. She laid the envelope on her desk and ran her thumb along its sharp edge.

She leaned back in her office chair and drew her hands over her face. Was this it? Would this letter finally help her and her family discover the truth about their father's death?

Six years before, her father, Sam Laidlaw, worked for Skyline Contractors as a tree faller. He was killed on the job under mysterious circumstances, and the only information his grieving widow and daughters had ever received was the official incident report the company released, which implied that Sam had died because of his own carelessness. But, Nadine knew better than anyone the care with which he had performed his work—safety was paramount for him, on and off the job. Although she didn't believe the company, she couldn't pursue her suspicions further.

Then, today, she received this letter with no return address and a cancellation marked "Prince George," which didn't exactly narrow her options. The anonymous letter gave no specific information but hinted at knowledge of the events surrounding her father's death.

Since the day of the accident, Nadine and her mother had fought to discover the truth. Though Nadine's younger twin sisters, Sabrina and Leslie, missed him badly, they seemed to have moved on.

But Nadine didn't let it die. Though she couldn't spend as much time on the case as she wanted, she was determined to clear her father's name, so to speak. Nadine had made phone calls, written letters, and gone to meetings with her father's supervisors and higher-ups in the company. But nothing, no budging from the company line: Sam died because he hadn't been careful.

This letter was Nadine's first break in six years. She only wished she could share this with her mother.

Six months ago, after a protracted battle with Lou Gehrig's disease, Brenda Laidlaw had died. Her determined nature could not help her conquer the illness any more than it could help her find out what had happened to her husband.

Nadine slipped the envelope into her knapsack, wishing her fingers weren't trembling, wishing she could release the tension the letter had created.

She snatched her suede bomber jacket from the coatrack against the wall and slipped it over her bulky knit sweater. *Fall clothes,* she thought, flipping her shoulder-length hair out of the collar and retying it into a ponytail.

She was dismayed to glance bits of straw still clinging to her corduroy pants, and she picked the pieces off, dropping them in the overflowing trash can under her desk.

This afternoon, she had roamed farmers' fields, taking harvest pictures for the newspaper. She could never stay tidy. Growing up, she was always the one with dirt on her elbows and rips in her jeans. Her twin sisters always looked photo-ready, with shining hair and coordinated outfits.

"Hey, Naddy, you still hanging around here?" Elaine, her friend and the office manager of the *Sweet Creek Chronicle*, stopped in the doorway, a laptop under her arm. Elaine blew her dark bangs out of her eyes and leaned in.

"Actually, I'm heading home." Nadine smiled up at her friend. "What's with the computer? You taking it home to play 'Minecraft' with Drew?"

"As if my husband would play." Elaine dropped into a chair across from Nadine's desk, still holding the laptop. "Clint wants me to go over the circulation records. He wants to bring some of the ex-subscribers back into the fold."

"You look tired too," Nadine said, noticing the faint shadows beneath Elaine's bright-green eyes.

"The big boss is a different general manager than Dory ever was," said Elaine with a sigh. "I have to get up to speed, that's all."

"Excuse me, can I come in?" The deep voice coming from the doorway made Nadine and Elaine both jump. Elaine threw Nadine a look of dismay and turned to face Clint Fletcher.

"I was just coming with the information, Clint."

"That's fine, Elaine. I'm in no hurry." Clint stepped into the room, his presence dominating it. A burgundy tie cinched the collar of his crisp gray shirt, his thick brown hair was attractively tousled, and his face was impassive as usual. His hazel eyes were on Nadine as he handed her an envelope. "I received this with my mail and mistakenly opened it. I wasn't aware it was addressed to you until I read it. I'm sorry."

Nadine took the envelope. "Thanks, Fletcher. I'm sure you were discreet," she said, unable to keep the flippant tone out of her voice. Clint always kept her on edge, and the sarcastic use of his last name was her favorite defense.

She stifled a flicker of concern as she shot a covert glance at the letter, wondering if it was more information about her father. Thankfully, it was simply another invitation to yet another event on building her connections with other newspaper professionals.

Pass.

"I was also wondering if I could see you in my office first thing tomorrow morning?" Clint said.

"Another editorial mini-summit?" Nadine laughed nervously, uncomfortable with the somber tone of his voice.

"You might say that," he said, expression still serious. He turned to Elaine. "Just bring the information to my office whenever it's convenient."

Then he left.

Elaine caught Nadine's gaze and raised her eyebrows. "I hope you're not in trouble. Again."

Nadine rolled her eyes at that last word.

Ever since Clint had started, the usual routines at the paper had been rearranged and turned end over end. Dory Strepchuk, the previous general manager, favored a looser editorial style and had let Nadine make a lot of her own editorial choices.

Clint, however, made it clear from the beginning that he wanted to be involved in the major editorial decisions of not only the *Sweet Creek Chronicle* but also its sister papers, the *Eastbar Echo* and the *Fort Henday Times*.

"I wonder if our esteemed boss knows I have a name?" Nadine said. "You get called a name," she said, "Wally has a name, Julie gets called by her first name. But somehow, he always avoids calling me anything."

"Doesn't help that you always call him Fletcher."

"He's been Fletcher to me for the past nine years. From the first day he went out with Leslie until he broke up with her and broke her heart," Nadine groused. She hefted her knapsack onto her back, still flustered by Clint's visit and his cryptic tone when he had spoken of their meeting tomorrow. "And what's with the suit and tie he always wears?" she huffed, still not finished with Clint Fletcher. "He never used to dress like that when he lived in Sweet Creek before."

"He's a big boy now. Not like you, wearing some of the same clothes from grade twelve."

"My mother knitted me this," protested Nadine, glancing down at the bulky cream sweater.

"And the pants?"

Nadine waved Elaine's comment off. She preferred her old, faithful jeans or cords. Usually, she dressed up only for church.

She disliked shopping for clothes. Occasionally, her sisters would come home and drag her off to a store. The two would laugh together, trying on clothes and having fun coaxing each other to buy new things. However, Nadine would resist as long as she could, buy something to keep her sisters off her back, then come home and hang her purchases in the closet, uncomfortable at the thought of wearing whatever it was her sisters made her pick.

"It wouldn't destroy your tough editor image to dress up once in a while," Elaine continued. "Put on a skirt; show off your legs."

"Give it a rest, Elaine. Pants are easier for climbing on tractors and over fences, anyhow."

"And fending guys off..." Elaine let the sentence trail, waiting a moment, as if to let the comment settle.

"Been there, done that," Nadine replied, fishing in her pocket for her car keys. Jack wasn't an experience she cared to repeat.

"Two years ago, I might add," Elaine admonished her. "I think it's time you put yourself out there again."

"Don't start," Nadine begged. "You sound just like my grandmother."

She was so not in a place to date again; Jack had been a mistake she preferred to avoid.

When she found out that a) he had gone out with her only so he could get an in with either of her sisters, and b) he'd been cheating on her for three of the four years they were together, she felt betrayed and like a dumb romantic, blinded by love.

She was also faced with the reality that not only had Jack been a mistake, her heart wasn't fully in the relationship. There was another that held a corner of her heart. Who had never returned her feelings. Who had also preferred one of her beautiful sisters.

Her boss. Clint Fletcher.

Elaine held up her hand. "Now you've crossed a line. I love your grandma a lot, but that's not a comparison I'd see as complimentary."

"You have her sparkling eyes."

"Devious eyes," Elaine returned with a grin.

"Thankfully, I have a few days' reprieve from her matchmaking. My sister Sabrina's not been feeling well since Megan was born. With any luck, Grandma will stay there and drive Sabrina crazy for at least a week."

"She'll be back," Elaine said. "Your dear grandma won't leave until you have a boyfriend or until you very firmly say, 'Barbara Laidlaw, time for you to go home.' And since you won't do either, you're stuck with her. So my advice to you is to get a boyfriend."

"Sure. I'll just head down to the nearest 'guy' store and pick one up."

"Well, there's lots of eligible guys in Sweet Creek."

"Besides the ones Grandma keeps dragging home?"

Elaine winked. "Our dreamy boss, for one."

Nadine's heart hitched, and she wondered if she had given anything away just now. "I'm not his type."

Elaine pursed her lips as she looked Nadine over. "How do you know? I think you would make a good couple."

Nadine tried to ignore the sting of Elaine's words. She had grown up a short, dark brunette, overshadowed by twin sisters a year younger than her. The fact that they were tall, slender, and blond *and* twins was a triple threat she couldn't compete with. Everywhere the three of them went, Sabrina and Leslie were the ones who drew people's attention. The twins had been the popular ones in school, the ones who guys watched walking down the hall while Nadine's presence was often ignored.

While Nadine loved her sisters dearly, she was so different

from them. Sabrina and Leslie loved going out, loved being with people, and were the life of any gathering. Nadine preferred staying home, helping her father, and puttering in the garage.

All of which had been fine with her.

Until Clint Fletcher came to Sweet Creek High. From the first day he started high school, he caught Nadine's attention like no other guy. He was tall, had a serious attitude that appealed to her. He shared many of her classes, and he was smart and focused.

But, like almost every other guy she knew, he was drawn to her sisters. Every time Clint came over, she hung back, secretly yearning that he would notice her instead of Sabrina or Leslie.

He never did. He flirted with Sabrina and dated Leslie for the three years he was in Sweet Creek.

Nadine had tried to forget him. Had even managed to find a measure of attraction with Paul, a boy she dated for a few months. For a time, she thought she had found a soul mate in Paul. But the last couple of weeks they were dating she sensed he wasn't fully committed so, to save herself the humiliation of being on the receiving end of a breakup, she beat Paul to the punch.

Unfortunately she still thought of Clint.

When Leslie broke up with Clint and Nadine started university in Edmonton, she thought that would help her get over him; but the first time she ran into Clint on Whyte Avenue—while she was on a date, and he was with another blond—her heart did the same jump it did in high school. And it annoyed her.

"I'm not interested. End of story." Nadine spoke the words with a new conviction. After dating Jack and being so badly duped, she was done with guys for a long, long time.

"Okay, no Clint. But what are you going to do about Grandma?"

"I should just tell her to move out," Nadine said, adding a fretful sigh.

Elaine laughed. "That sweet, tiny woman will just bat those blue eyes, smile at you, and hand you a plate of cookies. And then she'll tell you that she's having yet another single, totally unsuitable man over for supper."

Nadine groaned, thinking of the last two guys her grandmother had asked to come over. "I know. She's getting worse and worse. I seriously don't know what to do."

"Find a boyfriend. Or make one up."

"Like I could pull that off," replied Nadine. "I don't have a good enough memory to lie."

"The Lord helps those who help themselves."

"That's not even in the Bible."

"So? I'm an office manager, not a theologian." Elaine pushed herself to her feet, still holding the computer. "I'd better get my meeting with Clint out of the way. I promised my family real food for supper tonight. Want to join us?"

"Thanks, but tonight I'm going to enjoy being in an empty apartment, put on some music, and eat *two* bowls of cereal for supper."

As they walked out of Nadine's office and down the hall, Elaine wrinkled her nose and said, "Sounds like a big night." Elaine stopped outside Clint's office door. "See you tomorrow, wild thing."

"That's what they call me," Nadine teased back as she waved.

Nadine stepped outside, into the late-afternoon warmth of September. In spite of the shared laughter with Elaine, a feeling of melancholy washed over her.

It was a glorious fall day. She had walked to work this morning wanting to enjoy the last of the warm days.

Nadine ambled down the tree-lined sidewalks of her hometown, hands in her pants pockets, jacket hanging open, and knapsack slung over one shoulder. She scuffed her running shoes through the layer of leaves lying on the sidewalk.

It's a beautiful world, Nadine thought, squinting upward to the mountains that rose at the end of Main Street. Their granite peaks, dusted with snow, were etched against the sharp blue sky—

a bright contrast to the bright orange and yellow leaves of the aspen trees lining the street. Sweet Creek lay protected in the valley created by the Elk River flowing through the center of the town.

Nadine had grown up in the shadows of the peaks of the Twin Sisters, Hartley Mountain, and the ridges of the Kootenay range. In typical small-town-girl fashion, she had planned her getaway ever since high school started. Her plans had been to take journalism and photography courses, find a job with a city newspaper or small magazine, and work her way up to a position at a large city newspaper doing more investigative journalism. She'd had an internship at the *City Beat*—a small monthly magazine—a funky apartment in Edmonton, and a boyfriend. Then her father was killed and her mother became ill and needed help, forcing Nadine to give up all three.

For five years, Brenda Laidlaw fought Lou Gehrig's disease. When the disease was first diagnosed, the doctor gave her only three years, but he hadn't counted on Brenda Laidlaw's temperament or persistence. She vowed not to rest until she found out the truth about her husband's suspicious death. The saddest part of the disease was that while Brenda's body failed her, her mind still understood and still fought.

Six months ago, Nadine's mother lost the fight. While her death was not unexpected, Nadine was plunged into a deep grief that still materialized unexpectedly. And woven through was anger at the lack of caring from the company Nadine felt was responsible for her father's death.

Nadine drew in a deep breath of fall air, willing away the heaviness of heart accompanying thoughts of parents. Willing away the unwelcome loneliness that came with those memories.

While Leslie and Sabrina had husbands to help them through their pain, Nadine had her grandmother who, while wonderfully supportive, struggled with her own grief.

Nadine shifted her knapsack as she turned the corner to her

apartment, willing the dark mood away. At least she could look forward to a quiet evening at home, with Grandma still at Sabrina's.

Whistling softly, she approached her house, then caught sight of a small, red car parked in front of the two-story, red brick walk-up, and her heart dropped.

Grandma was back.

Just to make sure, Nadine looked inside the car. Sure enough, only her grandmother would drive a car that had granny square car seat covers. "Bought on eBay for dirt cheap," Grandma had told her.

Nadine glanced upward—seeking patience—shook her head, and unlocked one of the double glass front doors of her apartment. She walked down the hall to her suite, opened the unlocked door, and stepped inside. The mouthwatering smells of peanut butter chocolate chip cookies baking and chicken cooking drifted down from the kitchen into the entrance, beginning an ominous growling in her stomach, which almost—but not quite—made up for her grandmother's unexpected presence.

Nadine dropped her knapsack on the table in the side entrance, toed her runners off her feet, took a deep breath, and then stepped around the corner into the kitchen.

A tiny lady, no more than five feet tall, with soft, gray hair cropped short, was perched on a stool in the small, U-shaped kitchen area, singing softly as she rolled cookies, then laid them in precise rows on the baking sheet beside her.

Nadine cleared her throat, announcing her entrance.

Her grandmother whirled around, and the strains of "Nearer My God to Thee" faded away as Barbara beamed at her granddaughter. "Naddy! You're home." Grandma jumped down from the stool, walked over, and lifted her head for a kiss.

"Hi, Grandma. I'm surprised to see you back so soon."

What are you doing back here, Grandma? How long are you staying here, Grandma?

The silent questions unspooled through her mind.

"Sabrina was doing just fine and didn't really need help with the baby," Grandma explained, "so I thought I would come back here."

Nadine's heart sank as she stifled an unwelcome surge of frustration with her sister's recuperative ability.

"And from the look of the place, I'm not a moment too soon." Grandma shook her head. "Really, Nadine. Cereal for supper?"

Nadine ignored the reprimand and glanced around the kitchen for any changes her grandmother might have wrought. Sure enough, she had moved the kitchen table into the corner again. Barbara claimed it made the kitchen roomier, but Nadine liked the table directly under the chandelier. It shed a better light, with no shadows, which made reading the various newspapers she subscribed to easier.

And she had rearranged the living room.

Seriously.

The timer rang, and Grandma went back to her cookies. She opened the oven door to take out the next batch. "When I saw all those piled-up cereal bowls in the sink, I knew I shouldn't have left."

"Cold cereal is a well-balanced meal," huffed Nadine, shoving the high-backed, wooden chairs back under the table with one knee. "It says so on all the commercials."

Barbara dropped the trays on the counter, and tossed the oven mitts aside. "Goodness girl, would it kill you to buy some new oven mitts? These are almost useless."

Ignore, Nadine thought. *Do not engage.*

"Anyway, tonight I'm making you chicken and potatoes and carrots," Grandma said, lifting the lid of the frying pan and releasing another wave of aromatic spices. "So go wash up. I'll have supper on the table in a few winks."

"You're only staying for a while longer, right?" Nadine asked, remembering past promises blithely broken by her grandma.

Grandma gave her an innocent look. "I'll stay as long as you need me."

Nadine held that guileless stare, trying to decipher what that meant, but Grandma only winked at her. Nadine straightened the last chair and headed to the bathroom.

She glanced around the bathroom and wrinkled her nose. This morning, she had been rushed and had dropped her clothes and towels on the floor. Now, the bathroom taps sparkled, and clean, peach-colored towels hung on the towel bar, with a gray facecloth the same shade as the walls lying in a perfect triangle across them. The bathtub shone and a clean rug lay between the sink and the tub.

As she tugged a brush through her thick hair, she thought about her dear, sweet, intrusive grandma. And how she needed to get her to move back home.

When Nadine's mother had been in the first stages of Lou Gehrig's disease, Barbara Laidlaw moved when Nadine returned from Edmonton to take care of her mother—Nadine's sisters were already married and unable to do much. But, when Brenda was transferred to the hospital, Grandma stayed on. Barbara was perfectly capable of living on her own but preferred to rent her house out and stay to help Nadine.

Grandma "helped" Nadine by cleaning, baking, organizing, inviting "suitable" men over for supper, and regularly volunteering Nadine's services at church or any other community event that caught Grandma's fancy.

Nadine got a break from Grandma only when an anxiously placed call to one of her sympathetic sisters would result in a sham mission for Grandma. From time to time, Barbara would promise Nadine that someday soon, she would move back home.

But that day never came, as Grandma always insisted that poor Naddy still needed her. In Grandma's eyes, the biggest problem was that "poor Naddy" was still single, which was something that needed rectifying before she moved back to her own place.

Not that poor Naddy didn't have a chance at love and romance. She'd been dating Jack when her mother got sick. He encouraged her to move back to help her mother. Whenever he could, he came to visit her, always telling her how much he respected her devotion to her mother. They dated for four years, visiting back and forth.

Then, one afternoon, Nadine brought her mother to the city for an appointment and decided to drop in on Jack. Finding him with a tall, slender blond had been so much of a cliché, it still made her cringe. Then, discovering that this wasn't the first woman he'd been with made her feel like a complete fool.

Maybe if Nadine had been an alluring blond, he might have stuck around.

And perhaps the tooth fairy and Santa Claus would visit someday. Jack was a cheater—clearly he hadn't been faithful to any of the blondes he'd cheated on her with.

But still...

She checked herself in the mirror, analyzing. As always, she was critical of the tilt of her own brown eyes, the heaviness of her hair, the fullness of her jaw. It was, as her grandma would say when trying to console her, an interesting face.

Nadine looked away, ran the tap, and washed that interesting face with plain old soap and water.

When she was done, she stepped across the hall and checked the room that doubled as her bedroom and office and breathed a sigh of relief. The old roll top desk overflowed with papers, magazines lay in various piles around it. Grandma hadn't invaded her domain.

So far.

After changing, she stepped out of the room and, with a furtive glance down the short hall, opened the door to the spare bedroom across. In "Grandma's room," the suitcases were put away and the Bible lay on the bedside table. Framed family pictures filled the top of the dresser.

It looked as if Grandma was settling in for the long haul.

Nadine squared her shoulders and walked determinedly down the hallway. She would step into the kitchen, take a deep breath, and say...

"Sugar or honey in your tea?" Grandma set a steaming mug on the table just as Nadine marched into the kitchen. Her determined step faltered as Grandma caught her by the arm and led her toward a chair. "Supper's ready."

Nadine opened her mouth to speak, but Grandma had already turned to put food on the plates. Nadine sighed as Grandma set them on the ironed tablecloth and settled into a chair, smiling. "It's nice to be back again. I missed you, Naddy." She held out her hand. "Do you want to pray, or shall I?"

"You can." Nadine was afraid that she would ask aloud, her own questions about how to politely ask her grandmother to leave.

Barbara asked for peace and protection and a blessing on the food. When she was finished, she began eating with a vigor that never ceased to surprise Nadine. "So, what happened while I was gone?" Barbara asked.

"Not much," Nadine replied, thinking back over the quiet of the past few days. "Mark and Sheryl announced their wedding date. She asked me to be in the wedding party."

"Well, isn't that nice. Maybe at the wedding you'll meet someone nice."

"Grandma," Nadine said, a warning tone in her voice.

With a fatalistic shrug, Grandma plowed on: "I thought maybe that nice young man David might have called," she said with a lilt on her tone. "I can't remember his last name. We met him at the grocery store."

"David Branscome is unemployed by choice and lives at home. Hardly dating material."

Grandma appeared unfazed. "A good woman can make a huge difference to a man."

"David already has a good woman. His mother." Nadine finished off the food on her plate and laid her utensils on it. "That was delicious, Grandma. Mind if I pass on dessert? I've got some work to do."

"You work all day—surely you don't have to work all night?" Grandma asked.

"It's nothing really important. I just want to get it done before tomorrow," Nadine said, vague purposefully. She rose and picked up her dishes.

Nadine was hesitant to mention the letter. Sam was Barbara's son, and she was loath to raise any false hope that they might finally solve the mystery surrounding his death.

"I need to look over some information about Skyline," she added carefully.

Grandma turned to Nadine, her expression sorrowful. "Oh, honey, that always makes you so angry. Don't you have anything better to do?"

"They just received some government grants that are questionable," she said, keeping her tone light. Nadine took her dishes to the counter and set them down. "It won't take long."

She left the room before guilt over her evasive answers overwhelmed her. *I could never fib well*, she thought.

Once inside her bedroom, she closed the door and leaned against it, thinking of the mysterious letter and all it portended.

The letter promised some answers, possibly hard proof she could bring to Skyline. Once again, Nadine wondered at God's will in all of this. Why had the letter come now, after all this time?

With a shallow sigh, she walked to her desk and switched on the computer. While it booted up, she reread the letter.

Dear Ms. Laidlaw,

I've read your pieces about Skyline in the paper. I know you don't have any love for Skyline. Neither do I. You are right. I need to talk to you about your father. In person. I have some information that I think you can use against Skyline. I'll call.

CAROLYNE AARSEN

It wasn't signed, and there was no return address.

Nadine turned to her computer and opened Skyline's file, where she kept copies of every letter she wrote to the company's management, as well as to various government departments dealing with industrial safety. The correspondence netted her a few polite responses couched in the vague language of bureaucrats. These replies had been scanned into the computer and saved on file.

Nadine opened them all and read each one in chronological order to refresh her memory. Rereading the letters reminded her once again of what she and her family had lost: A hardworking father who loved her unconditionally; a father who listened with a sympathetic ear to her dating woes, who fixed temperamental bicycles and vehicles for daughters too busy to realize how fortunate they were.

Nadine leaned her elbow on her desk, recalling memories of Sam Laidlaw striding up the walk in the late evening, smelling of diesel and sawdust, swinging up each of his daughters in his strong arms and laughing at their squeals, and pulling Brenda away from the stove, only to spin her and envelop her in a tight, warm hug. Her father would whistle as he organized his tools, readying them for the next day's work. She loved helping him whenever he had a project—a bookcase for the living room, a new kitchen table. He loved working with wood in many forms.

Her parents never made a lot of money, but they had achieved a contentment that often eluded people with more. Sam was convinced of God's ability to care for them. Unfortunately, that conviction created a measure of laissez-faire over his personal dealings with banks and insurance companies, who were not forgiving.

Because her father was considered a contract worker, he had no company pension plan and no private life insurance. Neither was the loan against the house insured. The pittance paid out by workers' compensation barely covered expenses. Brenda Laidlaw

16

had worked for less than a year as a cashier in the local grocery store before her illness made her housebound. The house was sold, and the family moved into an apartment in the same building where Nadine now lived.

Nadine pulled herself back to the present and looked around the room, hers since the time her father died. With her mother gone, the apartment was too large for a single woman. She had her eye on a smaller, newer apartment in a complex still under construction. But, moving away from this place would feel as if she was breaking the last tie with her mother.

And you've got Grandma, she reminded herself with a sigh. Moving to a smaller place would probably be the best way to get Grandma to return home, but it seemed an unkind and disrespectful solution. When it came to facing down Barbara, too many memories intervened: Echoes of her grandmother reading devotions to her mother, singing while she carefully gave Brenda a sponge bath and fed her, and lovingly wiping her mother's mouth as Brenda's control decreased.

Grandma's service to her and her mother had been a blessing at the time, but now, seemed to suffocate her. Nadine didn't know how to shake free from Grandma's gentle grip of generosity without feeling ungrateful and unloving.

Nadine rolled her shoulders, rubbed her eyes, and turned back to the computer screen. Grandma and a new apartment would have to wait.

A gentle knock on the door interrupted her work.

"What is it, Grandma?" she asked, frowning in concentration.

"We have company," Barbara announced loudly.

Nadine glanced over her shoulder at her grandmother, who stood in the open doorway, smiling at her. "Who is it?" she whispered.

"Don't you want to do your hair?" Barbara whispered back.

"No," Nadine replied irritably. She would have preferred to

stay in her room, but it wasn't in her to be so rude to their unnamed visitor.

Nadine followed Barbara into the living room. The pewter table lamps shed a soft light. Nadine felt a measure of pride in the fawn-colored leather couch with matching chairs. Burnished pine-and-brass coffee and end tables complemented the warm tones of the leather. She had sewn the plaid valances that hung from the pewter curtain rods and the matching throw pillows herself.

A man stood with his back to her. He turned as they came into the room, and Nadine bit back a sigh.

"Nadine, I'm sure you remember Patrick Quinn. Didn't he live four houses down from us when we lived on 55th?"

Nadine smiled at Patrick, praying her pasted expression masked her seething frustration. She tried to suppress memories of Patrick as a boy—selfish, overbearing, and constantly teasing her about her hair, her chubbiness as a young girl, and the fact that she preferred to spend time with her father over her sisters.

"I remember you as a rough tomboy," Patrick said with a wide grin. "And you've turned into quite the surprise."

Really?

She had little choice but to sit down and try to make small talk. The talk turned out to be *very* small, with Grandma and Nadine asking Patrick polite questions about where he worked and lived. Patrick had changed little, or possibly had become even more boring.

After a while, Nadine had to escape. Stretching her leg under the coffee table, she nudged her grandmother.

Barbara didn't even flinch.

"Our Nadine is quite the little cook," Grandma continued, ignoring Nadine's next push, delivered with a little more force.

"I'm neither little nor a good cook," interrupted Nadine. She gave her grandmother a warning look, then glanced back at Patrick. "Grandma would love me to be more domestic, but for me, 'gourmet cooking' means putting brown instead of white sugar on my cereal."

Grandma didn't miss a beat. "She's such a joker, our Nadine."

"She always was," Patrick said, sending a wink her way.

Oh brother.

A painful half hour later, Patrick excused himself. He thanked Barbara and Nadine for a lovely visit and, with a playful smile at Nadine, left.

Barbara turned to Nadine. "He's such a nice boy. Don't you think?"

He wasn't then and he isn't now.

"He's not really my type," Nadine said dryly.

"He wanted to see you again. I can tell." Barbara bent over to put the mugs on the tray and then, as the clock struck, straightened. "Goodness, Nadine. You had better get to bed. I'll clean up. You need your sleep."

And with that, Barbara bustled to the kitchen.

Nadine shook her head. She had to do something about Barbara, or her meddling grandmother would take over her life.

She yawned a jaw-cracking yawn and glanced at her watch. But not tonight.

CHAPTER 2

*I*t was still early morning when Clint Fletcher stepped inside his office. The large window occupying almost the full wall looked over the neat grid of streets, shielded by trees turned shades of yellow and orange.

The sun had just risen over the mountains and lit the eastern sky outside his window, illuminating the office with a gentle light. His office, he thought with a proprietary air.

During the years he'd worked in the city for one of the large newspapers, he had been grateful to have his own desk in a large, crowded newsroom. Even then, he would often come back from an assignment to find it appropriated by a colleague whose computer was down.

Now, not only did he have his own desk in his own office but also his own phone, his own door, and an element of privacy.

And, thanks to his uncle, he had the chance to own a string of newspapers. When Uncle Dory had approached him with the idea and laid out the terms of the takeover, Clint could hardly believe his good fortune.

His uncle had been the father figure Clint never had growing up and his de facto guardian for his late-teen years. Clint's father,

Dory's brother, had spent most of Clint's youth fighting legal battles on two fronts—with Clint's mother and with the company he was suing. Both campaigns were nasty and brutish, and as a result, Clint was often left alone as his father holed himself in the study and his mother retired to her wing of their palatial home.

At the age of thirteen, Clint started roaming the streets in the evening after school, getting into fights and whatever other trouble he could find. When he got arrested for shoplifting at fifteen, he was fairly sure his parents saw the transgression as a good excuse to ship him to his Uncle Dory in the sleepy town of Sweet Creek.

That's when he met the Laidlaw twins. Both had flirted outrageously with him, but it was Leslie who pursued him the hardest. Back in Vancouver, he'd been one of the most popular guys. Here, he was starting over, and the Laidlaw twins were easily the most popular girls in Sweet Creek. It wasn't a hard decision to date Leslie.

But, when he started visiting Leslie at her home, he was intrigued by Nadine. She treated him with an aloofness he couldn't understand. They shared a few classes, and he found out she was smart and possessed a dry wit.

And not the least bit interested in him.

He took Leslie to prom with a vague hope that he might snag a dance with Nadine. But to his surprise and, he had to admit, disappointment, Nadine didn't attend. He never found out why. He and Leslie agreed to break up when his parents sent him on a six-month tour of Europe. When he returned, it was to find out his parents were divorced, and any money left was soaked up by divorce proceedings and the lawsuit his father lost.

He didn't see Nadine again until he accepted his uncle's generous offer to buy out the paper.

Clint shook off the memories, thankful as always for that dumb moment when he got caught in the convenience store.

Dory had given him a good home and a good example, and now, a good career.

Clint was determined to prove himself worthy of his uncle's trust, was determined to shake off the lingering bitterness of his parents' selfish actions.

He set his briefcase on his desk and walked to the window. Dory had occupied the office farther down the hall. It was larger, but Clint preferred the view. He liked to look up from his desk and see people in the park across the street or walking past the office, busy with their errands.

It had been Nadine's office, and he was sure she harbored some resentment over that. He still didn't know if it was enough to create Nadine's guarded looks or touchy attitude, nor did he understand why she still called him Fletcher.

She had always called him that. From the first time he sat by her in chemistry class and every time he came to her place to pick up Leslie. If she wasn't calling him Fletcher, she was ignoring him, her total concentration on the book she was reading. He wasn't used to being ignored. Consequently, he showed up earlier for dates, to talk to Nadine, to draw her out. He spent more time talking to Nadine about serious issues while he waited for her sister than he did with Leslie. He enjoyed their time together and thought Nadine did, too. But then life intervened.

He had gone out with several women when he left Sweet Creek, but none of them challenged him intellectually the way Nadine had. None had her appeal; nor did they ever keep him at arm's length as she did.

Now, she worked for him, and the intervening years—with all the sadness they brought—had helped her keep that prickly shell around her. He had returned to Sweet Creek hoping to see her again and raise their relationship to another level, but each of his overtures was rebuffed. After his first weeks here, he held back, sensing that Nadine still dealt with the grief of her mother's death.

Their relationship was cordial yet all business, but in the past few weeks, he saw glimpses of the Nadine who had always piqued his curiosity. An insightful comment from her about federal politics in the break room. A wry opinion on local politics or a funny, off-the-record anecdote about someone she interviewed.

Clint shook his head at himself. Regardless of his feelings for her, he had a job to do. He walked to his desk and pulled from his briefcase the letter he received yesterday from Skyline Contractors' lawyers. He didn't look forward to discussing it with Nadine.

~

"I made pancakes, Nadine," said Grandma as Nadine came into the kitchen early the next morning. "They're in the oven staying warm."

"Sorry, Grandma. I'm not in the mood for a big breakfast." Last night, she hadn't been able to sleep, instead wrestling with the implications of the letter she'd received. When she woke, her stomach was in knots.

"You never are," complained Barbara, looking up from the newspaper she was reading at the table.

Nadine tugged open the refrigerator door and pulled out a carton of yogurt and an apple. She set them on the table, then dropped into a chair, snagging a napkin from the holder on the table. The latest edition of the newspaper lay spread out on the table. Grandma had the first section, so Nadine grabbed the other.

She opened the pages, checking the stories she knew almost by heart, stopping at her kindergarten feature. She thought she had done effective work with the pictures she took. She had pasted them in a montage of children's faces: eager, expectant, and excited. The mix had energy and exuberance suited to the first day of a new venture. It was the kind of picture she knew parents cut out to put in their child's scrapbook.

"Listen to this item from the 'Court Docket,'" Grandma said, her voice scandalized. "Holly Maitfield fined for allowing her dog to roam the neighborhood unleashed. Again." She clucked anxiously. "They will put that poor mutt in the pound one day."

"They'll have to catch him first," murmured Nadine, skimming over the text opposite her feature. Halfway through, she sighed in frustration. Another typing error. Clint would be annoyed. Maybe that's what he wanted to discuss this morning.

"That's a lovely group of pictures," commented Grandma, leaning over to look at the paper.

Nadine glowed. In this line of work, people commented more often on what the reporter had done wrong, rather than right. Her grandma's compliment warmed her. "Thanks, Grandma. I had a lot of fun with this feature." She smoothed the picture with a proprietary air and turned it so her grandma could see it better. Nadine was about to turn the page when her grandmother stilled her hand.

"Wait a minute, I want to read 'About Town.'" Barbara held her hand on the paper while she read the bits of local gossip, gleaned from a variety of sources for the regular, anonymous feature. Nadine never read it. She couldn't be bothered, and anyway, she knew that Elaine wrote it. But Grandma read it faithfully. If she read it in "About Town," it had to be true.

Nadine polished off her apple, wiped her mouth, and prepared herself to face down Barbara Laidlaw.

"Grandma, I need to talk to you about last night."

Barbara blinked, put down her fork, and crossed her hands on the table in front of her. "This sounds serious."

"It is. I like organizing my social life, choosing my own friends. I don't think you need to invite young men over for tea."

"I didn't...invite Patrick. He asked himself over. He wanted to see you," Barbara insisted.

Nadine stared across the table at her grandmother, ignoring the remark. "I don't want you inviting anyone over for tea or coffee or cereal or anything; okay, Grandma? No uninvited men coming to this apartment."

Grandma Laidlaw smiled back at her, unperturbed by Nadine's pique. "I'm sorry, Nadine," she continued, her tone contrite. "I'm sorry you think I'm interfering in your life. I just want you to be happy and settled. That's all." She got up and took the teapot off the stove. "Do you want a cup of tea yet, honey? It's your favorite kind. I got it in that store on the corner, the one with that good-looking, young cashier."

"No, thanks." Nadine frowned, her anger fading. Her grandma had done it again. Taken the wind out of her sails and then changed tack.

"Well, you should get going. Make sure you're home on time tonight. We've got company for supper."

Nadine stopped, her frustration trying to find an outlet, trying to find words. "Who?" she sputtered, frustrated that she couldn't find the right words to make her grandmother understand.

"I know you said no more interfering, but I invited Dr. McCormack for supper a couple of days ago. I can't change that now, that would be rude," Grandma said quickly.

"I won't be home," she said firmly, not caring about the faux pas her grandmother was convinced would ensue.

"Why not? You're not working, are you?"

She wasn't, and she had to work fast to avoid a repeat of last night, and many other nights. "Actually, I'm going to..." What, what? She was going to do...what? Her mind flew over the possibilities and latched onto one in desperation. "I have a date."

"A date? With who?"

Oh, brother. Who? Name. She needed a name; she could see her grandmother's suspicious frown starting. "Uh...Trace."

Grandma frowned. "I've never heard of this Trace fellow. What kind of name is that? What's his last name?"

This was getting harder. Trace's name had just popped into her mind. Now he needed a last name, to boot. "Trace...Bennet," she quickly added. *Nice name, respectable name,* she thought to herself, and the names seemed to belong together. "He's a great guy. I met him two months ago at the Agribition in Edmonton when I was doing a story on the farm family of the year." She washed her hands and tossed her apple core in the compost pail—unable to look her grandmother in the eye—and bit her lip to stop the flow of drivel mixed with fibs.

"You never told me about this." Grandma sounded hurt.

Nadine shrugged nonchalantly, ignoring a stab of guilt. She reminded herself of the stories Grandma had spun to Patrick and the fact that Grandma had told her Dr. McCormack was coming over only seconds after Nadine specifically asked her not to invite prospective boyfriends.

"I'm meeting him in Eastbar," Nadine said, turning with a smile at her grandmother. "I have to do a review on a new movie showing there." She sucked in a steadying breath, knowing she had to quit before she got herself too mired in the fib.

Grandma sat back in her chair, almost pouting. "That's too bad. I was really hoping for you to meet Dr. McCormack. He's quite good-looking."

"Well." Nadine lifted her shoulders in a shrug, trying to look contrite. "Sorry, but I can't break a date with Trace." She brushed a quick kiss on her grandmother's cheek. "So long," she added, straightening.

Grandma caught her hand and squeezed it as Nadine straightened. "You never talked about him before?"

Oh, great, she sounded suspicious.

"I...wasn't sure how I felt..." which was true. How does one manufacture feelings about a fake guy?

"And how do you feel now? Do you like this man?"

Nadine almost relented at the sight of her grandmother's genuinely worried expression. *Grandma really did only mean the best,* she thought. But she remembered Patrick and Dr. McCormack and steeled herself, knowing Grandma's strongest ammunition was her concern and consideration. She would wear Nadine down with a smile, then turn around and arrange a meeting with yet another man.

She squared her shoulders, fighting her guilt and reminding herself to be strong. "We're just getting to know each other, Grandma. These things take time."

"Well, then, it shouldn't matter if I ask someone else over, should it?"

She just wouldn't give up, thought Nadine incredulously, holding her grandmother's gaze. Barbara's dogged determination reminded Nadine not to back down. Her self-reproach evaporated. "I have a boyfriend now, Grandma. You don't have to worry about me. You never had to." And with that, she turned and left before she had to lie again.

Trace Bennet, Trace Bennet, she repeated to herself as she walked out the door. *I've got to remember that name!* She stepped out and hurried down the walk, realizing she just stepped from the proverbial frying pan into the fire.

Clint stepped out of his office into the airy, spacious foyer. It still held that smell of fresh paint and carpet glue. He had ordered the renovations as soon as he took over, knocking out one wall and putting in a curved, chest-high divider that acted as a reception desk. The room was painted shades of cream and hunter green. The staff referred to it as the restaurant, but most agreed that the office looked more professional and inviting.

Julie was already at her desk, answering the phone, juggling things as usual. She looked up when Clint approached and covered her headset with one hand, raising her eyebrows in question.

"When Nadine comes, can you tell her I'd like to see her right away?" he asked.

Julie nodded, turning back to her call.

Then, just as he was about to return to his office, the front door opened with a jangle of chimes and Nadine stepped into the room, rubbing her hands. Her cheeks glowed, and her hair, pulled into its habitual ponytail, shone under the lights. She wore her usual jeans and a worn leather jacket over a loose sweater. On anyone else, the outfit would look sloppy, but Nadine made it look trendy—although he knew she wore that same sweater in high school.

A flow of cold air accompanied her and she glanced at Clint, then sharply away. He couldn't stop the nudge of disappointment at her reaction. It was no different than usual, but it still bothered him.

He cleared his throat. "When you've got a few minutes, Nadine, I'd like to see you in my office."

"Okay. I'll be there in a bit." Without giving him another glance, Nadine walked to Julie's desk and leaned on the divider. "Any fan mail for me?" she asked, her voice taking on a teasing lilt that she used with everyone but him.

"Stacks," Julie said, handing her a few envelopes. "And here's one with no return address. Be careful with it. Who knows who it's from? Maybe a stalker."

"You sound a little too excited about that. Besides, the trolls usually e-mail me," Nadine said, taking the envelopes. She flipped through them then took the one and quickly shoved it in her ever-present knapsack.

Finally, she turned back to Clint, her chin up as if challenging him. Clint bit back a sigh. Why did he even bother with this woman? She would never let down her guard. She would never come to care for him as he did for her. But, as he caught her eyes, he saw pain and weariness behind the challenge, and he felt the impulse to hold her, comfort her.

But he knew how she would react to that. The same way she did to every overture he made to her: a sarcastic comment and a dismissive shrug of her shoulder.

"You wanted to see me right away?" she said.

"If you have a moment."

"Better get me now before the phone rings."

Clint ushered her into his office, but before she sat down he offered her a cup of coffee, which she declined.

"You mean I don't even get to show you what a sensitive, caring guy I am?" he joked in an attempt to alleviate the mood.

She looked up, her face impassive. "I know what kind of man you are," she said.

Her voice held an edge that annoyed him. What had he done to her to make her so prickly around him?

And why did he even bother connecting with her?

"So what did you want to talk to me about?" she said, sitting back.

Clint took a breath, trying to find the right words, reminding himself that he was the general manager and protecting the newspaper was his first priority, not furthering his personal relationship with his editor. He rested his arms on his desk, knowing what he had to say next wouldn't help matters between them at all. "I wanted to ask you about an article on Skyline Contractors that I found in the computer archives. It was under your byline, but obviously not ready for press yet. Is it news?"

"I got some information from a former employee about some discrepancies in their accident reports..." she said slowly.

"Who verified it?"

"A former employee who used to drive Cat for them. Of course, the operative words are 'used to.' He heard a few things he shouldn't have, repeated them to me, and now he, too, is a former employee." She leaned forward. "Trust me, Clint. This is a story and it's good."

"I don't want you to write it."

"If you want to pull rank on me, Clint, that's fine. But before we go any further, I want to talk to the editors of other papers in the organization. They have as much a stake in this fight as we do. You know they'll take my part. I have to run this story."

Clint knew the history well. Uncle Dory had, in fact, pushed Skyline's buttons for years and all the editors of each paper followed suit. It had also now put him in a precarious position. He didn't have the resources to battle Skyline, but being against this company seemed to be the paper's stance.

"Skyline will kill themselves in the long run. Do you really think they need our help?"

Nadine held his gaze. "Well, it seems to me to be a good cause, so I say why not make the long run just a little shorter?"

Clint knew she was right, but he also knew that he had to make sure she wasn't setting out stories just for the sake of antagonizing a company that had their lawyer's number on speed dial. "Why not? Because this time they might take us to court." He pulled back his frustration. The newspaper business was a tough go and he was thankful for the loyal readership. He wanted to keep it that way. Lawsuits had a way of taking over lives and he didn't want to get pulled into that.

"Their lawyers make a lot of noise, but they always back down when we respond."

"Have you talked to anyone who works for Skyline now?" he persisted. "To corroborate?"

"C'mon Clint. The management likes me as much as you do."

Her comment puzzled him. "What do you mean by that?"

Nadine shrugged, not deigning to reply, looking anywhere but at him.

He got up from his desk, surprised that she should think that of him, and wondering if maybe that wasn't the key, the true reason she kept herself at such a distance from him. "Why would you think I dislike you?"

As he came to stand beside her, she stood as well, looking up at him, her dark eyes wide. And in their brown depths he caught a surprising hint of vulnerability. A momentary softening.

Did he imagine her leaning toward him? A hint of a smile on her lips?

Something seemed to shift between them and he felt an urge to touch her cheek, to run his fingers through that thick, dark hair...

"Matthew McKnight is on line two for you, Mr. Fletcher." Julie's voice on the intercom pierced the heavy atmosphere. Clint blinked, Nadine took a step back.

"Well, I'd better get going. You look busy," she said with a short laugh. She picked up her knapsack, slung it over her shoulder, and left.

Clint turned back to the phone, frustrated and angry at the intrusion. He punched the button and answered curtly, "Hello Matthew, what's up?"

"Not much. The usual lawyerly stuff. Torts, arguing, and writing briefs. Way too many briefs."

"Are you calling about getting together sometime?"

"Actually, no. Dad wanted me to take over your file from John."

"Oh." Matthew's father owned the firm Matthew worked for. If Clifton McKnight wanted his son on the case it must be serious.

"Yeah."

Though Clint was happy to hear his friend's voice, the fact that Matthew was calling him at the office during business hours did not bode well. He closed his office door and sat down by his desk, turning to look out the window. "So are you calling to be brought up to speed?"

"That and to mention that John got another call from Skyline's lawyers."

"Now what?"

"Nothing really. Just testing the waters. Asking if you got their notice."

Clint thought of the letter that Matthew had passed onto him.

The letter stating that they were unhappy with his paper's biased coverage of their company and what was he going to do about it?

"I did. I'll talk to Nadine again."

"Make sure you do. Those lawyers are sniffing around a lawsuit if she doesn't back down."

Clint rubbed his forehead with his index finger as if drawing out his thoughts. "I think she got the message," though even as he spoke his words he thought of the piece he had just talked to Nadine about. "It will be fine."

"I hope so," Matthew returned. "I don't want to have to go up against a company like Skyline. Deep pockets and a huge chip on their shoulder when it comes to your little newspaper."

"Thanks for the pep talk," Clint said.

"Just keeping it real," Matthew replied.

They chatted for a moment then Clint said goodbye. As he ended the call he glanced out the window at the mountains. He'd been glad to come back to Sweet Creek. Glad to move into the home that Dory Strepchuk had sold to him.

And though he had harbored some faint hope that he could make peace with Nadine, maybe even more than peace, he also knew he wasn't jeopardizing this opportunity so she could grind some axe she had with them.

CHAPTER 3

"*Y*ou actually did it?" Elaine stabbed her french fry in the ketchup with a grin. "My pure, unadulterated friend actually fibbed to her grandmother about a boyfriend?"

Nadine blew her breath out in a sigh and leaned her elbows on the scarred, wooden table of the Riverside Inn, glancing out at the people walking down Main Street. "It was a moment of insanity."

"Clearly."

Her friend's sardonic tone made Nadine defensive.

"I had to," she said, turning her attention back to her lunch, a salad. "First, it's Patrick Quinn last night for tea, then Dr. McCormack tonight for supper."

"Dr. McCormack?" Elaine grimaced and shook her head. "He's about fifteen years older than us, and, while I think bald men can be very attractive, on him it's not." She leaned forward. "What name did you give this pretend guy?"

Nadine closed her eyes, digging into her memory. She had to write his name somewhere, or she would blow it completely. "Trace Bennet."

Elaine pulled her mouth down. "Sounds like a country and western singer. What does he look like?"

"Goodness, Elaine. He's fake; I don't know."

"Knowing your grandma, she'll phone to ask about all the gory details. We need a biography on this guy." Elaine laughed. "We need hair color, eye color, backstory..." She pursed her lips, thinking. "Job, place of employment."

"Don't bother." Nadine waved a dismissive hand over the table. "I just blurted it out this morning because I was angry and wanted to keep her off my back. There's no getting around it. I need to toughen up and flat-out tell her, 'Grandma, go back home.'"

"Why don't you let her stay and you move out?"

"Because I'll lose my damage deposit, and she has a perfectly good house in Fort Henday." Nadine pursed her lips as she looked out of the inn's window, at the street she knew so well. Each brick building held some memory for her: The hardware store she and Sheryl used to visit to pick paint chips for their future houses; the library, down a side street, where she spent countless hours.

Some days it seemed as if her life stretched ahead like a prairie road. Predictable and the same—not that she needed high adventure. She was content here in Sweet Creek. She enjoyed her work and her life; she just wished she had someone to share it with.

She recalled her morning meeting with Clint and thought of the way he'd looked at her just before the phone call. For a moment, it seemed as if something was building between them. Nadine shook her head, dismissing the notion. Just wishful thinking. She wasn't his type.

She glanced up at the clock. "I should go. I promised Fletcher I'd get pictures of the rodeo."

"You going to be there all night?"

"Not much else going on."

"And tomorrow?"

This engendered another sigh. "I got tapped to do the review of the movie in Eastbar."

"Perfect," Elaine said with a wry grin. "You can tell your grandmother you're going with the handsome and very eligible Trace Bennet."

Nadine considered this a moment. "I could tell her that I'm going with 'someone,' and she would fill in the blanks."

"Look at you, learning to lie as you go."

"Learning self-preservation as I go," Nadine groaned. She finished her salad and pulled some bills out of her wallet. "This should cover lunch."

"If you want to call that lunch," Elaine groused.

"I can call it whatever I want," Nadine returned. She slung her knapsack over her shoulder and almost ran into their boss.

While trying to avoid him, she lost her balance and fell against the table beside her. To her dismay, Clint caught her by the shoulders, his grip solid.

Her heart jumped.

"You okay?" he asked, his dark eyes holding hers.

She swallowed and nodded, jerking back, frustrated again with her reaction to him.

"Yeah. I'm fine."

Before she could catch Elaine's eye, she hurried off. Headed to the rodeo—alone.

∽

The movie was a dud.

Bad enough that Nadine had spent the entire Saturday avoiding Grandma, now she had to end it watching this horrible waste of time? Nadine struggled to the bitter end, scribbled a few comments, and fled the theatre as soon as the credits rolled. Outside, the streetlights had just come on, competing with the setting sun. The evening still held vestiges of the day's warmth trapped by the mountains, but the changing colors of the trees were a reminder that winter would come whistling through the pass in a matter of weeks.

She should go home and work on stories for the next issue, but she had told Grandma she would be out tonight, and coming right back from a movie would be a dead giveaway.

And if Grandma found out she'd gone alone to the film, she would start matchmaking all over again. It was frustrating, not to mention humiliating. She had never been the flirtatious type, leaving that for her sisters.

Until Clint Fletcher came to Sweet Creek and she wished she could talk as effortlessly to him as her sisters managed to.

It had been hard to see how Leslie made him laugh, how comfortable she was flirting with him, when all Nadine could contribute was an opinion on the most ponderous issues of the day, or tell him how she and her father dovetailed the joints on the drawers of the new coffee table.

But, he wounded her sister's heart when he broke up with her and left on a tour of Europe. Nadine realized if Leslie couldn't hold him, she couldn't expect to.

Deep in thought, Nadine squinted at the darkening sky, past the streetlights of Eastbar. The crescent moon hung in the sky above her. A few of the brighter stars showed themselves in the blue-black sky. Beyond those lay more stars, more constellations, and other galaxies. She stared, aware of what a small part of creation she really was—a speck in the whole cosmos that God had created. She kept herself busy in the community and was involved in church. She enjoyed her work and liked being independent; but lately, when she came home, something was missing. Once in a while, a deep yearning for a companion waiting at home overrode her desire to be alone.

Her parents had it, thought Nadine, while giving an empty can a tinny kick. She remembered her big, burly father and his warm hugs. When his work required it, he would stay away for a week.

This was in the days when hand harvesting was more common—before machines took a week to chomp through what would have been a full winter's work. Nadine remembered how he used to grab her mother around her waist and swing her off the floor, singing loudly. Her mother would laugh, wrap her arms around his neck, and sing along. The waiting was over; the man of the house had returned. All was well.

Now, instead of life amidst her parents and sisters, all Nadine had at home was her dear, meddling grandmother.

Nadine thought of her conversation with Elaine and wondered if she could really put Grandma off the scent with her fake boyfriend. She knew beyond a doubt that she didn't have the resources to maintain the fib. This "date" would have to be a onetime thing, she mused, while pulling out the keys to her car. She was surprised she'd gotten this far.

Nadine glanced at her watch—too early to go home. It would have to be coffee at the Riverside Inn.

"I'll just have a coffee, Cory." Nadine smiled up at the waitress, who nodded and poured her a cup. "How is the catering business going?" Nadine asked her. Though Cory had been working at the Inn for the past half year, Nadine had heard that she and her mother had recently started up a catering service on the side.

"It's slow, but coming along. I've got a few events coming up. Thankfully Kelsey and her parents have been supportive. They let me use the kitchen at the Inn for larger events."

"They're good people. I also like what Kelsey's done now that she's taken over the day-to-day running of the Inn." The Inn was quiet and Nadine was willing to chat with Cory. She needed to kill some time. Her 'date' needed to drag on at least an hour longer. Hopefully Grandma would be in bed when she came home.

"She's created a great ambience," Cory agreed.

The entire interior was painted a soft yellow, and the windows were framed with rough pieces of wood that matched the heavy wooden tables. Vintage pictures of coal miners and logging crews covered the walls, along with early pictures of the town, with its classic brick buildings and metal lampposts.

"I like how she's collected stuff from people in the town and hung it on the wall," Cory added, smiling as she looked at the old menus, vintage keys, a couple of framed doilies, and other bric-a-brac that added to the homey decor.

"See those spurs there?" Nadine said, pointing out a rusted pair of tree climbing spurs hanging on the wall by her 'usual' spot. "My father gave those to her. They were used by my grandfather in the days when log fallers climbed up the trees to limb and top them before felling them."

"You've got history here," Cory said.

The melancholy in her voice caught Nadine's attention.

"I do. Been here for a few generations."

"That's a blessing." Cory gave her a smile then shrugged. "I should get going."

When she left, Nadine looked up at the spurs again, thinking of her father and the stories he would tell her of how agile and limber Grandpa Laidlaw was, scurrying up the trees like a monkey. When Nadine was very young, she had always imagined Grandpa Laidlaw as a chimp with a hard hat. She smiled at the memory.

"Share the joke?" The deep voice beside her broke her reverie. She jumped, her hand hitting the coffee cup and spilling half the contents.

She grabbed a handful of napkins and, while still mopping up, faced Clint Fletcher. "You scared me out of my wits," she accused him, her heart pounding.

"Now, that conjures up an interesting image. Nadine without

her wits," he said, still towering over her, with one hand in his pants pocket, the other resting on the table.

Clint hesitated a moment, then pulled out a chair. "Mind if I join you?"

She tried not to let his height intimidate her, tried not to notice how broad his shoulders looked in a suit coat. But mostly, tried to ignore the increase in her heartbeat at the sight of him.

She shrugged in answer. He could take that how he liked, but deep down, she faintly hoped he would stay, and then berated herself for feeling attracted to him after all these years.

"What story are you covering that keeps you out so late?" he asked as he sat down.

She fiddled with her cup. "I caught the movie in Eastbar, which was dreadful, and thought I'd kill time before I go home."

"I take it the review won't be favorable." Clint folded his hands on the table and leaned forward.

"Not likely." Nadine sat back against her chair. "I'll probably have Evan Grimshaw, the owner, accusing me of trying to put him out of business again."

"Who did you go to the movie with?" asked Clint, as he smoothed his tie.

"No one you'd know," she replied, realizing she needed to maintain some semblance of this fake date.

Clint nodded, and for a moment, Nadine was tempted to drop Trace Bennet's name. But, Clint with his quick, incisive questions would catch her in a lie.

"I'm guessing it wasn't your grandmother?" he asked with a careful smile.

"Oh my goodness, no. Grandma thinks movies and television are a waste of the good time God gives us."

"Does your grandmother still live with you?" he asked. "I know she moved in when your mother got ill."

Nadine traced her finger through the circles of moisture the mug had left on the table. "Technically, not," she replied with a sigh. "She's a dear old lady who thinks I need to be taken care of, but it's time for her to move back home. She gave me some reprieve when she stayed with Sabrina after she had her baby, but she came back. She thinks I need her...help."

And now she was talking too much. Clint could still make her nervous that way.

A moment of silence hung between them.

Clint cleared his throat. "How are your sisters?" he asked.

Nadine caught the tone in his voice and, looking up at him, caught a melancholy expression on his face. Did he miss Leslie? Regret breaking up with her? "Sabrina just had her first baby. Leslie is married and expecting as well and is quitting her job before the baby is born." As she talked, she held his gaze, as if challenging him—letting him know that in spite of his breakup with her, Leslie was doing just fine, thank you very much.

"Leslie always was a homebody. Just like you." Clint smiled at Nadine, his expression softening, and she wondered if he was thinking of Leslie. And why wouldn't he?

Just as suddenly, the moment was gone. He stood and straightened the cuffs of his shirt and once again became her boss. "Well, I'd better be off. I have a busy day tomorrow."

"Court docket." Nadine grinned at him. "A bit of a comedown for our esteemed G.M. to cover for Wally."

He paused, and for a heartbeat, looked as if he would say something else. "I don't mind. I like to keep involved in the day-to-day stuff too. Reminds me of why I became a reporter."

The small insight into his life surprised her.

"Do you miss working at a big paper? Living in the city?"

He tapped his fingers on the table for a moment, and his features softened. "Not really. I miss some of the drama, but I've had enough of that in my life."

Nadine wondered if he referred to his parents. She knew only what she'd heard from Leslie—that his parents fought a lot, and that, even though they had a lot of money, Clint wasn't happy with them. But she sensed Clint didn't want to extend the conversation so she simply gave him a polite smile in response to his comment.

"Have a good evening," she said.

He nodded, then, with a lift of a shoulder, he turned and left.

Nadine looked down at her half-full coffee cup. Suddenly she felt alone. *A lonely alone*, she thought as she dropped money on the table for Cory and grimaced at her watch.

Hopefully, Grandma would be in bed so she wouldn't have to make up any more evasive answers about her "date."

She stepped out of the inn, into the chill of the fall evening. Down the street, she heard a vehicle start, and then, it slowed as it drove by her.

Clint was looking at her out the window of his SUV, and for a split second, she felt it again, the curious lift of her heart he could always give her.

She shook her head as he drove away. She really needed to get past this silly attraction to him.

He didn't like the direction she took with her Skyline features, and she knew she needed to focus on finding out what happened to her father—not flirting with a boss who fought her on this.

CHAPTER 4

"C'mon Nadine," Grandma called down the hall of the apartment. "We will be late for church."

Nadine stifled a wave of impatience with her dear grandma as she straightened the cream-colored sweater she wore over her rust wool skirt. She would have preferred to wear the jeans she had spent the better part of the morning looking for. She suspected her grandma had pulled them aside, intending to patch the deliberate rips, as she had been threatening since Nadine bought them.

Now she was trying to get her hair, still damp from her morning shower, into an elastic. It snapped against her hand and her hair slid loose.

"Are you coming?" Grandma called again.

Nadine glanced at the clock and, with a frustrated sigh, grabbed her purse from the bed and slung it over her shoulder. She stopped at the bathroom long enough to grimace at the reflection of herself, feeling self-conscious with her hair down. A ponytail was far easier, but she could find no elastics in the bathroom, either. Down it would have to stay.

"Nadine." Grandma's voice was sharp, and Nadine threw the brush into the drawer.

"Coming, coming," she muttered as she ran down the hallway, wondering why she was even letting her grandmother get to her. They both had a car; they could both drive on their own. But, Grandma was on an environmental kick and had decided they would ride together and save the polar bears.

Grandma waited in the entrance, tapping her foot. "What took you so long?" she grumbled.

Nadine caught her car keys from the little pegboard hanging by the door. Without deigning to reply to her grandma, she stepped into the parking lot.

"You are certainly not in a Sunday mood today," Grandma chided as she stepped into the vehicle. "I thought you would be much happier after going out on your date."

As Nadine had hoped, her grandmother was in bed when she returned last night. And this morning, Nadine had grabbed an apple before Grandma was up and retreated to her room to work to avoid any cross-questioning.

"Sorry, Grandma," Nadine said automatically as she backed the car out onto the street. "But after you cleaned up the other night, I couldn't find the pants I wanted to wear." She chose not to address the 'date' and hoped dear Grandma would be distracted.

"Those pants are torn."

"That's why I bought them. Even though I probably paid too much." Now she was full-on baiting her grandmother. Somehow, Grandma had found the price tag in the garbage and had fussed about the cost of them all day. "And please don't patch them."

"Okay. I won't." Grandma folded her hands over the small purse on her lap. Staring primly ahead, she remained quiet for the rest of the trip.

Church was full again. Over the summer, attendance had waxed and waned with people leaving for holidays; but now, the children were back in school, the harvest was in full swing, and the congregation was back to full strength.

"You go on ahead, Nadine. I want to talk to Mrs. Phipps." Grandma gave Nadine a gentle push into the sanctuary. Nadine frowned at her, wondering what she was scheming now. She saw an elderly woman wave toward Barbara, and she relaxed.

"Don't wait too long, Grandma. Church is full," she warned.

"Don't worry about me," Grandma chirped as she walked to her friend. Nadine shook her head and let the usher show her to an empty spot.

Nadine dropped into the pew and scanned the bulletin that came with the order of worship. It was filled with the usual announcements. She read a few of the updates. Mark and Sheryl's wedding date was set and announced.

Nadine had been asked to be in the wedding party and had gladly accepted. She was happy for her friend.

While she read the rest, out of the corner of her eye, she saw Grandma stopping beside the pew, glancing backward down the aisle.

Nadine scooted over for them, turning the page of the bulletin as she did so.

"Come sit with us," she heard her grandmother say. Nadine glanced up to say hello to Mrs. Phipps—it wasn't the elderly lady who stood there.

It was Clint Fletcher.

He had one hand on the pew in front of them, the other in the pocket of a casual blazer. Underneath he wore a white shirt and a patterned tie in shades of deep gold and russet. Again, Nadine felt her heart lift at the sight of him, and again, she grew frustrated with her reaction.

"I was talking to young Clint," Grandma said to Nadine, "and I told him I wanted to catch up with him. Here, Nadine. Let Mr. Fletcher sit between us." As Grandma sat, she nudged Nadine over. Nadine silently fumed, but could do nothing without creating a scene. She moved aside so Clint could sit between them. So this was why Grandma didn't ask about her fake boyfriend and her 'date'—she had another victim in her sights.

Nadine picked up the bulletin, trying to ignore both her grandma and the tall figure seated beside her. It couldn't be done; Clint's presence exerted a force she couldn't ignore. So, she thought it would be better to do as always and face him head-on, hoping he wouldn't read anything into Grandma's little machinations.

"What brings my esteemed boss to church this morning?" she said, forcing a teasing grin.

He glanced sidelong at her. "Same thing that brought you."

Nadine couldn't resist. "You have a nagging grandma, too?"

Clint smiled and shook his head. "No. A nagging conscience."

Nadine was taken aback at his quiet admission. No quick reply came to mind, so she picked up her reading where she had left off. During the service, she couldn't forget what he had said, and she cast sidelong glances at him. His expression was, as usual, serious. He sang along with the hymns. As he listened to the minister, Nadine recognized that firm-jaw look that came over his face when he absorbed some particularly important idea.

His intensity surprised her. When they were dating, Clint had accompanied Leslie to church, but Nadine had never gotten the impression from him that his attendance meant anything. It was a way to keep Leslie mollified. She had challenged him once on his attendance, and had received a sarcastic remark. But he didn't look sarcastic right now.

When the offering was passed, he took the plate, dropped in an envelope, and handed it to her. He didn't let go, however. Nadine looked up at him, puzzled.

"Your hair looks nice like that," he whispered.

Nadine raised her eyebrows, almost dropping the plate. Flustered, she handed it to the person beside her, forgetting to put in her own contribution. She failed to stifle the flush that warmed her throat and crept up her cheeks.

Compliments from Clint Fletcher? That was something she had no defense for.

Nadine felt increasingly uncomfortable sitting beside her boss. She would bring her mind back to the sermon, but then he would shift his weight, move his long legs, or brush her arm with his elbow, and she would have to start all over again. Periodically, she caught a spicy hint of aftershave. Mentally apologizing to God, she took a deep breath, pulled out a notepad from her purse, and focused her entire attention on the minister. The reporter in her made it easier to remember sermons when she took notes.

When the congregation rose for the last song, she risked a sidelong glance at him. He looked down at her from his considerable height, and Nadine glanced away, feeling even more confused.

She was relieved when the organist and pianist began the postlude. It wasn't often that Clint could throw her for a loop, but his presence beside her and his unexpected compliment did.

As she made her way down the crowded aisle to the exit, she glanced over her shoulder. Clint was waylaid by Allen Andrews, Mark Andrews's brother and a local real estate agent who frequently advertised in the *Sweet Creek Chronicle*.

Nadine's step faltered as she saw him grin, then laugh. He was attractive enough when he was serious. Smiling, he became irresistible.

With a forced shrug, Nadine continued out to her car. Grandma already sat waiting, and Nadine slipped in behind the wheel.

"By the way, Nadine,"—she smiled, turning guileless blue eyes to her granddaughter—"Mr. Fletcher is coming over for lunch."

"*What?*" Nadine almost dropped her car keys. "But, Grandma..."

"I know what you said," Grandma interjected, "but he said he had nowhere to go when I asked. What could I do?" she asked innocently.

"Not invite him," Nadine groused. "I work with him, I don't need to see him on my days off."

"That's not kind. Besides, I think he was happy for the invitation. I'm thinking he'd like to see the place he visited when he was dating Leslie. And while Sabrina flirted outrageously with him, I think he secretly liked you the best," Barbara continued, undaunted by Nadine's expression.

"He kept that secret well," Nadine said dryly, looking away. "I never got that impression."

"Maybe because you were always so snippy to him. I'm sure he'd have spent more time with you if you weren't so uptight with him."

"May I remind you it was Leslie he was dating. Clint never looked twice at me," Nadine remarked.

"He has eyes for you, Nadine. I can tell," Grandma persisted.

"Grandma, I already have a boyfriend."

"Yes, I know. I keep forgetting." Barbara smiled at Nadine. "Someday, I'd like to meet him. For now, young Clint will be joining us for lunch."

Nadine glanced at her grandmother, but made no reply as she pulled out of the parking lot.

～

"What are you doing in the kitchen?" Grandma caught Nadine by the arm, frowning at her. "You go talk to Clint," she whispered.

Nadine laid out the cheese slices, quelling her irritation. "You invited him, you talk to him," she hissed.

Grandma would not be swayed. "I think Clint would like some coffee," she said loudly, smiling at Nadine. "I'll finish up in here."

Nadine counted to ten, grabbed the pot, and marched out of the kitchen.

Clint sat on the couch looking remarkably comfortable. He smiled up at Nadine as she filled his cup. Nadine straightened, still holding the pot. The smile surprised her. It was like he didn't mind being here.

To her surprise, she felt her own lips curving in a return smile. And her heart gently flipped as their eyes met. Held. The atmosphere felt like the other morning in his office, which hinted at a promise of other things to come.

"So, this place looks nice," Clint said. "You've made some changes since I saw it last."

"I've tried to make it homey." She glanced around the room, remembering too well what it looked like when her mother's hospital bed occupied most of the space. The steady hum of the oxygen concentrator had invaded the peace of the place.

After her mother died and the grief had settled to an easy throb, Nadine had done a complete makeover, painting the walls and purchasing new decor items—a fresh start and a way of easing away the sad memories.

"I think you succeeded." Still holding his coffee cup, he walked to the fake fireplace. Sabrina's and Leslie's wedding pictures were displayed on the mantel, as was the most recent picture of Sabrina's daughter.

"Your sisters look happy."

"They are."

Wow, she was really hitting it out of the park with the scintillating conversation.

He picked up Leslie's picture, and as he looked at it, Nadine caught a glimpse of sorrow cross his face. Nadine swallowed her reaction to him thinking of herself compared to her still-stunning sister. Still? Still, the fact that Leslie had caught his fancy could bother her? How foolish was she?

"She's as beautiful as she ever was," Nadine said, feeling a need to control the direction of the conversation. If she said it first, it wouldn't hurt as much as if Clint did.

"She is that," Clint said, a note of melancholy in his voice. "Is she happy?"

"Her husband is really good to her."

"I'm glad. She is...a sweet person." He replaced the picture carefully, as if reluctant to let go.

Well, there it was. He still missed Leslie. Which made her wonder again why Clint had broken up with her. Nadine had never discovered the reason from Leslie, because she never wanted to talk about it. She kept saying she just wanted to put it all behind her. She had been so adamant about it, Nadine never pursued it further.

"Lunch is ready," Grandma announced from the kitchen, and thankfully, the mood was broken. Clint finished his coffee then motioned for Nadine to precede him.

They sat down at the table where, no surprise here, Grandma had taken away the chairs on one side, so Nadine was forced to sit beside Clint. Nadine felt trapped, dreading the next hour, wondering what her grandmother was thinking when she invited Clint over.

"So, are you settling back into Sweet Creek, Clint?" her grandmother asked him as she handed him the tray with buns.

"I am. Sometimes it feels like I've never been gone."

"Yes. Not much changes around here, does it Nadine?" Grandma nudged Nadine's foot to encourage her to participate.

You invited him, you keep him busy, Nadine thought, not looking up. She kept her head down, focusing on getting exactly the correct amount of butter on her buns and meticulously arranging the cheese and meat so they didn't stick too far off the bun. Important work. Distracting work.

"And I heard your Uncle Dory will be coming home soon from his overseas trip?" Grandma continued.

Clint nodded, wiping his mouth with the napkin. "Yes. In a couple of weeks."

"I'm sure he'll have lots to talk about."

This gained Nadine another foot nudge, which she also ignored.

"And now that you're living in his house, where will he be living?"

"He's bought one of those condos that just went up a year ago."

"Nice for him. I understand you also went overseas after you graduated," Grandma put in, gamely carrying the conversation.

Nadine knew she was being obstinate but wasn't sure how else to let her grandmother know her behavior today was unacceptable in so many ways.

"I did," was all Clint said. "My parents insisted that I go after graduation. I...I wasn't keen on the idea, but in retrospect, it was the right thing to do."

His blasé comments made her uneasy. The right thing to do? After breaking her sister's heart?

Nadine was in college at the time, but that summer, she came home whenever she could. She remembered how restrained Leslie was. How she looked thinner. How quiet she was about the whole breakup.

Finally, in September, her sister pulled herself together and moved to Calgary to start over.

And now Clint was so casually stating that it seemed the right thing to do?

"Was the trip the reason you broke up with Leslie?" The question jumped out before she could stop herself.

The regretful way he looked at Leslie's picture bothered her. And now he acted like breaking her sister's heart was no big deal. The way Leslie was talking before Clint broke up with her, marriage was in the cards. Now he was passing it off like it was some silly high school crush.

He didn't look her way; instead, he carefully pushed his salad around the plate. He shook his head. "We were pretty young at the time."

"It still hurt Leslie quite a bit," Nadine returned, unable to deny his comment.

At that, Clint turned to her, a frown creasing his forehead. "Sounds like you're still upset about that."

Nadine held his gaze, trying to figure out what he meant by that comment. "No one likes to see their sister's heart broken."

"Did she talk much about it? Our breakup?"

Nadine couldn't believe his nerve. "Why do you want to know?"

Clint held her gaze a moment, as if trying to delve into her soul. "I just thought she might have said something to you. After all..." he shook his head.

"She only told me that you broke up with her, and that she didn't want to talk about it. She was adamant about that."

Clint nodded slowly, then turned back to his lunch. It was a stilted affair after Nadine's comment. Grandma gamely tried to forge on, but Nadine could see that Clint was only being polite, until he could politely leave. After another few agonizing minutes, he made a show of glancing at his watch, the universal sign for "I'm out of here."

"I'm sorry, but I should go." He wiped his mouth, gave Grandma a polite smile, then got up. "Thanks for lunch," he said. "I appreciate the invitation."

He didn't look at Nadine, and as he walked away, Grandma shot her an angry look.

Nadine didn't care.

However, the manners her mother had drilled into her and her sisters took precedence over her own awkwardness. She got up and walked Clint to the entrance.

"Thanks for coming," was all she said as he went to open the door, realizing how empty the polite words sounded, even to her.

He held the knob a moment, and then shot a look over his shoulder, holding her gaze.

Was that regret in his eyes? Sorrow?

The emotions were so fleeting, she was sure she had imagined them.

"Yeah. Tell your grandmother thanks again."

He opened the door and left.

As the door closed behind him, a mixture of emotions coursed through her. Had she pushed too hard? Did it really matter what he did to Leslie all those years ago? She was happy now, as she had told Clint.

Or was there a deeper reason behind her frustration?

"You could have been nicer to him."

Her grandmother's reproachful voice behind her made Nadine turn around.

"I was just telling him the truth."

Barbara's shoulders lifted in a heavy sigh. "And now he's gone. Seriously, Nadine. I try, I really do."

"You don't need to try, Grandma. I'm fine on my own."

This netted her a puzzled look. "But I thought you went on a date with that Trace fellow. Didn't it turn out?"

For a moment, she was ready to tell her everything: that Trace wasn't real, that she was just trying to keep Barbara off her back. It was too much work to remember everything.

"Well, you'll just have to be nicer to Clint if I invite him over again," Grandma said. "But before I try that again, I was thinking of having Conrad come—the fellow who works for Mark Andrews."

Nadine wanted to scream. This was really the limit.

"I had a lovely time last night," she told her grandmother, reminding herself that if she didn't push back, Barbara was going to drive her around the bend. "Trace and I will be seeing each other again."

She held her grandmother's wary gaze, look for look, simultaneously praying for forgiveness.

Don't back down. Don't give in. While she doubted her grandmother could convince Clint to come again, there was no way she would be subjected to yet another debacle like she had just weathered.

"So just stop, because it's not fair to Trace," she pushed.

"Will I get to meet him?"

"If you behave and stop inviting over other young men, or old men, or any kind of man."

Grandma pursed her lips, and as she seemed to consider the ultimatum, Nadine wondered how she would produce Trace.

"I'll wait two weeks," Grandma said. She yawned and glanced at her watch. "I'm tired, Nadine. I think I'll lie down for a nap. Can you clean up? Thanks." With that, Grandma walked away.

Nadine watched Barbara close the door to her bedroom. Then, she turned to the kitchen, full of leftovers and dirty dishes, and was left to wonder how Grandma had finessed her way out of both the dishes and another confrontation.

And wonder why Clint had accepted her grandmother's invitation to lunch.

CHAPTER 5

*C*lint leaned back in his chair with the most recent edition of the *Sweet Creek Chronicle* in his hands, taking a moment to appreciate the new format they were using. It was a struggle to update the fonts, clean out the deadwood, and encourage the reporters to be more creative. Some had resisted change, but others were eager to take a different direction. Slowly, the editors of all three papers were coming around.

The front page had a half-page, color spread of a horse in full buck, a cowboy in midair, fringes of his red chaps fanning. The audience was a soft blur, setting off the action.

He'd have to let Nadine know that he really liked it. Maybe a compliment would put him on her good side.

He snapped open the paper, skimming the other stories, not reading as much as measuring impact. All in all, it was a clean, sharp-looking paper.

He turned to the editorial section and was immediately confronted with a picture of the one who wasn't coming around.

Nadine Laidlaw.

Clint studied the grainy picture on the top of her column. Her large eyes stared back at him, her full mouth unsmiling. The photo didn't do her justice, but at the same time, her somber expression was too familiar.

Sunday, when Barbara Laidlaw had invited him to lunch, he thought it would be a chance to ease the tension between him and Nadine.

Yeah, that went well.

After he left her apartment, he thought of a hundred other ways he could have answered Nadine's question about Leslie, without breaking the promise he'd made to her sister.

Sunday was one of those times when the convictions that Dory had instilled hampered more than helped him. As Nadine seemed to grill him about his breakup, he wanted nothing more than to tell her the real reason he and Leslie had broken up. He wanted to tell her about broken promises, and the guy who Leslie had been fooling around with and who Leslie was terrified Nadine would find out about. When Clint discovered who it was he told Nadine he had to break up with her even as she pleaded for a second chance.

Clint knew there was more to his breakup than Leslie's infidelity. His heart had never been truly engaged in the relationship.

Still looking at Nadine's picture, he blew out a sigh and wondered why he thought things would have changed between them—even though, it seemed, Grandma Laidlaw was on his side.

Plus, she didn't seem to be above a little matchmaking. While he was pleased to have such a strong ally in his corner, he wondered if it even helped.

And he wondered why Nadine still held his attention.

He turned the page to "About Town," giving it a cursory glance. He had wanted to cut it when he came, but the letters from the readers convinced him otherwise.

This week, the column was the usual boring chitchat. The name of a town councilor seen at the golf course during one of the meetings, other well-known people and their goings-on. Local reporter Nadine Laidlaw spotted at the theater in Eastbar with...

CAROLYNE AARSEN

"What?" Clint shook the paper, as if to bring the name into focus. "Who in the world is Trace Bennet?"

He suddenly realized he had spoken aloud and glanced through the open door to see if Julie had noticed. Thankfully, she wasn't at her desk. He looked back at the paper and reread the piece. Was this Trace guy a boyfriend?

And why was that name so familiar? Maybe Nadine had mentioned it when he'd met her the other day at the Riverside Inn. Thinking back, he remembered she had been evasive about whom she'd been with.

He suddenly felt very foolish. She already had a boyfriend and kept making it clear that she wasn't interested in him. No wonder she'd been so cool to him on Sunday. What an idiot he was.

Julie was now at her desk. She looked up and smiled as the door jangled open. "Hey, Nadine," he heard her call out.

Clint couldn't help the tingle of awareness as he heard Nadine's name. He straightened as she entered the main office area and dropped her knapsack on the reception desk. Her cheeks were ruddy from the morning air. Unfortunately, her thick, dark hair was pulled back into the ever-present ponytail. On Sunday, as she wore a skirt and her hair hung loose on her shoulders, she had looked softer, more approachable. Less the sassy reporter and more womanly.

He let his eyes travel over her face. She had a firm mouth, offset by unique eyes that tilted upward at the corners, accented by narrow eyebrows. Her striking features drew him again and again. He had been attracted to her from the beginning, yet was put off by her prickly manner. Somehow, the intervening years had softened her features. Sorrow granted her an air of vulnerability he was sure she was unaware of.

Nadine seemed to sense his gaze and met his eyes. Clint felt once again the spark of awareness he experienced each time their eyes met. She blinked and jerked her gaze away.

56

"Let's see the latest news from the bustling metropolis of Sweet Creek," Nadine said.

Julie slapped a paper into Nadine's outstretched hand, and she laid it out on the counter, eyeing the front page. She glanced Clint's way and, holding up the paper, her smile shifted into a polite expression. "Nice shot, eh?"

He sauntered over, hands in the pockets of his pants holding back his jacket. "Looks great, Nadine. Good job."

Nadine smiled. "Thanks, my sartorial boss." She turned back to the paper, flipping the pages as he had done a few moments ago. Clint could tell by the way her soft brown eyes traveled over the pages that she was looking at them the way he had. Not reading but checking for overall impression.

"Cute little piece in 'About Town' on your trip to Eastbar," he gibed, needing to know about this boyfriend.

She frowned and turned to the section. As she read the piece, he could tell—to the second—when her eyes hit her name. A flush shot to her hairline. She swallowed and, without looking at him, slapped the paper shut, caught her knapsack with her other hand, and marched down the hallway.

Clint raised one eyebrow in surprise, his curiosity further aroused by Nadine's reaction.

∾

"You did this. I know you did," Nadine hissed, shaking the paper in front of her friend's face.

Elaine rose and shut the door to her office. "Of course I did," she said, giving Nadine a broad grin. "I know your grandma always reads that section. Doesn't she?"

"But...the paper," Nadine sputtered. "To put it in the newspaper..."

"Oh, c'mon. Most people know it's idle gossip. But your grandma puts as much stock in it as anything she hears from the pulpit on Sunday. I knew if she read it, it would bolster your cause." Elaine walked over and patted her friend on the shoulder. "Trust me. It's for the best."

Nadine looked up at Elaine and then back at the paper. "What do I do?"

"Nothing, you ninny. Grandma will read it, believe what you told her, and then she'll move out. Which, I might remind you," Elaine said, her voice stern, "was the point of this whole exercise."

"But she wants to meet this guy, eventually. I have to do something."

"Just hope that this little piece in the paper will be enough. Send her on her way and tell her you'll bring him for Thanksgiving." Elaine sat on her desk, her arms crossed. "Just before Thanksgiving, you 'break up' with him. Easy as can be."

"Easy for you to say, that is." Nadine looked once more at the offending section, shaking her head. "I still can't believe you did this."

"Hey, I could have put in Clint Fletcher's name."

Nadine shot her a murderous look. "You dare."

"Hey. You could do worse," Elaine said with a laugh. "Clint's pretty easy on the eyes, and whether you like to admit it or not, I think you agree."

The problem was, she did agree; she agreed most wholeheartedly. Even after the debacle of Sunday, seeing him could still raise her heart rate.

But after Sunday's mess, she doubted he would want to have anything personal to do with her anyhow.

"Well, thanks to this, whether I agree or not, he probably thinks I'm taken."

"Maybe he'll get jealous."

Nadine released a hard laugh. "Too much history there. Besides, he's my boss, and he doesn't like some of the things I write about."

And she was sure if she followed through on the letter she had received the other day, he would be less than happy with her.

~

Nadine was scribbling notes on a pad of paper when a knock on the door caught her attention. She looked up to see Elaine standing in the doorway, a pained look on her face.

"Do you have a few moments? Someone wants to see you," Elaine said.

Her voice was strained.

"Can you tell me who it is?" Nadine wondered if it was someone from Skyline. Clint would have a fit if it was.

"Um...Okay..." Elaine stepped into her office and closed the door.

"What's wrong?" Nadine's radar was on full alert now. "Who is this person?"

"Promise you won't stab me with your letter opener?"

"Tell me why I might do that?"

"Just bear with me. There's a guy in the reception room..."

"Okay," Nadine said, rotating one hand impatiently.

"His name is Trace Bennet."

"What?"

"He says he's Trace Bennet."

"Is this a joke?" Nadine struggled to find her breath.

Elaine leaned further back as if afraid Nadine might, in fact, attack her with an office supply. She looked a bit green. "He said his name is Trace. Trace Bennet."

Nadine had to shake her head to settle the questions and thoughts.

"You sure he's not pulling your leg?"

"He gave me a business card, and he's kind of cute," Elaine added with a feeble smile. "I don't think he's a stalker either. He seemed sincere."

Nadine sighed and pressed her palms to her cheeks. "Okay. Okay, send him in."

"Do you want Wally or Clint around? In case he is trouble?"

"You told me you don't think he's a stalker, though right about now, I'm mistrusting your judgment." Nadine stood. "Just send him in already."

Elaine scurried out of the office, leaving Nadine to wonder what in the world she had started with her "boyfriend."

A moment later Elaine appeared at the door with a tall, rather good-looking man. He had wavy red hair and gray eyes that seemed to sparkle with amusement. His grin underlined the humor in his eyes.

"So, Nadine, this is Trace. Trace Bennet."

"I'm so glad to finally meet you," Trace said, holding out a hand to her, while a dimple appeared in one cheek. He wore a loose sweater and blue jeans and looked very self-confident.

And not at all like a stalker.

Nadine forced a smile and then took his outstretched hand. "Sure. Yeah."

Elaine stood behind Trace, lifting her hands in a what-can-I-do gesture.

"I'm a little confused here," Trace said.

That makes two of us.

"Well, we can see what we can do about that," Nadine said with a shaky laugh. "Please, sit down."

"I think I had better check on some coffee." Elaine took a few steps backward, bumping into the door before she beat a hasty retreat.

Nadine sighed and looked once more at Trace Bennet. What coincidence had caused her to come up with this man's name? This man who was very handsome and frighteningly real, now seated in a chair, smiling hesitantly at her?

"I have to apologize, Mr. Bennet..." Her usual interviewing skills disappeared.

"That's okay." He smiled and leaned forward. "I'm guessing it was a coincidence. I had to come to this office this morning, anyhow. When I noticed my name and yours in the paper, I thought maybe I should talk to you."

Nadine was puzzled, his name echoing from some other source in her mind. "Why did you have to come to this office?"

"I'm starting a new business and needed to talk to you, as the editor, about covering our opening day. I had sent you some information."

Nadine looked at him, and suddenly it all fell into place. There'd been a letter. A new farm implement dealership. With his name on the e-mail. "That's where I got the name."

"Pardon me?" Trace looked confused.

"The papers you sent me. I must have pulled your name from there. That night, when Grandma…" She shook her head to clear her thoughts.

"When Grandma…" he prompted.

"It doesn't matter," Nadine replied, embarrassed. "It's a long story, and you're a complete stranger who, unfortunately, got caught up in a bunch of lies. I'm very, very sorry."

"Don't be. Nothing bad came of it." Trace smiled. "I'm glad I came down to the office today."

The door opened and Elaine bustled in, carrying a tray bearing two steaming mugs of coffee and a plate of some broken cookies. "Sorry," she said. "I had to rescue the bag from Wally." She set the tray on the desk by Nadine and was about to execute another hasty exit when Nadine reached over and caught her friend by the arm.

"You've already met Elaine, but I bet she didn't tell you she was instrumental in this whole business." Nadine forced a smile at her friend, squeezing her fingers on her arm.

"What?" Elaine sputtered. "You're the one who came up with the name." Elaine turned to Trace, pressing one hand against her chest. "Honest. I just worked with the raw material provided by my friend Nadine. What I did was just embroidery."

Nadine let go, shaking her head at her friend's duplicity. "I didn't think you'd put it in the newspaper for everyone to read…"

"No. I put it in the newspaper for your grandma to read." Elaine turned to Nadine, an exasperated expression on her face. "That was the point, wasn't it? To let Grandma know you had a boyfriend so she would move out of your house and leave you alone?"

"Somehow, it worked out that the whole county got to read that little tidbit, as well…"

"Excuse me, girls," Trace interrupted with a laugh. "It's really not a problem."

"No?" they both said at once, turning in unison to him.

"Not at all. I'm new in town." He lifted his hands in a gesture of surrender. "I wanted to meet Nadine anyway. On a purely professional basis. When I saw that we had attended the movie in Eastbar, well, I was intrigued."

"That's great," Elaine said to Nadine. "Here's your boyfriend. All you need to do is bring him home to Grandma."

"Just a minute, Elaine…" sputtered Nadine, seeing an instant need to take control of the situation. "Mr. Bennet is a stranger. He's here to do business." She sat back, feeling overwhelmed.

Trace Bennet clasped his hands behind his head, looking perfectly at ease. "Why don't you tell me the history of this little episode? I think it's the least you can do," he added in a teasing tone.

Nadine bit her lip, looking contritely at him. "If I had known…"

"I said it's okay," he said, grinning. "So, I gather there's a grandma in this sordid tale."

Elaine sat down beside him, appearing more than ready to fill him in.

"Elaine, maybe you had better see if Julie needs any help out front?"

Her friend frowned, then, taking the broad hint, stood, but gave Trace one more quick smile.

When the door closed behind her, Nadine pulled in a long breath, trying to steady her racing heart, hoping the embarrassed flush on her cheeks wasn't too obvious.

"Anyhow, the story," Nadine began again. "My grandma has been living with me for the past five years, ever since my mother got sick. I've always been very thankful for what she's done, but she was never content to sit back and let other people live their lives. The problem is, she won't rest until her only single granddaughter, being me, is married or, at the least, settled down with a boyfriend."

"Which was supposed to be me," Trace said with a grin.

"Which was *supposed* to be a fictional character," Nadine said. "Your name popped out one day when I found out she was inviting all kinds of single men over for supper." Nadine lifted her hands in surrender. "I'd had enough and told her I had a date that night, and somehow—I guess from skimming over the material—your name came to mind. Elaine ran with it and this is the result."

"Believe me, I'm not one bit sorry that our names were linked in the newspaper. The next question is, where do we go from here?"

"We break up, of course." She had to put an end to this for Trace Bennet's sake and her own.

Trace stroked his jaw with one hand, his eyes still on her. "But why? You need a boyfriend, and I could use the help of someone who knows the people of this town. Maybe make some helpful introductions to prospective clients. I don't think we should end such a compatible match over such a little misunderstanding." He smiled, a dimple winking at her from beside his mouth.

Nadine felt a softening. Trace had a gentle charm about him, and she felt guilty about using this man's name. But the thought of hoodwinking not only her grandma but also the citizens of the town she lived in made her hesitate.

And what will Clint think?

Nadine wished she could dismiss that thought.

"If we went out together, you wouldn't be lying to your grandmother," Trace continued, sounding far too reasonable for a man who had just been hoodwinked.

"You're not a stalker, are you?" Nadine asked.

"Considering how things happened, that would be a question I should be asking you." Trace's dimple appeared again, and Nadine had to concede.

"Besides, dating a beautiful girl like you would hardly be a hardship." Trace stood up, his hands in his pockets. "I don't mind, if you don't."

"No," squeaked Nadine. "Not really."

"Good. We can start off with dinner tonight at the Riverside Inn. You can fill me in on the town and its occupants."

Nadine nodded, feeling once again as if someone was taking control of her life. But as she looked up at Trace's handsome face, she thought that maybe, this time, things might work out.

"Great." He reached out a hand, and automatically Nadine caught it. "It's a deal, then. I'll pick you up from your place tonight, and we'll celebrate our first official 'date.'" He winked at her. "Where do you live?"

Nadine gave him her address, then he left, and she stared at the closed door, feeling bemused, overwhelmed, and oddly satisfied. Trace Bennet was a charming, fine-looking man. And the thought of spending an evening with him made her feel wanted.

Okay, Lord, was this it? Was this the answer to my prayer? She smiled. She would find out in time.

CHAPTER 6

*A*s Nadine poured herself some tea from a miniature silver pot, she looked across the table at Trace, studying him as he stirred his coffee.

He glanced up at her and smiled. "And what is Nadine Laidlaw thinking of now?"

"Actually, I'm wondering why you wanted to take me out." She stopped, realizing how that sounded, then added, "I mean, after what we did to you."

"I'm lonely, I'm new in town, and I want to get to know you better." He set his cup down, lowering his voice to a more intimate level. "I've been wondering about you for a while."

"What do you mean?"

"I've been subscribing to the paper since before I came. Scoping the place out you might say. I knew our dealership would make a move here, and I wanted to find out more about the community. What better way than the paper?"

"You are very thorough."

"I try. I've read your articles. You are a very principled person. You've got strong values that come out in your writing." He leaned closer. "I think that little mistake your friend made wasn't just a mistake. I think this meeting was meant to be."

Nadine blinked, trying to absorb his words. While his declaration had been pleasant, it created a feeling of discomfort she couldn't put a finger on.

He smiled then, easing the intensity of the moment. "I feel it is only right we spend this evening getting to know each other better." He picked up his coffee and took a sip. "Why don't we start with you?"

"I don't know," she said, gathering her thoughts. "There's not much to tell."

"Try me."

Nadine lifted her hands and then, with a laugh, started. "I was born here in Sweet Creek, went to school here, left and got my journalism degree, came back when my father died, and my mother became ill. Got a job at the *Sweet Creek Chronicle,* moved from reporter to editor, where I am now."

"That was a concise résumé."

"I've had a concise life." Nadine shrugged. She took a sip of her tea as she looked past him—just in time to see Clint Fletcher get up from the table where he had been sitting. How long had he been there?

Just then Clint looked around, catching her gaze. Disconcerted, she watched as he paused, then, to her dismay, sauntered over.

"Hello, Nadine." He turned to Trace, and Nadine had no choice but to introduce them.

"Trace, this is Clint Fletcher, my boss. Fletcher, this is Trace Bennet." She forced a smile. "Trace is starting an implement dealership in town."

Trace stood and held out a hand to Clint. "Pleased to meet you," Trace said. "Would you like to join us?"

But to Nadine's relief, Clint shook his head. "No. I have to be on my way." His mouth was curved in a polite smile. "Thanks for the offer, though."

"I'll have to make arrangements to talk to you sometime," Trace said, sitting down again. "You can tell me all about Sweet Creek."

Clint glanced at Nadine. "Nadine has spent her entire life here and can fill you in better than I can on the goings-on of the town." He jingled the change in his pocket a moment. "I hope you two have a pleasant evening."

"And I hope it is to be the first date of many," said Trace, a touch of humor in his voice.

"The first?" Clint asked. Nadine's gaze flew up to his, then she looked away, blushing again. Of course Clint would catch that little slip; he was a reporter after all.

"I guess Trace doesn't count the movie as a date," she said.

Clint nodded, then turned and walked away.

"Your boss has quite a forceful presence, doesn't he?" Trace remarked.

"When he wants to," she said, her tone abrupt.

"Has he lived here long?"

"No. He moved here when he was in grade eleven and came to live with his uncle and my old boss, Dory Strepchuk. He used to own the paper, and Clint took over from him." Nadine took another sip of her tea, now cool, and set it down with a grimace. She didn't want to talk about her boss. She could still feel his eyes on her, his assessing of Trace. For some reason, she didn't want him to see her and Trace together.

"But you seem to know him well."

"I should." Nadine laughed shortly. "He dated my sister."

"You have sisters?"

Nadine spun her teacup. "Two. Sabrina and Leslie. Twins. Both tall, blond, gorgeous. Which I am not."

"Why do you put yourself down like that?" he asked.

Nadine shrugged, uncomfortable with his scrutiny. "It's not a put-down, merely the facts."

"You're a very attractive person. You have such beautiful, deep brown eyes, and such lovely hair." He paused as he looked her face over.

Nadine tried not to feel uncomfortable, tried not to let herself believe what he was saying.

He sighed a moment. "You have an earthy beauty..."

"Wholesome." Nadine couldn't keep the dour note out of her voice, nor was she able to stop the faint flush that crept up her cheeks at his kind words. "You can stop now."

"I will. For now." He winked at her. "So, now I know you have two sisters and a grandma. How about your parents?" he prompted.

Nadine looked down at her tea, curving her fingers around the cup as if trying to warm it up. "My father was killed in a logging accident about six years ago. My mother died about six months ago."

"I'm so sorry to hear that."

"She had ALS, Lou Gehrig's disease. It was better." She looked away, anxious to change the subject. Her mother's death wasn't news, but lately, it seemed to bring up sorrow and regrets she didn't want to deal with; not in front of a stranger, no matter how kind he might be. "And what about your family?" she asked as a way of deflecting any more questions.

And Trace told her about the Bennets. They still lived in the Fraser Valley and had a dairy farm. Trace had worked for an international implement dealer, and from there, had moved up. Now he was poised to start his own franchise. He had been scouting likely locations for the past year and had settled on Sweet Creek.

"But I've been looking for more than just a place to build a dealership." He winked at Nadine. "I sure didn't expect to find such a good-looking date this quick."

"Let's not talk about that one, okay?" she pleaded.

"How many times do I have to tell you? I'm enjoying myself."
He shook his head. "Now you have to tell me more about yourself.
What about your hopes, your dreams?"

Hopes and dreams? Had she even an opportunity in the past
years to figure out what she wanted?

"Stuck?" he prodded.

She shook her head. "I've spent so much time taking care of
my mother and working that I haven't had a chance to hope and
dream." She looked back at Trace and dismissed her melancholy
with a light laugh. "I guess I just want to make a difference."

"That's a good goal."

"What about you?"

He chuckled at her question. "Ever the reporter, aren't you?"

"Occupational hazard," she said.

He sat back and started talking. Their conversation then
ranged from the town to politics, books they had read, movies
they had seen.

The rest of the evening went by far too quickly, and soon it
was time to go. As he pulled up to her building, Nadine noticed
one light burning in the living room of her apartment. Grandma
was waiting up.

They walked into the building and Trace stopped at the door
to her apartment, stretching out their farewell.

"Will I be able to see you next time I'm in town?" Trace picked
up her hand, playing with her fingers.

"Sure," Nadine said, suppressing a thrill of anticipation.
"Thanks for a lovely evening. I enjoyed it thoroughly."

The door behind them creaked open. "Nadine, are you still
out there?"

Nadine stiffened at the sound of her grandmother's voice. "Yes,
Grandma."

"You should come in," Grandma stepped out into the hallway,
wrapping her fleece robe around her. "It's late."

Nadine glanced back at Trace, who, thankfully, hadn't changed expression at the sight of this diminutive woman.

"Trace, this is my Grandma Laidlaw. Grandma, this is Trace Bennet."

Grandma kept her hands around her waist and only nodded in acknowledgment. "So I finally get to meet you, Mr. Bennet."

"Pleased to meet you." Trace held out his hand to Grandma. She took it begrudgingly and shook it. "And please call me Trace."

"I will." She looked him over once and then gave him a polite smile. "It's late, Nadine, and I'm sure both you and Mr. Bennet have an early day at work tomorrow."

"I'll be in shortly, Grandma," Nadine replied in a warning tone. Grandma was talking to her like she would a teenage daughter late for curfew. This was really stepping over the line.

Barbara was unrepentant. She glanced once more in Trace's general direction. "Nice to meet you," she said, her tone conveying anything but. As she left, Nadine turned to Trace.

"Sorry about her. She takes notions. And the notion she has in her grip tonight is that she refuses to like anyone she hasn't picked for me herself."

"That's okay." Trace slid his hands into his pockets, hunching his shoulders. "But I still want to see you again." He grinned at her and straightened. For a moment, Nadine thought he would kiss her, but he only touched her cheek with one finger. "I'll call," he whispered. Then he left.

Nadine watched him go, a sigh lifting her shoulders. She walked to the glass doors and watched as he drove away.

After she'd dropped Jack and come back to Sweet Creek, she had no time to date. Since her mother's illness she hadn't gone on a real date until tonight.

Nadine wrinkled her nose and laughed shortly—even this date had been manufactured.

"Special delivery for you, Nadine." Julie breezed into Nadine's office two days later carrying a huge bouquet of white roses.

Nadine reached for the flowers, surprised and pleased. "Who are they from?"

"That's what I'd like to know. Here, this came with them." Julie handed Nadine an envelope. She opened it and pulled out the small card, then smiled. Trace.

She went in search of a vase, carrying the roses with her. She found a jar and was returning to her office, her nose buried in the bouquet, when she literally bumped into Clint Fletcher.

He caught her by the elbows and steadied her, then glanced at the bouquet.

"A secret admirer?" he said, his expression serious.

"This one's not a secret," she said with a self-conscious smile. "They came from Trace."

He cocked an eyebrow at her, still not smiling. "The boyfriend?"

Nadine didn't appreciate the ironic tone of his voice. "Yes. I got them this morning," she answered.

"He's certainly expressing his affection in an atypical fashion." Clint flicked a finger at the flowers. "I always labored under the impression that red roses were the flower of choice in a romance."

Where does he haul out that language from? "Well, labor no more, Fletcher. These days, anything goes." Nadine took a noisy sniff of her flowers, her eyes on Clint.

"It would seem that way," Clint said dryly.

"Boss, can you come here a moment?" Wally, the other reporter, called out from the end of the hallway.

She turned and watched him go, puzzled at his comment and his attitude.

Shrugging off Clint's reaction, she returned to her office. She had a few calls to make, some follow-up work to do, and mail to go over.

And it was Clint's and her turn to "Face Off."

The weekly column was Dory Strepchuk's legacy. Each week, two of the staff of any of the three sister papers took an opposing view on a controversial subject. This week, by some twist of fate, she and Clint had to go head-to-head on the topic "Should the government bail out large companies?" Thankfully, Clint had chosen the "yes" side.

And that was okay with her.

Her phone was ringing as she stepped into her office. It was Trace.

"Get my flowers?" he asked.

"I did. Thanks so much. They're beautiful."

"Not as beautiful as you are." Trace chuckled. "That's a pretty corny line, but it's true. And you're simply supposed to say 'thank you.'"

Nadine tried not to take his compliment seriously. "Thanks, Trace. They are very lovely."

"Got them because. I miss you, you know."

"We only met two days ago."

"But I feel very comfortable with you, Nadine," he said, his tone serious. "I feel like I know you very well."

For once, Nadine didn't know what to say. Trace seemed almost too good to be true.

"I'm coming to town on Thursday. There's a new movie showing in Eastbar. I thought we could go out for supper and then hit the movie. Just like we did last week." He laughed. "What do you think?"

Nadine couldn't help the smile that curved her lips. "Sounds wonderful."

"This might sound silly, but I think we're meant for each other, Nadine. I'm looking forward to getting to know you better."

"Me, too," was all she could say. "Me, too."

"Why do we allow our government to bail out megacorporations," read Nadine out loud, "while ignoring the daily bankruptcy of small, home-based businesses, owned by families and in financial difficulty because of circumstances beyond their control? Is their plight less important than that of large companies?" Nadine folded the papers with a grin and set them on the table at the Riverside Inn. "And my column goes on to make many more very scintillating points."

"Very well done," agreed Elaine, pulling a sprout out of her bagel. "Emotional, but well done."

"Of course, it's emotional—it's an editorial. And I'm facing off against Clint. I need to make my point."

"Well, you do tend to make very pointy points whenever you write about anything even remotely connected to Skyline, who, I'm guessing, is the megacorporation you're nattering about."

Nadine frowned, lifting her chin in a defensive gesture. "They've received a ton of bailouts. You know it isn't right."

"So have lots of other companies. And they do employ a lot of people who would otherwise lose their jobs. That isn't right either."

"But that doesn't make it any better." Despite her brave words, Nadine felt a quiver of anxiety.

"No, but you do seem to make a point of zeroing in on them."

Nadine caught an underlying emotion in her friend's voice. "I'm sensing some sub to that text."

Her friend wrinkled her nose and shrugged, then held her gaze. "I know why you want to do this, and I used to think it was admirable. But, your ongoing fight has been taking over your life since your mother died."

"What are you saying?"

Elaine set her bagel down, wiped her hand, then reached across the table and held Nadine's hand. "I know you feel bad that you couldn't get further on your father's case, and that you wanted it resolved before she died, but nothing has changed."

Nadine thought of the letter she had received. She felt as if she was on the edge of a huge change.

She couldn't tell Elaine.

"I think you'd be a lot happier if you let it go. Let it stop defining you."

Nadine let her friend's words rest in her soul, and for a moment, she was tempted to give in. To let go. To stop fighting.

"It won't bring your father back," Elaine said.

"I know that," she said, unable to keep the prickly tone from her voice. "But, I feel, in my heart, they were responsible. I can't let the company that I think callously ignored my father's death get off scot-free."

Elaine nodded. "And what about Clint?"

"What about him?"

"You know he'll end up in trouble over this."

"I had an empty spot I needed to fill," Nadine said defensively. "With the 'Face Off' column, it's a perfect fit. Skyline has been on the receiving end of a few kickbacks and government grants." Nadine smiled feebly, trying to erase the unease Elaine's words created. "Besides, I needed something serious to balance photos of beaming farmers holding up monster vegetables."

"Why don't you leave poor Clint alone?" Elaine continued. "He's got enough on his plate."

"What do you mean by that?"

Elaine took the last, tiny bite of her bagel, frowning. "A nagging partner, a potential lawsuit, and a stubborn employee who won't listen. That's more than enough," she mumbled. She finished her bagel and wiped her fingers off with a napkin. "But you don't want to talk about Clint or Skyline, so tell me about your date with Trace instead."

Nadine gladly took up the change in topic. "He's very nice. He's funny. He's good-looking."

"And Grandma?"

Nadine blew out her breath. "She's coming around." Which was a huge exaggeration.

"Now that she's met your boyfriend, is she going to give up? Move out?"

"She hasn't said."

"I gather he doesn't meet her full approval."

Nadine shook her head and finished her sandwich.

"What are you going to do?"

"I don't know." Nadine wiped her fingers and sighed.

"I can't understand why you have so much trouble with her." Elaine leaned forward, smiling. "Goodness knows she's smaller than you."

"She's also incredibly stubborn and obtuse. When I try to get a definite date, she gently reminds me of all she did for me and my mom." Nadine set her napkin aside. "That's where I cave."

"That's easy enough. Take some of the stuff you dish out to Clint and save it for Grandma. Might work."

"What is *with* you?" Nadine asked, surprised at the return to her boss. "What comments are you talking about?"

"Those snide comments you're always tossing at him. You could use them on Grandma."

"I wouldn't do that. I love my grandma."

"And you dislike Clint?" Elaine asked.

"I don't dislike him. We just seem to strike sparks off each other." Sparks that made her uneasy.

"I think you do more striking than he does."

"Where does that come from?" asked Nadine, uncomfortable with what her friend inferred. "How come suddenly you're on his side?"

"I'm not on anyone's 'side.' I've just been watching you and him, and if I didn't know any better, I'd say you had a crush on the man," she said as she pulled her debit card out of her purse.

"Are you crazy?" Nadine scrambled to her feet, dragging her

camera bag along with her. "Where in the world do you come off saying something like that?"

"If you don't like him, why do you pay so much attention to him?" Elaine walked to the front of the inn. Cory was already behind the register. "I got lunch," she said to Nadine as she swiped her card and punched in her number.

"Thanks for that, and just for the record, I don't pay that much attention to Clint."

"Have a great day, Cory," Elaine said, sauntering out of the inn, leaving a confused Nadine and an obviously interested Cory.

Nadine caught up to her friend.

"Okay. What were you talking about back there?" Nadine jogged up beside Elaine.

Elaine stopped. "I was talking about the way you treat Clint. You can't resist any chance to give him a dig or a snide comment."

Why would Elaine say that? "I don't treat him that bad," she protested. She thought back to her comments to Clint, trying to see them from Elaine's viewpoint. "Considering that he broke my sister's heart."

"Why do you still care? That was eons ago."

Nadine caught a note of reproach and thought again of her confrontation with Clint at her apartment. She'd had time to regret it, but it was done now.

"Besides, what has he ever done to you?"

Nadine looked away, rubbing her hand along the strap of her bag, trying to remember. "Give me a couple of days; I'll come up with something." Saying aloud the other reason she struggled with Clint would make her look small and petty. The fact that he preferred her sister to her, like every other guy?

Elaine nodded. "The truth is you can't think of any one incident. If you can't think of any time he's been miserable to you, you might want to wonder why you pay so much attention to him." She winked at Nadine and stepped into the office.

CHAPTER 7

"*Y*ou're wearing a skirt, Nadine?" Grandma set her cup of tea down and stared at her granddaughter as she stepped into the kitchen.

"Trace is picking me up right after work for a date tonight."

She had topped the skirt with a loose sweater and, in a fit of whimsy, wound a gauzy, patterned scarf around her neck and tucked the ends in. She had curled her hair and taken time to brush her eyelashes with mascara and her eyelids with a faint dusting of gold eye shadow. Nadine couldn't recall when she'd purchased the rarely worn makeup—maybe for Leslie's wedding? Or was it Sabrina's? Nadine was surprised that the mascara hadn't dried up.

"You look very nice," Grandma said approvingly. "The makeup looks good, as well. Sets off your pretty eyes."

"Thanks, Grandma." Nadine laughed as she bent over and kissed Barbara's cheek. "I'm trying not to feel fake," she admitted, sitting to breakfast. She wondered if she would make it to the end of the day before the hair hanging around her jawline drove her nuts.

"Well, you will turn a few heads, I'm sure." Grandma nodded

77

her approval, and Nadine felt a little better. "Clint Fletcher won't recognize you."

"I didn't do this for my boss," Nadine said more sharply than she had intended.

"Of course not." Barbara smiled. "I'm sure Trace will like the way you look."

Nadine was mollified by her grandmother's encouraging comments. "Thanks, Grandma."

They ate their breakfast in silence, Grandma reading the paper and Nadine reviewing her notes for tomorrow's interview. When Nadine left the apartment, she felt ready to face the world.

"Good morning, Julie." Nadine breezed into the office, pausing at the desk to check for any mail or messages.

Julie looked up from an ad she was writing with a smile that froze on her face when she caught sight of her editor. "Nadine?" she said, her voice weak with surprise.

Nadine grinned back and flipped a hand through her hair. "Do I look *that* different today?"

"Different enough." Julie shook her head. "The Nadine I know wouldn't wear a skirt except to church, and she certainly would never put on eye shadow."

"People change," she murmured, taking her mail out of the slot.

"Do they ever." Clint's disbelieving voice behind her made her head snap up.

Nadine kept her eyes straight ahead, feeling suddenly self-conscious about how she looked.

What does it matter to you what he thinks?

She curved her lips into a smile and turned to face Clint, who stood in the doorway of his office, with one shoulder propped against the doorjamb and eyebrows raised.

A sharp retort to deflect his comment came to mind, but on its heels, Elaine's admonition. She hesitated, catching his eye. Clint's expression became serious as the moment stretched out. He straightened, his eyelids lowering and his lips softening. She couldn't look away and, for some puzzling reason, didn't want to.

Flustered, she shuffled through the envelopes, dropping a couple. As she bent to pick them up, other hands beat her to it. Without looking up at Clint, she took them from him and escaped to her office.

What is wrong with you? she chided herself as she dropped her knapsack on the floor. She shook her head, as if to rearrange her thoughts and laid the mail on her already overflowing desk. *Clint Fletcher is your boss, you are Nadine Laidlaw, and you dressed up for your date with Trace.*

She walked around her desk to turn on her computer. She had set today aside to clear off some paperwork and finish up some of the columns she had written. With a little luck, she would be finished by the time Trace came.

Over the course of the morning, she looked over her articles, skipped lunch, and headed out to do an interview.

Trace phoned while Nadine was away and left the message that he would pick her up from the office a little later than he had originally planned.

She spent the better part of the afternoon looking over the résumés of people who had applied for the other reporter's job. She and Wally were each doing a job and a half to make up for the vacancy, and it was wearing both of them down. Clint helped where he could, but the workload was still too much.

The day flew by. When Nadine finally pushed herself back from her computer, she was surprised to see it was almost five forty.

Blinking, she lifted a hand to rub her eyes. Just in time, she remembered her mascara and stopped herself.

Nadine clicked her mouse to save the file she was working on, and then shut down her computer. She didn't want to work anymore. Trace would be coming for her at any moment.

She rolled her neck, looking with satisfaction over her desk, pleased with the empty spaces she could now see. She had another interview to do tomorrow, and Saturday, a volleyball tournament to cover. Thankfully, this one was in town, so she wouldn't have to travel. Trace wanted to take her out that night as well.

She went to the bathroom and checked her makeup, brushed her hair, and tried to still the butterflies in her stomach.

After all these years, she was going on a date. She grinned at herself in the mirror. And not a date of Grandma's doing, but a date with someone who wanted to be with her. Nadine tilted her head as she studied her reflection. She wasn't a vain person, but that someone wanted to be with her made her take another look at the young woman in the mirror. She winked at herself and walked out.

Half an hour later, Trace still hadn't come. Nadine had busied herself with odd jobs—she cleaned out the coffee room and gathered a few mugs from different places in the office—trying to quell her nervous tension. *What if he wasn't coming?*

She tried not to, but periodically she walked down the hall to the front door to see if Trace was waiting outside. Nadine wondered how long she should wait.

She brewed a fresh pot of coffee and leaned against the counter, waiting for the machine to finish dripping, an unwelcome feeling of melancholy coming over her. Fifteen more minutes and then she would...

What? Her stomach tightened at the thought of facing her grandmother, telling her she had been stood up.

The soft hiss of the coffee machine broke the stillness of the room. Nadine used to dread this time of the day. For the past year, any free evenings she had were spent at the hospital. The last few months of her mother's life were fraught with tension and wondering. Each time the phone rang, Nadine and her grandmother wondered if this time it was the hospital calling with bad news. Her sisters came and helped out whenever they could, but Nadine knew they didn't have the time she had. That meant the bulk of the visiting and doctor's consultations fell on Nadine's shoulders.

The memories always brought tears, and tonight was no exception. Nadine felt the nudge of pain and closed her eyes as it drifted over her. She tried to fight it, but couldn't.

I miss her, Lord, she prayed, pressing her hand against her mouth, tears sliding down her cheeks as the pain increased. *I know she's better off where she is, but I still miss her so much.* She drew in a deep breath, wishing she could stop the tears.

A noise behind her broke into her sorrow. She whirled around, her heart pounding.

"Sorry." Clint stood in the doorway of the coffee room, his tie loosened, his cuffs rolled up. "I didn't know you were still here."

Nadine turned away again, surreptitiously wiping at her cheeks. "That's fine," she replied, looking around for a napkin, anything to get rid of the mortifying tears.

"Nadine." He came toward her, his deep voice tinged with concern. "Is something wrong?"

She snatched up some napkins and swiped at her eyes. "Do you want some coffee?" she asked, her voice muffled by the napkin.

"I can get it," he replied, stepping past her and thankfully not glancing her way. He stood with his broad back to her, his shirt pulling across his shoulders as he reached up for a cup. He poured himself some coffee and then glanced over his shoulder at her.

"I'm sorry if I embarrassed you." He turned to face her. "I don't mean to intrude."

Nadine looked down at the crumpled napkin, now smeared with mascara. She shook her head at her own clumsiness. "I'm fine" was all she could manage.

"Has something happened?" he persisted.

"No. Nothing." She didn't want him to see her like this.

"Really?"

Nadine hesitated, her previous encounters with Clint creating a barrier. She remembered once again Elaine's comment. He had been a visitor in their home many times, had met her mother, and knew Grandma. He had been a large part of her life for a time. She had to concede he was the kind of old friend who could be told the truth.

"Nothing happened," Nadine said with a shaky smile. She took a deep breath to steady her voice. "I just...miss my mother." She bit back another soft cry and could speak no more. Another set of tears drifted down her cheeks.

Clint said nothing, and for that Nadine was thankful. He stood —quiet, waiting, listening; his gaze serious and interested. Sympathetic, yet with no trace of pity.

Nadine inhaled deeply, studying the smeared napkin. "Silly, isn't it? She's been dead six months, and it seems like I'm sadder now than I was when she died."

"Six months isn't that long," he replied. "I would think it takes years to get over the death of someone you love."

Nadine nodded. "I remember my mom crying over my dad up until a couple of years ago."

"I think it's an inspiration, the way your mother loved your father." Clint laughed shortly. "You were lucky to see that while you were growing up."

"You were...never close to your parents, were you?" she asked.

"Hard to be close to a couple who seldom talked to each other, let alone their son." He sounded a bit bitter.

Nadine wiped her nose with the napkin, surprised at his admission. She said, "But they sent you on that trip to Europe."

"Spending money was the easiest solution to any of my parents' problems."

"Leslie told us you came to Sweet Creek because of some trouble you'd gotten into."

Clint released a harsh laugh. "That was part of the reason. Truth was, I think my parents saw that as a way to get me out of their mess."

"Mess?"

Clint held her gaze a moment then shook his head. "Doesn't matter. I just know that when I met your family, I was jealous."

His voice took on a faint yearning tone, and once again, Nadine felt confused. "We didn't have much."

"You had everything anyone could want."

"And that was?"

"Parents who cared about their kids. I always admired your mother's strength," Clint continued, setting down his coffee cup. "She did a good job raising you girls, teaching you the right things. I'm sure she must have been proud of you."

Nadine shrugged. "Well, at least Sabrina and Leslie got themselves married."

Clint said nothing to that, and Nadine sniffed once again, wiping at her eyes.

"You have nothing to be ashamed of," Clint said finally. "Jack was a fool to let you go, and I hope Trace is worthy of you."

Nadine looked up at that, blinking away more tears as she caught Clint's steady gaze. She looked at him again as if seeing him with new eyes.

"Were you a fool to let Leslie go?" she whispered, unable to let go of that.

Clint pulled in a long, slow breath. "We both decided it was the right thing to do," he said.

"Both?" This was the first Nadine had heard of this. According to Leslie, the breakup was all Clint's doing.

"If you want to find out more, you should ask your sister," Clint said, giving her a rueful smile.

"Why don't you tell me now?" Nadine asked, sensing there was more to the story than what her sister had always told her.

A sudden knocking on the front door startled them both. "Hello, anybody there?" Trace's muffled voice drifted down the hallway.

"Well. Looks like your date is finally here," Clint pulled away, his voice dry.

Nadine turned to leave, but was surprised when Clint caught her arm to stop her. "Just a minute," he said, picking up a napkin. He tugged her arm to bring her closer. "Your mascara is smudged," he said.

Nadine felt a most peculiar sensation as she looked up. His hazel eyes drew her in. She felt the warmth of his hand encircling her arm and of his fingers brushing her cheek as he wiped a smudge away. She raised her hand to rest it on his shoulder as she felt herself drift toward him.

Another loud knock on the door broke the moment.

"You better go before your ardent suitor breaks down the door," said Clint dryly, letting her go.

Nadine nodded, feeling breathless. She stopped at the doorway, and looked back at Clint. But he had his coffee in his hand and was sipping it, his eyes downcast.

Shaking off the feelings he had aroused, she ran down the hallway.

"Wow. Do you ever look terrific," Trace greeted her appreciatively. "I didn't think you could get even more gorgeous."

Nadine smiled, passing off his compliments with a dismissive gesture.

Trace caught her hands. "I know what that means, you silly girl. Hey, sorry I'm late," he said. "I got stuck at the bank." He pulled her closer and kissed her on her cheek. "Forgive me?"

"I was wondering if you were standing me up."

"Are you kidding?" Trace pulled her close to him. "A guy would have to be crazy to do that to someone like you." He kissed her again. "The movie just started. We can grab supper later."

Nadine ran back down the hallway and got her purse from her office. She stepped out of her office, and, pausing a moment, walked back to the coffee room. Clint still stood at the counter, his coffee cup in his hands.

He looked at her. "Still here?" was all he said.

Nadine bit her lip, unable to pass off what just happened, unsure of what to make of it. "Thanks," she said finally, hoping he understood what she meant. "For everything."

Clint nodded. "Any time, Nadine," he replied softly. "Any time at all."

"C'mon, gorgeous," Trace called. "The night isn't getting any younger."

"See you Monday," she said, then turned and left.

Nadine checked the picture she had taken as the noise of the winning team roiled around her. It was Saturday night. The home team had won their invitational volleyball tournament and was celebrating in the true manner of high school champions.

They were screaming their fool heads off.

Nadine checked the last few shots then turned her camera off and dropped it and the other one she had looped around her neck into her large camera bag. She would load the pictures onto the computer tonight and see what she could do with them before deadline on Monday.

"There you are." Trace's voice behind her made her whirl around in surprise. He wore a denim jacket, blue jeans, and cowboy boots. He looked like a rodeo poster boy—rugged and almost too handsome.

"Hi." She smiled up at him, and he reached out and tucked a strand of hair behind her ear. "You're early."

"I was even earlier than you think. I watched the final game."

"They're pretty good, aren't they?"

"I wouldn't know." He took her bag from her and winked at her. "I kept getting distracted by this cute reporter on the sidelines snapping pictures."

Nadine just shook her head at his lavish compliments and

slung her knapsack over her shoulder, leading the way out of the gym. As they passed the group of celebrating teenagers, a few of the girls cast admiring glances Trace's way. Nadine knew she shouldn't feel proud, but she did. Nothing boosted a girl's ego more than knowing that other women, no matter how young, thought your escort was good-looking.

She looked up at him and caught him smiling down at her. "I missed you, Nadine," he said.

Nadine looked away, her feelings uncertain. On the one hand, she felt inundated with his charm, his obvious attraction to her, yet she couldn't help but feel uncomfortable with how quickly he'd laid a claim to her. His intensity didn't seem right, for a reason she couldn't put her finger on.

They walked out to his truck and as they did, Nadine's cell phone rang. She pulled it out and answered it. It was Grandma.

"I'll be home in a while, Grandma. Don't wait up for me." Nadine rolled her eyes at her grandmother's response, then ended the phone call.

"Handy things, aren't they?" Trace said with a grin as he unlocked the door and opened it for her.

"Not really. I wish I didn't have to carry it around, even though it is a great tool for a reporter." Nadine got into the car and laid the phone on the seat as she buckled up.

"Where do you want to go tonight?" Trace asked as he started up the car and backed out of the school parking lot.

Nadine shrugged, stifling a yawn. She had been busy all day and hadn't given a thought to dinner.

"You look tired," Trace said as he pulled into the street. "How about someplace quiet?" He grinned at her and, gunning the engine, headed down the street.

Once again, they ended up at the Riverside Inn. She ordered soup and a salad, and Trace ordered a burger.

Nadine felt a little better once she'd eaten. Trace was stimulating company, and he made her laugh. The talk stayed light, something for which Nadine was grateful. She was also thankful when Trace said he had to leave early.

She was also thankful Clint wasn't at the inn tonight as he had been the last time.

"Looks like your grandma is still up," he commented as they walked up to the apartment.

"She usually goes to bed." Nadine shook her head knowing that since she started "dating" Trace, her grandmother stayed up until she got home. "I'd invite you in, but with Grandma still up..."

Trace shrugged. "I don't want to bother her. Besides, I hope to come here tomorrow after church. If that's okay," he added quickly.

Nadine smiled back, a feeling of well-being bubbling up in her. "I'm looking forward to it."

Trace caught her close, and he lowered his head to kiss her. A cough sounded in the hallway behind them.

"Nadine, are you coming in?" Barbara demanded, her voice querulous. Her gray head poked into the hallway.

Trace pulled back and winked at Nadine. "I should let you go." He ran a finger down her chin and then looked past her. "Hello, Mrs. Laidlaw. How are you?"

"Tired," said Grandma. This time, she sounded a little more friendly; maybe she was warming up to Trace.

"I'm sorry." Trace looked back at Nadine. "I guess this is goodnight?"

Nadine nodded, curiously glad Grandma had shown up. She felt once again that Trace was moving too quickly. Too quickly for her, anyway.

Trace flashed her a grin. "I'll see you at church tomorrow?"

"I'd like that," she said softly.

"Good." He winked at her and then, with a quick wave at Grandma, left.

Nadine watched as he pulled open the doors and sauntered

down the walk. He got in the truck, waved at Nadine, and drove away.

"So," Grandma said from behind her. "Why didn't he come in?"

Nadine sighed and turned to face her grandma. "I think he's afraid of you."

Barbara snorted at that. "He looks a little too polished for my liking."

"How can you say that? He wears blue jeans and cowboy boots."

Barbara shrugged and sat on a kitchen chair. "It's just an impression."

Nadine turned on the tap and filled a glass with cold water. "I don't know why you dislike him."

"I don't dislike him, Naddy. What a thing to say." Barbara sounded hurt.

Nadine gulped down the water and set the glass on the sink. "You don't treat him very well. The last time he stopped by here, he asked me what I had told you about him."

Barbara fingered the belt of her housecoat, her eyes downcast. "I don't trust him, Naddy," she mumbled. She looked up, her blue eyes softened with concern. "I'm just not comfortable with him. I would much prefer it if you were to go out with..."

Nadine held a hand up. "Stop right there, Grandma." She tilted her head, studying her grandmother. "I think you don't like him because you didn't handpick him for me yourself."

"I already said I don't dislike him," protested Barbara.

"Well, treat him better tomorrow, because he's coming over," Nadine announced, a warning note in her voice.

"I will, Nadine. I'm not rude."

"No, you're not," conceded Nadine. "But I know how you can smile and sting at the same time."

"I'll be kind and considerate."

But Barbara didn't have to exert herself because Trace didn't show up at church the next day and consequently didn't come to the Laidlaw residence for the Sunday lunch Nadine had risen so early to prepare.

Nadine tried to hide her disappointment and Barbara tried to hide her triumph—neither was successful. As a result, Sunday was not the blessing it should have been.

CHAPTER 8

*N*adine spread the latest edition of the *Sweet Creek Chronicle* out, propped her elbows on her desk, and began her Tuesday-morning hunt for typos. It didn't matter how up-to-date the technology or how eagle-eyed their copy editor, on a good day only one typo slipped through, on a bad...

Nadine sighed, pulled out her red pen, and circled the spelling mistake that jumped off the page at her.

She glanced over a few more articles, turned a few more pages, then stopped at her article on Skyline. She skimmed it, then reread it to make sure she had been balanced and fair.

Nadine tried to read it critically, which was difficult when the words were so familiar. It had taken her a couple of drafts to get it just right.

"Their labor practices are questionable, and when asked for a copy of their safety code, this reporter was brushed off. What do they have to hide? And why do they continue to obtain government grants by fair means or foul..." Nadine read. And it got stronger after that.

Because when it came to Skyline, she had emotion to spare.

Nadine sat back and closed her eyes, reliving the helpless anger and frustration and grief of her father's life wasted by a company that lied. So much had been taken away from them, with so little explanation.

I want to bring these guys to justice, Lord, she prayed, as she so often did when she thought of Skyline and all the sorrow their actions had caused. *Show me the right way; show me how to do this.* But the prayer brought no peace, no answer. She knew only that she felt better doing *something* instead of sitting back, a helpless David facing down an indifferent Goliath.

"Call for you on line one, Nadine," Julie's voice came over the intercom. "It's Trace. Oh, and some woman phoned for you a few minutes ago. Didn't leave her name."

"Thanks, Julie." Drawing in a deep breath, Nadine picked up the phone. "Hey Trace."

"Hey girl. How's things?"

"Good. I missed you Sunday," she said.

"Yeah. Sorry about that."

He didn't sound as repentant as he should, considering all the work she had gone through to make lunch.

"How are you otherwise?" she asked.

"I have to bail on seeing you tonight. I have to run into Edmonton to meet with one of the company execs I'll be working with."

"What time will you be back?"

"Not sure. Sorry." This time he sounded more contrite.

Nadine sighed her disappointment. "Okay," she said.

"Hey, Nadine, I'm really sorry."

"Of course you are." She was unable to keep the sarcasm out of her voice as she recalled Sunday's also-broken promise. It shouldn't matter as much as it did. She still wasn't sure how she felt about Trace, but it was so wonderful to be wanted, to look forward to being with someone. "I'll see you when I see you then."

She hung up the phone and fell back against her chair. *Not an auspicious start to the week,* she thought. And tomorrow she had to head off to the FoodGrains project, which would keep her tied up all day. Normally she didn't mind, but the paper was still short-handed and Wally was supposed to go with her.

Wally was a good writer, but had a hard time staying focused when he was out and about in a large group. He spent so much time chatting up people, he often forgot to take notes.

An abrupt rap on the door made her sit up. "Come in," she called, folding up the newspaper.

The door opened and Clint stepped inside.

He dropped the newspaper on her desk and stood in front of her, his eyes narrowed.

"I thought you weren't running the article," he said tightly.

Nadine looked at the paper folded open to her story on Skyline. "That was your thought, Fletcher, not mine."

"I called you into my office last week and asked you not to run the story." His voice was even, but Nadine could hear the suppressed anger.

Nadine steeled herself to look up into Clint's irate eyes so close to hers, trying not to remember their time in the coffee room; that small moment of connection.

"The article is correct, and the facts have been verified by enough people that I feel more than justified in running it," she replied, her own anger building. "I also told you that we could call an editor's meeting and make a diplomatic decision on whether to run it or not."

Clint looked down at her, his hand resting on her desk. "It shouldn't have to come to a showdown of authority, Nadine."

"Maybe not," she acknowledged, "but an editor of a paper should be just that—an editor. Last I checked, that gives me certain authority in what goes into the paper."

"And last I checked, my name is on the masthead as well." He straightened. "As the owner." He held her challenging gaze. "I wish we could work together on this, Nadine," he said with a sigh.

Nadine watched him, her heart doing a slow flip. He looked vulnerable. For a moment, she felt a stirring of pity, mingled with attraction. It bothered her more than she cared to admit. It hearkened back to numerous daydreams she had spun over him years ago—and if she dared to admit it, even more recently.

And now, to her dismay, all those dreams and emotions threatened to undermine her. She was determined to see her self-appointed job to the end, and her ever-changing feelings about Clint shouldn't interfere.

Taking a deep breath, she concentrated on Skyline and the pain they had caused her family. "I don't know if we can," she said, her voice sharper than intended. "Skyline has blood on their hands. Men have died working for them. We have a responsibility to stop them."

"Your father, among the lives lost," he said.

Nadine nodded.

Clint blew out his breath and rubbed his neck. "This will help?" he asked, indicating the open newspaper.

Nadine stood and reminded herself why she was doing this: Justice. "I intend to serve notice to them, indicating that we report on more than just local sports and library board meetings." She leaned forward as if to emphasize her point. "We have a duty to expose companies like Skyline. They're crooks and liars, and if they did the same thing anywhere else, they'd have a pack of reporters on their back and lawsuits coming down their throat." She drew in a breath, afraid she was beginning to sound shrill. "I need to do this, Clint."

Clint looked across the desk at her, his features softening. "I understand why, but..."

Nadine waited for him to say more. Their gazes met, locked, and it seemed that all else, for that moment, drifted away. Nadine felt gripped by the same curious feeling from the other evening in the coffee room. Once again, she felt the tug of attraction and the pull of his personality, and she knew the feelings surfacing were the same ones that had plagued her so long ago.

She forced herself to look down and break the intense connection, busying herself with the newspapers on the desk.

She refolded his newspaper and handed it back to him, her eyes going no farther than his dark tie cinched around the collar of his gray shirt. "Here's your paper," she said.

Clint cleared his throat. "Thanks," he said as he took it. He tapped the paper against his thigh, still towering over her.

He hesitated, then finally left.

When the door closed behind him, Nadine pressed her fingers to her eyes as unwelcome tears rushed her. She dropped her face into her hands, and in the privacy of her office, allowed the confusion of her emotions to overwhelm her.

She missed her father, she still grieved her mother. She felt alone though surrounded by people who cared for her. She had been put off by Trace for the second time in two days.

And now she was falling for Clint Fletcher all over again.

How do these things happen? How can a heart work so independently of a mind?

Was she an idiot? How could she fall for a man whose presence intimidated her so much that she resorted to deflecting his attention with cutting comments?

She looked heavenward. *Why, Lord? Why am I falling for this man? He doesn't like me that way, never has. Please take away these feelings. Please.*

She stopped, as if waiting for something, anything: a feeling of reassurance, a still, small voice guiding her. But she felt nothing, heard nothing. Nadine felt as if her prayers went only as far as the ceiling above her.

And later that evening, as she sat alone in the inn, pretending to be on her date to keep her grandma off her back, she wondered what she had done to deserve the loneliness that seemed to surround her.

∾

"Two cameras, notebook, recorder." Nadine scooped her hair away from her face and retied her ponytail, pencil stuck in her mouth. Looked like she was ready to head out.

For the past few years she had been covering the local Food-Grains Bank project, a joint effort of the Sweet Creek community to grow food for people in impoverished countries. Every year it was a celebration of coming together and this year, for a change, the weather was picture perfect.

She glanced over at Wally who stood in her office door, looking pale.

"I think I've still got the flu," Wally mumbled.

"I thought you were finished with that."

"Maybe it was your article on Skyline that brought it back on," he joked.

Nadine didn't think that was funny. She and Clint had avoided each other since their standoff, but the tension between them was palpable through the whole office.

Wally groaned again and doubled over. "I think I'd better get back home," he said as he clutched his stomach.

"Okay," she grumbled, annoyed at him for still being sick and feeling guilty at her reaction. The project often required two reporters and two photographers. That's how she'd always done it. It showed the people on the project that the paper took this event seriously. "I'll drop you off on my way. Can you make it to my car?"

He nodded and slowly got up.

Nadine zipped her bag shut. "I need another SD card and a battery. I'll meet you outside."

Wally only groaned in reply and stumbled out the door.

Nadine snagged what she needed then followed him down the hall.

As she closed the door behind her she met Clint walking up the hallway, a frown on his face. "What's with Wally?" he asked.

Nadine swallowed and willed her beating heart to slow down. This was the first time since yesterday morning they had spoken. "The f-flu...I think," she said.

"Didn't you need him today?" he asked with an impatient frown.

"I guess I'll have to do without him."

"You were headed out to the FoodGrains project, weren't you?"

Nadine only nodded, wishing she could just leave. Her discomfort around Clint before the Skyline article was bad enough; since yesterday her awakened feelings had made it worse.

Clint tapped the sheaf of papers he was carrying, his lips pursed. "Do you need help?" he asked, his voice casual.

Nadine's head shot up. Why would he want to come, especially after everything that had happened? "No, no," she said hurriedly. "I'd just as soon do it on my own."

Clint nodded and Nadine realized that it sounded as if she was brushing him off. Elaine's reprimand warred with her own confusion around her boss as she forced a smile at him, and she amended her statement. "I mean...that's okay. I don't want to bother you. You've covered Wally enough the past few days."

"I don't mind. I could stand to get out for a while. Besides, I know you always do it with two people."

Nadine glanced at his suit and tie, and he looked down as well.

"Don't worry. I'll change," he said.

Nadine chewed her lip, wondering what it would be like to have him around an entire morning, wishing he'd be called to a sudden emergency. But, he was the boss. If he wanted to come, she could hardly say no.

"Sure," she said, forcing a cheerful note into her voice.

"Okay." Clint nodded without smiling. "I'll meet you at Mark Andrews's place in about an hour."

Nadine's eyes met his and once again, in spite of everything that had happened between them, she felt a pull of attraction. Their gaze held until she glanced away.

She had to be careful. Letting herself fall for this guy would be a mistake.

Besides, she had a boyfriend. Didn't she?

CHAPTER 9

*C*lint watched her go back to her office, feeling torn, wishing for a moment that he hadn't volunteered. He knew Nadine was only letting him come because she was stuck.

Part of him wanted to exert his authority, and part of him was looking forward to the first reasons he became a reporter: To be enmeshed in a story and to find an angle that would connect with the readership.

He wanted to participate in a community—something he'd only experienced here in Sweet Creek.

And what about Nadine?

He stifled a sigh, thinking of that contrary girl, wishing he could dismiss her from his thoughts. He knew coming to Sweet Creek would mean working with her. In the past, he hoped to start something special with her. But, from the first day he stepped into the office, she kept him at a firm arm's length.

He wondered why he still harbored some faint hope she would soften toward him.

Two things precluded that—her boyfriend and her opposing stance on Skyline. He had gone to her office on Tuesday morning hoping he could try once more to talk her out of the latter, and if not that, at least try to get her to tone down her rhetoric. But she was stubborn as always, and he was frustrated as always.

Matthew McKnight had called today with predictable news. He had just come out of a meeting with Skyline's lawyers. They were threatening another lawsuit if the paper didn't soften its stance toward them.

The newspaper made a comfortable living for all involved, but not a huge profit—not enough to defend against a company like Skyline.

Nadine had put him in an awkward situation. He would lose no matter which way he turned.

Because, for better or worse, he was unable to change his feelings for Nadine Laidlaw.

And he knew she wasn't letting this case go.

He had to think of his father, holed up in his study, going over strategies with his lawyer in an ongoing lawsuit against a partner he felt had shorted him of his shares.

It had consumed him, taking over his life and casting a long, dark shadow over their home life. When his father wasn't railing against the injustice, he was at court trying to defend his position. Anger had taken over to the point that Clint was ignored and his mother retreated. Money drained from the family's finances.

He was afraid the same thing would happen to Nadine if she wasn't careful; and, in the process, she would take him and his newspaper along.

He had always been attracted to her, but she'd always made it clear what she thought of him. And now, with her frustration over his breakup with Leslie returning, he wished again that he dared tell her the truth.

What would that do to her? What would that do to her relationship with her sister?

Lately he had caught a hint of vulnerability, a softening that drew him in and made him want to peel away the sarcastic outer shell.

He knew what he would find beneath that. He read her articles, sensed her deep, unwavering faith, caught the wry humor that permeated her writing. When she wrote, she showed a side of herself that she was wary to show him.

He just wished he could separate his attraction to her with his need to keep his paper afloat.

Clint shook his head as if to dislodge the thoughts. Nadine was like an itch he couldn't scratch, a puzzle he couldn't solve. He had to let go and move on.

He slowed down and turned at the entrance to the farm. As he did, in spite of his lovelorn state, a smile pulled on his lips. Tall, columnar poplars lined the driveway, creating a stately entrance and opening up to a large, log home situated on a hill overlooking the valley and the mountains beyond.

When his parents shipped him off to Uncle Dory all those years ago, it was with the hope that the calm, straightforward man would be able to turn their son around. What Dory did was keep Clint very busy.

As well as three newspapers, Dory owned eighty acres, ten cows, three horses, chickens, rabbits, potbellied pigs, and six dogs. Clint had been responsible for feeding the animals and cleaning the barns and stalls.

In time, he enjoyed the horses nuzzling him as he doled out their grain ration, nickering to him when he came to fork hay for them. He took more time with his daily chores. Working with the animals brought about a sense of satisfaction that had been missing from Clint's life in the city.

He and his patient uncle had worked well together—soon Clint helped with other jobs. Together, he and Uncle Dory finished renovating the comfortable story-and-a-half home, and Clint took as much pride in it then as he did now.

Clint slammed the door of his vehicle and strode up the gravel path to the house. He skirted the bushes nestled against the front entrance and unlocked the heavy wooden door, then shed his suit jacket and loosened his tie as he ran up the carpeted stairs to his bedroom. He turned to his cupboard to dig out more suitable clothes for a trip to the harvest project.

He selected jeans and an old corduroy shirt, carryovers from his backpacking days. He slipped on the worn clothes, feeling as if he was going back in time. Clint generally favored a more formal look for work: Ties and crisp monochrome shirts as opposed to worn sweaters and corduroy pants. This matched his preference for tight writing with newsworthy stories instead of breezy, loosely written articles that meandered all over the map like his Uncle did. It was all his way of making a statement.

Clint had put his own stamp on the newspaper. It took time to clean out the deadwood and make the changes, but on the whole, things were going well. His biggest problem was also his biggest asset.

Nadine Laidlaw. His editor and, it seemed, constant critic.

And there she was again. Stirring up trouble.

He had to stop thinking of her. Especially if she continued with this Bennet guy.

For some reason, he didn't trust Trace. He was a little too ingratiating. Too over the top.

He knew Nadine's grandmother felt the same way. She had called him up the other day to ask his opinion about the guy, loudly and clearly stating her own. Brash, overconfident, and too smarmy for her. Clint had to laugh, but he also had to agree with Barbara Laidlaw.

Not that his opinion mattered. Nadine was a big girl. She could look out for herself.

He dug through the cupboard to find his own camera and bag. Even though Nadine would take most of the pictures, he liked to hone his own skills. He checked the camera, making sure the battery was still charged, packed some extra lenses, then slung the bag over his shoulder. He walked down the stairs, pausing at the bottom as he wondered once again if he should have offered to help.

Was it her obvious frustration as she stood contemplating a sick reporter? The fact that she worked extra hard the past few weeks, covering for a reporter who had suddenly quit?

Or was it the notion of spending a morning with her, away from the office and the politics of manager and editor?

Clint blew out a sigh. It didn't matter. He had offered and now he was committed.

∼

Five combines lumbered down the field, the roar of the large diesel engines thundering through the peace of the surrounding countryside. Grain dust swirled upward and the sun shone like a benediction in a promising blue sky.

Nadine glanced again over her shoulder at the gravel road, mentally calculating how long it would take Clint to get here.

The combines had already made one full round, and she was itching to go. She couldn't wait for him and didn't want to admit that she was.

Finally she grabbed her camera bag and jumped out of her car, jogging to one of the grain trucks that stood ready to relieve the combines of the harvest.

The driver was leaning against the truck. "You're from the paper, aren't you?" he asked, pulling on the bill of his cap.

Nadine nodded as she pulled her camera and light meter out. "And I'm taking your picture." She took a quick reading, adjusted the settings on her camera, focused on the driver, and snapped her first picture. Nadine guessed from the bright logo emblazoned on his obviously new cap that the hat had been a freebie from one of the various implement dealers in the area.

Trace's competition. Once more she wondered what had happened last night. Or for that matter, Sunday. He hadn't called to explain, and she wasn't about to chase him down. She did have some pride.

An SUV pulled in behind hers. She couldn't stop the renegade beat of her heart, and when Clint stepped out of the vehicle, it was as if time had turned back.

He wore a brown corduroy shirt that hung open over a plain white T-shirt. Jeans hugged his long legs, and cowboy boots finished the look at odds with his usual tucked-in shirt and tie.

Nadine's heart slowed, then began a dangerous thumping. He looked like the old Clint Fletcher that took up so many of her dreams.

He sauntered over, notebook and pen in one hand and camera slung over his shoulder. The wind lifted his hair, making it fall carelessly over his forehead. He stopped beside her. "How long ago did they begin?"

Nadine swallowed and returned her attention to her camera, fiddling with the lens. "Just started," she muttered.

Her discomfort made her take refuge in her usual caustic comments. "Brought your own camera in case I muck up?"

Clint shook his head. "It's just for myself."

Nadine opened her mouth to apologize, then looked up at his handsome features. A soft smile played around the corners of his mouth, making him even more attractive than usual, and she changed her mind. Her sarcasm was her only defense against him.

She continued, "I should get going. I just got here and need to get some pictures. Haven't taken any yet..." *And now you're babbling, you ninny,* she reprimanded herself. *Just because he shows up dressed in jeans doesn't mean you need to make a fool of yourself.*

Besides, you have a boyfriend.

"Talk to you later," she said, then turned and ran down the field toward the combines, her heart banging against her chest. *You idiot,* she fumed, *he's just Clint Fletcher, the man you love to torment.*

Nadine took a steadying breath and lifted the camera to her

face. Five combines crested the hill, their bulky shapes silhouetted against the sharp blue sky. The thunder of their engines gave Nadine a thrill.

The combines roared toward her, gobbling up the thick, fragrant swaths that lay in readiness on the golden stubble. Grains of wheat spun through various screens inside the combines. Straw spewed out the back—it would lie there as mulch for next year's crop. Once the combines were full, the trucks would pull up alongside, and the hopper of the combine would spill its bounty in a fountain of grain destined for people in other countries who had so much less.

Behind the combine, the field looked swept clean. All that was left was stubble strewn with finely chopped straw, looking like a buzz cut on a young boy.

She had done a lot of harvest pictures over the past couple of weeks, but this particular annual harvest held a special place in her heart. The FoodGrains Bank project was a cooperative effort of the community. A large map of the quarter section or sections was displayed in the local co-op store and divided into parcels. Anyone who wished could purchase a parcel to help pay for the costs of seeding and fertilizing. The use of the land was donated, then the land was planted, sprayed for weeds, and harvested by volunteers.

The grain went to Third World countries, where it was exchanged for work from the people of the country they were assisting.

Nadine had done a piece on it each year since she first heard about it and felt as much a part of it as any of the organizers. She always bought her own acre and helped keep track of the progress of the combines, cheering when "her" part was done.

The FoodGrains Bank project always had an air of celebration about it. Local implement dealers donated combines and members of the local church prepared a lunch for the volunteers; some people came just to spectate. The project became a way of

recognizing the good things God had given the farming community close to Sweet Creek and a chance for farmers to share their
harvest with the needy.

One by one the five combines mowed down wide swaths of
grain. Once filled, they spilled out the wheat, filling the huge
truck. The truck pulled away, and the combines returned to their
swaths.

Nadine took many shots of the entire process. Then she
glanced over at the group of people standing around the huge
map of the quarter section. Clint was talking to a few of the
volunteers, smiling and nodding. He held a cup of coffee, and his
notebook was stuffed in his pocket and camera now hung around
his neck. Mark Andrews came to join him. He must have made a
joke because Clint laughed, his eyes bright, the deep timbre of his
voice warming her soul like sunlight.

Nadine felt time still, pause, and turn back. She hadn't seen
this side of Clint since he had returned to Sweet Creek a couple of
months ago. He always insisted on a measure of aloofness, always
held his emotions in reserve. But the Clint who mingled and
mixed with people on the edge of the field was so much like the
Clint who lived in Sweet Creek so many years ago, her step
faltered in reaction.

She was falling for him all over again in spite of her
"boyfriend," in spite of what he had done to Leslie.

What kind of sister falls for the man who broke her sister's
heart? And hers?

Leslie is a big girl. Married. Happy. Surely it was time to
let go?

Nadine squinted at the men standing against the white grain
box of the truck. It would be a tricky shot with the sun glaring off
the background. She raised the camera, analyzing the composi-
tion with one part of her mind even as the other part tried to
analyze her own life.

It was self-preservation that kept Trace at a distance, she

concluded, snapping a few pictures and zooming in closer as she adjusted her aperture setting. It was the same thing that kept her sniping at Clint Fletcher. Trace, she let get a bit close because she knew she could deal with him, but her heart wasn't fully engaged with him. Something about him made her keep her distance.

Clint was another story.

Nadine repressed her thoughts, concentrating on her job. She moved the camera along the group of men. They were the implement dealers and would appreciate having their picture in the paper, so she got a few more frames of them.

She stopped as Clint's face came into view. Nadine held her camera steady, unable to move on. She adjusted the zoom, pulling the picture in and adjusting the focus. Clint's mouth was curved in a crooked smile, his eyes squinted against the bright sun. A soft breeze teased his hair, softened its usual crisp style. Unable to stop herself, Nadine snapped a few pictures. Then he turned her way and—through the eye of the camera—she saw him look at her, his gaze so intent, it seemed as if he was directly in front of her instead of fifty feet away.

Nadine's breath slowed. She lowered the camera, still looking at him. He didn't turn away.

Even across this distance, awareness sparked between them.

Then she turned away, resisting the urge to look at the pictures on the camera's display. She took a few more of the combines.

Nadine had intended to spend about an hour there, but was chivvied by the organizers into staying for lunch.

"There's more than enough," said Freda Harper, wife of one of the implement dealers. She pulled Nadine over to the table, set up in the shade of a grain truck. "Besides, I understand elk burgers are on the menu."

"Sounds intriguing." Nadine's stomach clenched with hunger as she caught a whiff of the food on the barbecue. She checked out the table, spread with salads, buns, a few vegetable platters and squares. "And it sure looks good."

"Well, dish up." Freda smiled at Nadine as she helped herself to some potato salad. "We've had such a beautiful fall," Freda continued as she worked her way down the table. "I'm so glad the weatherman co-operated today, too."

"It sure has been a blessing for all the farmers and ranchers in the area," replied Nadine with a smile.

Freda nodded, her red hair glinting in the sun—a bright contrast to the yellow sweatshirt she wore—then leaned closer. "You know, I've always meant to write you a letter, but I'm not much for doing that." She smiled apologetically. "I've always wanted to say that I sure appreciate all the support you give this project. Douglas, my husband, got involved because of an article you wrote. How it's a chance for us, who have so much, to share." Freda scooped up a spoonful of salad and paused a moment. "But even more than that, I appreciate your honesty. How you're not afraid to take on who you do."

Nadine couldn't stop a niggle of unease. She knew one person who wouldn't agree with her.

Her thoughts piggybacked on what Elaine had said to her. About backing off. About how her quest to bring Skyline to justice had become detrimental to her happiness and well-being. How Nadine was letting this battle define her.

And yet. Freda's comment seemed to fuel Nadine's quest.

"Thank you," she said. "That's good to know."

Freda grinned back at her. "I imagine writing what you do is quite a contrast to volleyball scores and hockey summaries."

"Your daughter plays volleyball, doesn't she?"

Freda nodded, and the talk moved to sports and children. Nadine found out that Freda had two girls in volleyball, one in senior high and one in junior high. They also had one foster child and one adopted child. The Harpers were a giving, loving family, and Nadine had lots of questions for Freda.

By the time they got to the end of the line, they were chatting as if they had known each other much longer than the ten minutes they had spent together, and Nadine's busy reporter's mind had another idea for a feature article.

But even as she plotted, even as she thought, her eyes couldn't help drifting to Clint.

Couldn't help think, again, of what Elaine had said the other day.

Could she, for his sake, let go of the battle she'd been fighting so long?

What would she gain?

And what would she lose?

CHAPTER 10

"Sorry Nadine, but I told you I was stuck in a meeting..."

Nadine tried to smile as she shifted her phone to her other hand. "You have quite a few meetings, Trace."

"It's this new business. It's a lot of work to set up."

"Whatever." Nadine tucked the phone under her ear and squatted by her filing cabinet. She tugged it open with an angry jerk, an expression of the uncertainty that had been dogging her the past few days.

Uncertainty about Trace and, even more, about Clint.

"Really, Nadine. I'm not trying to put you on. I'll be in town in the morning. Can I come then?"

"No. I've got to interview a reporter for the opening here."

"What about Thursday night?"

She hesitated, not sure she wanted to chance the loneliness that could be created by Trace's unreliability.

"C'mon," he said, his voice wheedling. "Don't make me suffer."

"Why do I have such a hard time believing you?"

"Nadine. I really wanted to come last night."

Still she hesitated, unable to shake the feeling he had been avoiding her.

"Once things slow down, I'll have way more time. I've got a few loose ends to tie up, and once that happens, I'm all yours. You have to believe me."

Nadine didn't know if she was imagining the pleading tone of his voice. She thought of Clint and the time they had spent together earlier that day. Going out with Trace would give her the emotional distance she needed from Clint. Trace was becoming less important, while what she felt for Clint could hurt her more in the long run. She and Clint were on the opposite sides of a fight she was determined to win.

"We'll aim for tomorrow night," she said with a sigh, hoping she wouldn't regret this.

"Great, that's just great," he enthused. "I'll pick you up at five o'clock. I can't wait to see you."

She fiddled with the phone cord, frustrated with her wavering attitude. "I'll see you tomorrow, Trace."

"For sure, Nadine. I won't let you down."

"I hope not," Nadine said. She ended the call and dropped the phone in the cradle, pulling a face at it as she did so. *My life and welcome to it*, she thought. *Another potential loser "boyfriend."*

With a shake of her head, Nadine picked up some papers from the desk and shoved them into the appropriate folder in the file cabinet. She was acting in such a typically feminine fashion, even if she didn't dress the part. She glanced down at the blue jeans she wore today—and most every day. Running her finger over them, she remembered Clint's reaction when she'd worn a skirt. Remembered the surprised look on his face, and the way his eyes had seemed to linger.

So different from his usual, penetrating look. When he dropped that aloof manner, his eyes could sparkle, his usually firm mouth would soften, and he was suddenly charming, infinitely appealing.

She recalled this morning—how the wind had teased the groomed line of his hair, how his eyes had crinkled as he smiled.

Her hands dangled between the file folders as she relived each time their gazes had locked, each time they'd seemed to make a connection.

The tinny ring of the phone broke her thoughts and Nadine pulled herself up short, mentally giving herself a shake. *What in the world is wrong with me? Getting all dreamy over Clint Fletcher.*

She was losing it, she thought as she got up and picked up the phone. "Hello," she said curtly, pushing shut the door of the filing cabinet with her foot.

"Is this Nadine Laidlaw?" a woman's harsh voice asked on the other end of the phone.

"Yes." Nadine frowned as she tried to place the caller.

"I sent you a letter. The one about Skyline. Did you get it?"

Nadine felt her breath leave her as she fumbled behind her for a chair. "Okay. I remember. You said you knew something and wanted to talk."

"I can't tell you over the phone. I want to meet you somewhere. Will you be at the volleyball tournament next week?"

Nadine hoped a new reporter would be hired by then and the new person would cover the game. But, she couldn't chance this, not after all this time. She had to meet this woman wherever and whenever she asked. "If you are talking about the one at the high school, the answer is yes." She scribbled a note on a pad, her hands shaking.

"Good. I have a son on the team. I'll be there."

"And who is this?"

"It doesn't matter." The woman sighed. "It doesn't matter who I am. I'll be wearing a green sweatshirt and gray pants." A pause. "I don't want to do this, but I have to."

Nadine swallowed, her heart pounding with a mixture of excitement and fear. "I'm glad. I'm glad you're willing to talk to me." Nadine wiped a damp hand on the leg of her jeans. "I'll see you at the tournament, then."

A sharp click in her ear signaled the end of the conversation.

Nadine slowly replaced the handset. Her heart refused to slow down, her thoughts spun. Six years she had speculated on the circumstances surrounding her father's death. Six years she had asked questions and received no answers.

And now.

Now she was so close, so close.

She felt a deep conviction that now, finally, she would find out the truth.

It was what Nadine had been striving for. She longed to be finished with the struggle. As her grandmother and Elaine chided her for her near obsession with Skyline, a small part of her knew they were correct. Even while her mother was alive, there were many times she had been tempted to quit, let it all go and realize there would be questions that would not be answered. Then she would come home or visit her mother in the hospital. Brenda would be lying in her bed, barely able to speak, but always able to make it understood that she wouldn't have peace until Skyline was exposed.

Once she talked to her mysterious tipper, she might be able to work something into an article. She knew Clint would hit the roof. She didn't want to antagonize him, but the new information was a chance for her to assuage the guilt that clung to each thought of her mother's death.

But for now, she had pictures to edit and a few articles to write up.

Nadine pulled out the camera and removed the SD card. If she didn't edit the pictures now, her time would get eaten by phone calls and paperwork. She held the SD card in her hand, and slipped it into her laptop instead of her desktop computer. Then she walked down the hall and up the stairs to the employee lounge. Her new office had no windows, and after spending the day outside, she didn't want to feel boxed in.

She walked up the stairs, thankful for the changes that Clint had made when he came to the *Sweet Creek Chronicle*. One of the first things he had done was empty out the upstairs storage room and turn it into an employee lounge. It was a welcome addition, as it had large windows that looked out over the valley. Everyone had pitched in to buy a new coffee machine and a local furniture store exchanged a couple of couches for some free advertising.

With a heavy sigh, she dropped onto the couch, kicked her shoes off, and, sitting cross-legged on the couch, opened the photo editing software.

As the pictures loaded into the program, she heard feet coming up the stairs, and then Clint stood in the doorway with his own laptop under his arm.

"I have to do some editing," he said, giving her a sheepish smile. "I don't have the software on my desktop computer in my office. And this is where the coffee is."

"You don't have to make excuses to me," Nadine said with a nervous laugh. "This all belongs to you."

"Technically it belongs to the bank," Clint replied with a tight smile. "But I'll go back downstairs. I don't want to bother you."

"No, please don't do that," Nadine said hurriedly. "I can move."

"Or we could just both sit here," Clint said.

Nadine replied to that comment with a faint shrug. It wasn't what she wanted, but he was the boss, and she really didn't feel like working in her office.

So she stayed where she was, working on the pictures.

As she tilted, cropped, and enhanced, she was far too aware of the man now sitting across from her. She didn't want Clint, of all people, to have that kind of control over her.

The silence between them was heavy. Nadine felt she should say something, anything, but it was as if her mind had shut off.

She moved on to the next picture, her eyes on her screen, but her entire body aware of Clint.

"I thought today went well," Clint said, breaking the silence, his eyes on his own laptop.

"Yes, it did."

"You're keeping quite late hours today, aren't you?"

"Have to." Her voice sounded small.

"I imagine your grandma will be waiting."

"Yes." *Brilliant conversation, Nadine,* she scolded herself, trying to come up with anything to say. She nudged the color bar on the picture, bringing out the blue.

"She's quite the go-getter," he continued.

"She can be a little overwhelming."

"She was always really friendly when I came over," Clint said quietly.

"Yes, she was." Nadine almost groaned at her lame response, resisting the urge to smack herself on the forehead. *What's the matter? You spend the morning with him, then he corners you in the break room, tosses a few lame questions at you, and you freeze up.*

Even as she formulated the thought, she knew why. It had to do with the daydreaming she had indulged in a few moments ago in her office and with seeing him all morning. It had to do with a sudden and unwelcome awareness of Clint as an attractive man. It had to do with old emotions and old feelings. With new emotions, too. And she didn't like it.

The silence lengthened. Then Clint cleared his throat. "I never gave you proper condolences with the death of your mother. I can tell it's been hard for you."

Once again Nadine's chest tightened as still-painful emotions clenched her heart. "Yes, it has." She sniffed and reached into her pocket for a tissue, but her pocket was empty.

"Are you okay?" Clint's voice was a soft, rich sound.

"Yes." She swallowed, blinking; then, to her dismay, a tear drifted down her cheek.

He set his laptop aside, got up, and tugged a tissue out of the box beside the coffee maker. "I'm sorry. I didn't mean to make you cry." He handed her the tissue, and she awkwardly swiped at her cheek. But another tear fell, and another.

"I'm sorry. I don't know why I'm still so sad."

"It's only been six months," Clint said quietly.

She sniffed again, grappling with emotions that threatened to swamp her. She couldn't allow herself to lose control in front of him.

A sob crawled up her throat, followed by another.

Then Clint's arm slipped around her. His warm fingers cupped her shoulder. He gently drew her toward him, cradling her head in the welcome refuge of his arms. She kept one hand pressed against her lips, as if to contain her sorrow, but her other hand gripped his shirt.

"It's okay," he said, his hand stroking her hair. "Of course you miss your mother."

The sorrow she had held for such a long time finally found a place for release. The bitter loneliness and emptiness from her mother's death had been sequestered and stifled. No one could comfort her, until today.

She closed her eyes and let the sorrow take over.

Her body wracked with sobs, and she allowed the waves of grief to wash over her.

And all the while she cried, Clint stroked her head, whispering that he was here, that it was okay.

Finally the last sobs shook her body, and she took a deep breath, her head aching.

She knew she should pull away, but it felt so good to be here, held by the man who occupied so many of her thoughts.

She shifted her head to look up at him. His eyes were mere inches from her and she lost herself in them.

His fingers gently pushed her hair back from her face and lingered on her cheek. Her breath caught in her throat, and then, as if inevitable, their lips touched with tender hesitancy.

His arms tightened around her, and the kiss deepened. She cradled his head with her hand, tangling her fingers in his thick hair.

Time wheeled and slowed, and Nadine willed this moment to last forever.

The shrill ring of her cell phone broke the moment. Nadine jumped and pulled back.

She thought she should apologize; yet, she wasn't sorry.

Her phone rang again, and Clint gave her a wan smile. "Are you going to answer it?"

She didn't want to; she wanted to be back in his arms, but this wasn't the time. There was too much between them right now.

As she looked at the number on her cell phone, her heart sank. She also had this so-called boyfriend.

What was she doing? How could she do this to either Clint or Trace?

"I guess I should take this," Nadine turned away from him, her heart pounding. She got up and turned her back to him as she answered. She had waited too long. There was no one on the other end. She kept her back to Clint, trying to regain her composure and sort out which emotion she should feel.

Clint had been such a huge part of her life; it was hard to know where to put him now. They were both in different places in their lives. Much had happened since that high school crush.

And yet...

"I'm sorry, Nadine," Clint said as she turned to talk to him.

"Excuse me?" she said, not sure she had heard right.

"I was out of line. I was just...feeling sorry for you, I guess."

He couldn't have hurt her more than if he tossed his laptop at her.

Sympathy. He was only feeling sorry for her, that's why he kissed her.

A rush of anger surged through her—anger born out of deep emotions and a pain that had nothing to do with her mother's death, and everything to do with the death of hope.

"Of course. I'm sorry I dumped on you. I should have been more circumspect." She gave him a tight smile, and then, because she couldn't think of anything else to say, she picked up her phone and dialed Trace's number.

"No. That's not—"

"Hey, Trace," she said with a false brightness as Trace answered the phone, cutting off another apology from Clint. "Sorry I missed your call." She looked at Clint, holding his gaze, a hardness coming over her. "No. Not doing anything important at all."

Clint lifted his chin, his eyes narrowing. Then he gave her a tight nod, grabbed his laptop, and left the room.

Nadine swallowed a knot of pain as she watched him walk away.

Trace was saying something, but she couldn't concentrate. Pain and betrayal gripped her. She wanted to run after Clint, but she did have some pride.

There was no way she wanted anything to do with a man who only kissed her out of pity. Besides, she had a boyfriend who was talking to her right now.

Yet, even as she brought out all these reasons, she knew things between her and Clint had shifted, and she could never go back.

When Nadine woke the next morning, her first thoughts were of Clint.

Then Nadine groaned and dragged her hands over her face as his words echoed through her weary brain.

I was just feeling sorry for you.

Yesterday, she had been so angry and hurt when he said that. And then she became more upset with her reaction to it all.

What made it all even more pathetic was that despite her anger, she could resurrect the feel of his lips on hers and of his arms around her. She hadn't slept well as a result, and when sleep finally caught her in its soft grip, it was a restless venture.

She pushed herself up and trudged across the hall to the bathroom, grimacing at the tangled nest of hair and the rings of exhaustion under her eyes. She knew Grandma would notice and would comment, and she didn't have the energy to deflect the questions.

The shower revived her. As she brushed her hair, she reminded herself that she had a date, with someone who liked her and found her attractive, and who didn't feel sorry for her.

So she spent a few extra minutes blow-drying her hair, brushing and curling it. Then she walked across the hall and sifted through her wardrobe, looking for exactly the right outfit. It had to be appealing and attractive, and had to show Clint that he hadn't just broken her heart.

She found a soft sweater and skirt that looked good with tights. A pair of low boots and a drapey scarf finished her outfit.

She looked at herself critically in the mirror. Short where her sisters were tall, athletic where her sisters were slender, and dark where her sisters were light.

It shouldn't matter, even after all these years, but somehow Clint's kiss had resurrected all the old feelings she thought she had dealt with.

How was she supposed to face Clint now?

And what was she going to do about Trace? Even though Clint's motives for kissing her were questionable, she couldn't let go of the memory.

Too much to think about. She stepped across the hall and stopped. Silence greeted her.

"Grandma?" she called out.

But no pert voice replied. Nadine felt a flicker of fear as she hurried down the hallway. Had something happened to Grandma? Nadine hadn't heard her come home last night.

"Grandma," she called out again, and then her racing heart stilled when she saw the table set for breakfast and a note pinned to the apple on the plate.

"Had to leave early this morning. Hope things are okay with

you." Grandma had drawn a heart below that, and, in spite of her own confused emotions, Nadine had to smile.

She pulled the pin out of the apple and ate it while she got dressed. She ate the boiled egg Grandma had left for her and made herself a piece of toast. Then, when she couldn't put it off any longer, she cleaned up, grabbed her knapsack, and left the apartment.

The closer she got to the office, the quicker her heart pounded against her ribs, the shallower her breaths came. She wanted to be angry, but it still hurt too much.

But just before she got to the alley to the employee parking lot, a silver SUV turned onto the street and drove away.

Clint.

Relief sluiced through her; thank goodness he would be gone.

She walked through the back door, and as she headed down the hallway, Julie met her.

"Oh. You're here already," she said, sounding puzzled.

"I'm not late."

"You never are. It's just I saw Clint go storming out a few moments ago, looking like thunder. I thought you might have said something or done something to tick him off."

Quite the contrary, Nadine thought, taking a deep, calming breath.

"Haven't had time to do that yet, and the paper isn't out for a few more days." And there wasn't a Skyline article in sight.

"Okay. There's a girl here named Allison. Says she's here for her interview for the reporter position?"

Nadine stared at Julie a moment, comprehension fleeing as her brain scrabbled through her obligations. Then it all snapped back into focus.

"Right. I forgot about that."

"Seriously? You'd been cribbing at Clint since he came that we need another reporter."

Yet another reason for him to be annoyed with her. Shame

slithered down her back as she thought of how she had reacted yesterday to his kiss. How she had responded.

What an idiot.

"Send her in," Nadine said, moving to her desk and dropping into her chair.

A few moments later, a sweet young girl was sitting across from her, long blond hair slipping over her shoulder, eyes bright, holding a notebook and a pen. She looked adorable and she was blond. Clint would like her.

Nadine pushed the unkind thought aside.

"So, I understand you're here for the job?" Nadine said, standing up to shake her hand.

"I am. I'm very excited to work for this paper."

"You do realize it's just a small-town paper," Nadine reminded her.

"Of course. I came from Eastbar. I know the *Sweet Creek Chronicle*. It used to be kind of boring, but since Clint Fletcher took over, I think it's gotten more focused."

Nadine gave her a second look. "You've been doing your homework."

"All part of being a reporter."

"Good for you. Sit down and let's get at it."

It only took her ten minutes to know it wasn't worth Nadine's time to interview other applicants even though Allison was the first she had spoken with. She was smart, witty, and asked all the right questions. There had been six applicants for the job, and only two were interview material. Of the two, Allison had the more impressive credentials—three summers' work for a weekly paper in southern Alberta, and two years at another. Nadine had also been impressed by Allison's clips.

"You know, we could go on for another half an hour," Nadine said with a smile, "but I'd like to offer you the job."

Allison Edlinger leaned forward, her long blond hair slipping over her shoulder. "Seriously?"

"Very seriously."

She grinned, clutching her notebook to her chest like the young thing she was. "This is great, just great. Thanks so much. When can I start?"

"Yesterday?" Nadine joked at Allison's enthusiasm. "Actually, you can start as soon as possible. We've been just swamped." Nadine indicated her desk, which was full again despite a few long evenings attempting to clear it. "If you want, I can show you around today. We've got deadline on Monday. Our paper comes out on Tuesday."

"That's a little unusual for a weekly," Allison commented.

"Yes. Most come out on Monday, but Clint changed the date so we didn't have to work Sunday to get the paper out. At least, not as much."

Nadine rose and ushered Allison out of her office. They walked to the back of the building, where the two typesetters worked at their computers. She poked her head over Wally's cubicle on the other side of the large, open room, but he was gone. "This is where you'll be working," Nadine said, pointing to the cubicle that abutted Wally's.

Nadine introduced Allison to Avis Harper, whose office was across the hallway.

"Hey there," Avis said, not looking up from her computer and merely granting them both a quick wave.

"Avis is our ad person. She usually words the ads, helps set them out," Nadine said, getting the message that Avis wanted to be left alone. They walked past Nadine's office, and Elaine's across from hers was also empty. "Empty building today," Nadine commented as they walked to the reception area. Nadine leaned on the counter. "And this is Julie, our receptionist, ad taker, and sometimes copy editor."

"And answerer of phones and giver of messages." Julie handed Nadine a piece of paper. "I'm guessing Trace called about your date tonight."

"I'm guessing he would be. Let's hope he shows up," Nadine said.

"Why wouldn't he?" Julie asked.

Nadine pushed away from the desk and walked over to Clint's office, effectively cutting off conversation with Julie. She felt uncomfortable talking about Trace. She wasn't sure what to do with him.

Nadine turned and gestured to the door that faced the open foyer. "And this, Allison, is our boss's office. Thankfully he's gone for the day, so I'll just let you have a peek into the inner sanctum."

Nadine opened the door.

"No, he's not—" Julie interrupted, but she was too late.

Nadine almost jumped at the sight of Clint bent over his desk. He looked up and Nadine backed away. "Sorry. I was just showing our new reporter around. I thought you were gone." She reached over to close the door, but Clint was getting up from his desk.

"Just needed my pen."

"I d-didn't want to interrupt you," Nadine stammered, suddenly self-conscious of her skirt, her hair, her makeup. All dressed up for a date.

"It doesn't matter," he said, his eyes holding Nadine's. "I wouldn't mind meeting her."

Of course he wanted to meet a new hire. How dumb of her. Nadine stepped back, taking a breath to compose herself.

Nadine made the introductions, and Clint reached out to shake Allison's hand. Allison smiled up at him, her blue eyes shining with appreciation. It seemed to Nadine that the light from the front windows caught Allison's blond hair, making it sparkle. Her dress emphasized her delicate shoulders and skimmed her narrow hips.

Ah, yeah. She was exactly his type.

"Allison is starting today," Nadine announced, her voice sounding falsely bright. "She's originally from Eastbar, moved to

Vancouver, but has lived here for a couple of years already, and knows all about our little paper."

She was talking too much.

"Nice to have you with us, Allison," Clint said. "I hope you'll be working with us for a while."

Allison fairly simpered, and Nadine resisted the urge to roll her eyes. "I hope so, too," she said, a coy note in her voice.

"We should go back to my office," Nadine said to Allison. "There are a few things I want to go over with you—camera allowance, travel, that kind of thing. And then Elaine will need you for the payroll forms."

It seemed to Nadine that Allison had to tear her gaze away from Clint's.

"Sure," Allison said. "We can do that." She hesitated a moment, then followed Nadine back down the hall. When she opened the door to her office, Nadine wasn't surprised to see Clint still standing in the doorway of his office, watching them.

Always was partial to blondes. She closed the door behind Allison.

Nadine walked around her desk and slipped into her chair, pulled an empty pad toward her, and found a pen that still wrote. "First, I need to get your address and phone number."

Allison said nothing and Nadine looked up.

"Earth to Allison."

Allison jumped. "I am so sorry," she said. "I have to confess that I'm still a little surprised."

"At what?" As if she didn't know, but politeness dictated to ask.

"At how handsome the boss is." Allison shook her head as if she was still trying to absorb it. "He's so good-looking, and what dreamy eyes."

Nadine stopped, her pen poised over the pad of paper. "He *is* your boss, I'd like to remind you," she said, her tone more sharp than intended.

Allison sighed, then smiled at Nadine. "Sorry. I didn't mean to sound like some drippy teenager, but I sure never imagined meeting someone like him in a town like this."

"Well, these unfortunate incidents happen," replied Nadine dryly. "Now, I'd like to get on with this."

Someone rapped on her door and Julie stuck her head in. "Accident just came in on the scanner. Truck rolled over on the highway."

"Where's Wally?"

"Can't raise him on his cell phone. I'm pretty sure he's covering that event at the museum."

Nadine jumped up and grabbed her camera bag, checking it for the necessary supplies. She glanced at Allison. "Are you ready for your first assignment?"

Allison looked surprised, then nodded. "Sure."

"Great." Nadine looked back up at Julie as she zipped up her bag. "Where are we headed?"

"Secondary highway, 498, toward Eastbar."

"Leaving now. Any more info on who's involved?" Nadine asked as Julie stepped quickly aside for her.

"The trucker..." Julie hesitated as Nadine headed out the doorway. Nadine stopped and glanced over her shoulder.

"What?"

Julie bit her lip. "He was driving for Skyline."

CHAPTER 11

"*I* couldn't believe how ticked that guy was when you took pictures," Allison said to Nadine as they returned to the office. "I thought he was going to pull your camera out of your hand."

"There's more to that story," Nadine said grimly. She was surprised herself at how quickly the administrative people from Skyline had come to the scene of the accident. Nadine snapped some pictures of the paramedics working on the injured truck driver before the workers from Skyline blocked her.

"I'll have to wait and see what happens to him," Nadine continued. "We have a standing rule not to print pictures of actual fatalities. If he doesn't make it, we'll make an editorial decision as to which pictures we'll run."

"He looked like he'd make it to me," Allison said. "The truck looked in worse shape than he did."

When Nadine had seen the crumpled semi lying in the ditch, she felt an initial reluctance to photograph the scene. Thankfully the paramedics were already there, and from what she could see, he wasn't too badly injured.

"I'm fairly sure he will, but I still want to be certain."

"I'd say run the ones of the Skyline people trying to block you taking the picture," Allison said as they stopped at Nadine's office.

"That won't win me points with the boss." She smiled up at Allison. "Do you have a place to stay for the night, or are you going back home?"

Allison shrugged. "I'm staying at a friend's tonight. She promised she would help me find an apartment if I got the job."

"Good, because it looks like you'll be hunting for a place to live." Nadine let her camera bag drop to the floor. "You'll be covering a livestock show in Eastbar tomorrow afternoon. I suggest pants."

Allison looked down at her dress. "We sure looked a pair, rushing out of your car, both of us dressed to the nines." She glanced at Nadine's legs. "I don't know how you kept your panty-hose from running."

"Just as well. I'm supposed to be going on a date tonight."

"If you'll excuse me, you don't sound too enthusiastic," Allison said.

"Probably not," she admitted.

"Personally, I'd ditch him and make a play for the boss," Allison said with a grin. "I haven't been here long, but if a guy looked at me like he looked at you, I wouldn't waste my time on someone I didn't like."

"Time out," Nadine said firmly. "First of all, he's your boss and *mine*; and secondly, Clint Fletcher looks at me like he'd like to fire me but doesn't know how to."

Even as she spoke, Allison's words produced an unwelcome thump of her heart. In spite of his sympathy kiss, she hadn't been able to stop thinking of him. And she didn't like it.

"Sorry," Allison said, suddenly contrite. "I didn't realize you felt that way about him."

"I don't feel any 'way.' He is my employer, and that is the only relationship we have." *Don't we sound prim.*

"Again, I apologize. Not exactly a good footing to start out on, is it?"

"No, I'm sorry," Nadine reassured her, frustrated with her lapse. "I always get uptight after covering an accident." Nadine glanced at her watch. "Well, I have to do some work yet, and you should head out to your friend's place." She looked back at Allison and held out her hand. "Thanks again. I think it will be a good article."

Allison smiled in relief and shook Nadine's hand. "I hope so. And thanks again for the job." She tucked her notebook in her purse and walked down the hall, her blond hair swinging with each step.

Nadine watched her go. Allison thought Clint looked at her a special way. Did he really?

Nadine shook off the thought and went into her office. Pulling her chair up to her desk, she flipped through a pile of message slips and began returning the calls.

By the time she was done, the office was empty. She had told Trace to pick her up from the office, as Nadine didn't feel like dealing with Grandma's blatant disapproval of Trace. So, she opened another window on her computer, ostensibly to work on a story, but instead, she ended up playing a computer game.

Entirely appropriate. Once again, it's just my computer and me.

With a sigh, she closed the game and put her computer to sleep.

She glanced at the clock: Six-thirty. Trace was late again. She called his cell, but was sent to voicemail. There was no way she was leaving a message.

She lifted her bag onto the desk, shoved some papers into it, which she would look over at home, and zipped the bag shut, all while gritting her teeth as she felt the unwelcome and all-too-familiar prickling in her eyes. She had never been the weepy type, but since her mother died, her emotions stayed close to the surface.

Trace ditching you is nothing to cry over, she castigated herself. *He's not that important.*

But it seemed that she was crying more and more, and she disliked it intensely each time it happened.

Except once, she thought. When Clint had dried her tears.

Nadine's stomach clenched at the reminiscence of Clint's hands on her face, his gentle comfort. For a brief moment, she allowed herself the luxury of remembering his touch, the scent of his aftershave, and his hovering nearness.

Then, with an angry shake of her head, she dismissed the memories. It was only pity that made him do what he did.

Sure didn't feel like pity.

Nadine hefted her bag onto her shoulder and got ready to leave, yet hesitated as she turned the doorknob.

Going home meant Grandma and her unsubtle "I told you so" looks. It would be too humiliating to have Grandma see her come home after another canceled date.

Then what? Another solitary movie in Eastbar had no appeal, and eating alone had even less.

Nadine dropped her bag in frustration. She wouldn't go out by herself, yet she wanted her grandma out of her house. She wanted to be alone, and when she had the chance, she felt lonely.

Wishy-washy. That was what she was. Easily pushed around, and easily taken in. Trace was a case in point. How many dates had he kept as opposed to the ones he had broken?

Not that it mattered that much, Nadine thought as she dropped into her chair. She had felt uncomfortable with Trace from the start. The whole relationship was contrived and fake.

She still felt uneasy about him. Something about their relationship just didn't seem right. Yet, she was loath to call it off altogether. What would she have then?

And what do you have now? She reminded herself, rocking back in her chair. *You're all alone in this office. You were supposed to go out with him, and again he's a no-show.* Nadine sighed and pushed her chair away from her desk. She didn't feel like writing up the Skyline story and didn't want to go home.

She got up and wandered around the deserted office. Even Clint was gone. The thought made her unaccountably lonely.

Each step seemed to drag, each step echoing in the empty building, as if mocking her own lonely state.

I've tried, Lord, she prayed, stepping into her small office. *I've tried to be happy with what I have. What's wrong with me?*

Wasn't she supposed to be a liberated woman? Hadn't she shown that she could compete with a man, could do the same job? Wasn't that supposed to be enough for a woman these days?

Nadine sat in her chair, letting her head fall backward, her eyes closed. Deep down, she wanted what her friends had: A husband, children; a home. She wanted to sit in church and frown at fidgeting kids, sing with her husband. She wanted to have windows to sew curtains for, laundry to wash. She wanted a house with an office that she could work out of, part-time. She wanted to hear a door open and close, feel a lift of her heart as her husband came into the house, feel the same sense of completion as when her own father would come home and fill up the man-space that had been empty since he had left that morning. And she wanted that man to be Clint.

Who did she think she was fooling? She was frustrated with where her thoughts so easily went. She remembered all too well the contrast between her and Allison this morning, how Clint couldn't seem to keep his eyes off Allison.

She and Clint were obviously not meant for each other. Nadine figured she was destined to become one of those old newspaper ladies, who ended up heading to South America to do features on Mayan temples for travel magazines.

Or maybe she would become a dedicated single missionary who would work in faraway mission fields, then come back and do church tours and slide shows, drumming up support for evangelism in faraway locales.

Lately, she felt events slipping out of her reach, with deadlines always looming. They were shorthanded too long, and it had drained her.

The sorrow from her mother's death was still too fresh, and her guilt over being unable to find more about her father's death still haunted her.

Nadine pressed her hand against her chest as if to keep the sorrow contained. She pulled the Bible out of the drawer and laid it on her desk.

She drew in a deep breath, then another. God had answered her scattered prayers about her search for justice for her father. The phone call yesterday was confirmation that she was given another chance to find out what happened to him.

She idly flipped through the Bible, trying to find something to connect with.

And then she found it: Isaiah 55.

Nadine stopped, carefully running her fingers along the familiar lines:

Come all who are thirsty, come to the waters.

Why spend money on what is not bread and your labor on what does not satisfy?

Seek the Lord while He may be found.

You will go out with joy and be led forth with peace.

Drawing in a slow breath, she read on, reading warnings and comfort and promises.

She waited a moment to let the words settle into her worn and weary heart. Then she pulled in a deep breath, knowing she couldn't stay here any longer.

Time to go and face Grandma.

The ring of the phone made her jump. For a moment she was tempted to let it ring, but her innate curiosity led her to answer.

It was Trace, spilling apologies and promises to come over right away, but Nadine cut him off.

"Doesn't matter, Trace. It's over." As she spoke the words, she felt a momentary shaft of panic. Was she crazy? Was she deliberately trying to sabotage any chance she would have at a life's partner?

But, as she heard his protests and listened to his excuses, she realized that the longer she allowed the relationship to go on, the worse it would get. Trace wasn't reliable, wasn't the kind of man she wanted for herself.

"No. I've thought it over," she interrupted. "You're just too busy and I don't like being stood up."

"Nadine, don't do this. Tonight was a blip, unexpected."

"Like your visit with your banker?" Nadine put heavy emphasis on the last word as if to tell him she didn't believe his excuse of the other day, either.

"I was talking to Allan Andrews. Give him a call." He sounded out of breath. "Please, don't do this, Nadine. Please."

Nadine had heard his begging before and found it a little embarrassing. If she was to have a meaningful relationship, she wanted it with someone dependable and trustworthy.

If she was to have a relationship. She closed her eyes as the words taunted and echoed in her mind. Being married wasn't everything. She had a challenging job and lived in a good place, and she had her faith and her church community. As lonely as she sometimes felt, she wasn't desperate enough to settle for a man who showed her such little respect. She respected herself far too much for that.

She listened to more of his protests and false promises, waiting for a suitable time to end the conversation. It was a relief when she could finally say, "Goodbye, Trace," and hang up the phone.

As she did so, she shook her head. For a moment, she felt a pang of sorrow, but behind that, a feeling of empowerment. She—plain, ordinary Nadine Laidlaw, single woman—had broken up with a very handsome, eligible man.

Nadine walked toward the front of the office. She might regret the impulse in the morning, but for tonight, she was in charge. She turned on the security, locked the main office door, and went back down the hallway to the parking lot, turning lights off as she went.

Maybe Grandma would have fresh muffins made, Nadine thought as she pulled out the keys to her car. *To sweeten her I-told-you-so's.*

Headlights swung down the alley and momentarily blinded her. Nadine stepped back toward the office. An SUV pulled up beside her car, and with a start, Nadine recognized Clint's vehicle.

The SUV stopped and Clint got out, walking around to meet her. "Hi, there," he said. "Going out?"

Nadine shook her head, a sense of shame mocking her newfound confidence. "No, just home."

"I thought you had a date..."

"I did." Nadine shrugged, fully aware of her boss standing beside her, his height overwhelming. His hair was tousled and his tie was gone, causing Nadine to recall the way he looked the day they'd covered the FoodGrains Bank project together.

"And," he prompted, "he broke it?"

Nadine shook her head, fiddling with the end of her scarf. "No, I did. I didn't feel like waiting anymore." She looked up at him, only to catch his gaze on her. She looked down again. "What are you doing here?"

"Forgot some papers I needed." He jingled the change in his pants pocket. "So, what are you going to do?"

Nadine shrugged. "Go home. See if Grandma has any supper left for me."

"I see." He made a move to leave, checked himself, and came back. "I, uh..." He stopped and cleared his throat. Nadine glanced up at him, puzzled. He seemed hesitant, unsure of himself. "I haven't eaten, either. We could grab a bite."

"Because you feel sorry for me?"

As soon as the words popped out, she wished she could take them back.

Clint blew out a sigh.

"I know saying I'm sorry about my apology only underlines the stupidity of what I said that afternoon, but I didn't have a chance to explain."

Nadine frowned. "What do you mean?"

"I was about to when...well...Trace called."

Her thoughts shifted backward, and she remembered now.

"I got interrupted, and I didn't get to finish. So...can I try to make it up to you? By taking you out to dinner? There are a couple of things I need to talk to you about."

Nadine paused in surprise, her hands no longer fiddling with her scarf. "Okay," she agreed, hardly knowing what else to say and wondering what he wanted to say to her.

"Good." Clint took a step backward and whacked his leg against the fender of his vehicle. He steadied himself, straightened, and held his hand up to Nadine. "Sorry."

She didn't know what he was apologizing for, but his unexpected—and uncharacteristic—clumsiness gave him a sudden vulnerability.

"So. Do you want to ride with me or take your car?" he said.

"I'll drive my car." She wanted the option of being able to leave on her own. "I'll meet you at the Inn."

He nodded and took another step back. "Okay. I'll see you soon." He jogged up the walk to the office, leaving Nadine to wonder what had come over her usually calm and collected boss.

Briefly she recalled his touch yesterday, his concern. With a laugh, she dismissed her foolish thoughts. He said he had a couple of things he wanted to talk to her about. She was afraid one of them was Skyline.

But, as she backed out of the parking lot behind the *Sweet Creek Chronicle*, she couldn't help remembering his grin when she'd said yes.

∾

Clint settled himself behind the table and glanced across to where Nadine sat. Her gaze roved around the restaurant as she looked everywhere but him. For a moment, he regretted asking her. She seemed ill at ease, even though she had agreed to come.

He couldn't get her off his mind lately. Each day he tried to seek her out, tried to connect with her in some way.

"Menus or just coffee?" Tess Kraus stood by the table, grinning as she looked from Clint to Nadine, giving him a knowing look. "Or time alone?"

"Coffee and menus," Clint said, slanting her a warning look.

Tess Kraus was one of those waitresses who seemed to know everything and loved to keep it that way.

"Eating it is," she said, pouring them both a coffee with one hand and laying the menus in front of them with the other. "I'll give you two a moment, and then I'm coming back."

Why did she make that sound like a warning?

"I guess it's orange hair streaks for Tess this week," Nadine said, taking the menu and glancing at it.

"She's a character, that's for sure."

"I wonder if I could pull colored streaks off." Nadine fingered her own thick, brown hair, now hanging loose, framing her face and softening her features.

Not at all unusual. Nadine never seemed comfortable whenever he was around; that in turn created a measure of tension within him. He didn't like it. He wanted her to be as relaxed around him as she had been around the people on the afternoon of the Food-Grains Bank project. He wanted her to look up at him with a smile brightening her eyes, the way her smile had that day.

"I can't think why you would want to," Clint said, giving her a smile that he hoped would alleviate the tension.

He wasn't that hungry and had asked Nadine out for supper on an impulse—partly because he wanted to explain about that stupid moment when he made that lame apology for kissing her. But, he also had another important reason. Skyline. Again. He wished she would just lay off, wished she would stop poking them. Each time she did, he had to pay the price, and he hated being in conflict with her. And now, after the accident that involved a Skyline employee, he was afraid she would go on one of her editorial rants.

"So. What will it be for you two?" Tess returned as promised, her smile still holding a faint smirk.

"The chicken burger and potato salad," he said.

"I can highly recommend both," Tess returned. "And for madame?"

"I'll have a bowl of beef barley soup," Nadine said, granting Tess the kind of smile Clint wished she would give him.

"Also excellent." Tess took the menus then left.

"So, all you're ordering is soup?" Clint asked, trying to keep his conversation with Nadine light and casual.

For now.

"Not really hungry," she explained, tapping her thumbs against each other, then looking around the restaurant.

They sat in a strained silence that Clint knew would be up to him to fill.

He didn't want to talk about her sisters. Not after the last time he got hammered for dropping Leslie, despite the extenuating circumstances.

"Do you think Allison will work out for the paper?" he asked, shifting to a safer topic.

"I think she will. She's smart and quick and eager." Nadine fiddled with the cutlery in front of her. "I have her covering the livestock show in Eastbar tomorrow. If that's okay with you."

"You're the editor," Clint said, holding up his hands in a gesture of surrender. "It's your call."

"Glad to know."

He wasn't sure if that was a sarcastic tone in her voice, so he ignored it.

He unrolled his own utensils, wishing he knew where to go from here. Straight to Skyline? Or the mangled apology he gave her after he kissed her?

"So, how long was your mother sick?" he asked, hoping he could get her to talk about her, and from there, he could explain why he said what he did without making himself look too foolish.

After he had left her that afternoon, he couldn't forget that kiss and how she responded to him. If he could get the awkwardness out of the way maybe...

Nadine pursed her lips, picking up her napkin and playing with it. "Most ALS sufferers live anywhere from one to three years after diagnosis. In my mother's case, it took a little longer."

"How come?"

Nadine pleated the napkin as if weighing her answer. Then she looked up at him, holding his gaze. "My mother's mission to discover what happened to my father kept her alive longer. That mission included Skyline Contractors being brought to justice." Nadine stopped abruptly and bit her lip.

Clint absorbed this piece of news with a heavy heart. Looked like he would deal with his apology and Skyline in one fell swoop.

He reminded himself that he was her boss, and that Matthew was pushing hard at him to rein her in. That another lawsuit would cost too much, and that this time, Skyline would do more than threaten.

"I know your father died while working for Skyline, but I've never heard how it happened." Even as he spoke the words, Clint thought he might be fashioning his own noose. But, he wanted to find out what drove her to keep up the battle for so long.

"Didn't Leslie tell you?"

"She only told me that he died at work."

"Do you want to hear the official line we got or what I think?"

She looked away, then at him, her expression troubled.

"Tell me both." He leaned forward, wishing he could forget about his paper, wishing he dared give in to a sudden and intense need to protect and support her. Wishing he could kiss her again.

She unfolded the napkin again. "The line we got from the company was that my father was out in the bush by himself. He was working on a nasty hill that was too difficult for the mechanical logger to get to. They claimed he was using a practice called domino felling. That means cutting a tree so that it hangs up on another standing tree. Then the faller cuts that tree until it leans against another, and so on. Then you cut the last main tree, which falls all the way, and because all the trees are leaning against each other, the rest come with it. It's illegal according to many labor standards and extremely dangerous but very effective. Lots of hand-fallers have gotten killed that way. According to Skyline, this is what my father did, and he was killed by a hung-up tree coming down on him." Nadine stared up at Clint, her brown eyes intense. "My father was the most careful man I know. He would never do anything as dangerous as that. He'd gotten many safety commendations from the company."

"What do you think happened?"

Nadine held his gaze a moment, then looked down again. "That's what I've been trying to find out. I've talked to as many employees who will talk to me, other subcontractors. I've heard rumors that my father went in behind another young guy to clean up the mess he had made and they were working together. And I've heard that my father's death was just a tragic fluke." Nadine held up one hand, ticking off her fingers with the other. "I haven't gotten any names, any times, any sign of other vehicles, or any verification of the rumors, at least not from anyone who was willing to commit. Nothing."

"The bush is a pretty wild place."

Nadine released a harsh laugh. "Not when there's a logging show or two in an area. You go out there, it's like a little community. If my mom wanted to bring my dad supper, and we made a wrong turn, all we'd have to do is drive up some logging roads until we saw a skidder or Cat operator. They always knew who was working where. But in my father's case...nothing."

Clint didn't know what to say. Nadine's voice took on a note of authority that showed him that she knew of what she spoke, and how important it was to her.

"How did you find out about his death?"

"My father didn't come home that night, and my mother called my dad's supervisor. He went back up the mountain to the cut block he was working. It took a while because he wasn't working in the block he had been assigned to. At least, not according to the supervisor's information." Nadine folded the napkin again, her eyes intently focused on it. "He was found lying underneath a tree. Dead."

Clint covered her hands with his, squeezing them, wanting to pull her close and to comfort her. "I'm so sorry to hear that. You must have cared for him a lot."

Nadine looked down at their hands and tightened her grip on his. "I did. I was especially close to my father." When she looked back up at him, her eyes were clear but pensive. "Seems kind of wrong," she said with a soft laugh. "I had my mother around longer than my father, but sometimes it's as if I miss him more." She shrugged, then pulled her hands away from him.

"Your mother was a lot of work for you and your grandmother, wasn't she?"

Nadine waved the comment away with a graceful turn of her hand. "I resented it at first, but then I wondered if it wasn't God's way of giving me a chance to get to know her better. I always spent so much time with my dad." She smiled, her eyes looking over his shoulder as if she had disappeared into another place and time. "I always helped him with his projects in the shop. We would go out to the bush on Saturdays to cut firewood. The twins stayed at home with mom." She smiled softly. "He called me his little tomboy." She shook her head and looked back at Clint.

"I always remember him as a kind man." Clint folded his arms, leaning his elbows on the table. "Whenever I came over, he would always ask what me and Uncle Dory were working on at the acreage."

"He liked you."

"I liked him. He was a man of integrity, content with his life." Clint couldn't keep the bitter note out of his voice. "Unlike so many others."

"Others being..." prompted Nadine.

Clint rubbed his thumb along the inside of his opposite arm, concentrating on the tabletop. "My parents."

"And," Nadine prompted, "what about them?"

Clint shrugged, hesitant to tell her even after all these years. "They both worked hard to collect enough money to buy more things. They were going to give me a car when I graduated high school."

"But you didn't get it."

"No. I blew it. That's how I ended up at Dory's. I was caught stealing a flashlight from a hardware store, a very deliberate act of rebellion." He looked up at her, his mouth curved in a wry grin. "My parents didn't understand what was happening because they never took the time to."

"You wanted them to notice you."

Clint caught Nadine's look of surprise, as if she had just discovered something new; and, he conceded, she probably had. At that time, he hadn't told too many people how he had ended up in Sweet Creek. It was embarrassing to admit to anyone who he wanted to impress that he had gotten into trouble over something as unimportant as a flashlight. As he got to know the Laidlaws, he said nothing—as much because of his shame over the ease with which his parents had sent him away as the guilt over his actions. "That's exactly what Uncle Dory said," he mumbled.

"And where are your parents now?"

"Dad's in Rome and Mother shuttles between Toronto and New York." Clint smiled at her as if to negate the bitterness that crept into his voice. He had forgiven his parents the same time he had become a Christian, but he still struggled with it.

"I take it they're divorced."

"You take it correctly."

"But it still bothers you."

Clint lifted one shoulder in a negligent shrug. "It doesn't matter what the marriage counselors say, it's always hard on kids when their family breaks up. At any age." Clint looked back up at Nadine, surprised to see a gentle understanding in her expression. "Your family was one of the first I saw that worked together and cared about each other. I've always wanted that for myself." He hesitated, wondering if he should tell her more. If she would understand how his family had been impacted by the lawsuit his father pursued for so long.

A bit heavy-handed maybe?

Too obvious?

Nadine looked down, and Clint thought he had overstepped some unknown boundary. One never knew with Nadine, and he had been talking more in the past few minutes than he had in days.

"Which makes it harder to hear about your father's death as well as your mother's."

Nadine was quiet a moment, and then she looked up, her eyes soft. "Thanks for that."

"And how are you feeling now about losing your mother?"

"Don't worry. I won't start crying again."

"No. No. Of course not. And about the other afternoon-"

Nadine held her hand up to stop him. "It's okay. You don't need to apologize again."

"I don't want to apologize again," he said. "I want to explain."

She frowned in confusion. "Explain what?" Her voice held a wary tone, and he would have to tread carefully with her. Especially since she still assumed he had broken Leslie's heart so long ago.

"I didn't want you to feel like I was taking advantage of you...of your sadness," he amended. "I felt bad that you had to deal with it and I wanted to comfort you. But, then..." he let his voice drift away as he struggled to find the right words.

Thankfully she said nothing to fill the silence, so he plowed on.

"I like you. I'm attracted to you. And the kiss was part of that." He held her gaze, hoping she understood what he was trying to say.

She blushed and looked down at the napkin she was folding and re-folding.

"I wasn't sorry about the kiss," he continued. "I was just sorry about the circumstances. I wished it could have happened another time."

For a moment, she said nothing, then her lips curved into a gentle smile.

"Me too," she said quietly.

Then, to his surprise, she took his hand. He wound his fingers around hers, wishing he could leave everything here. Wishing they could just carry on like this—just Clint and Nadine without all the other stuff, past and present, clinging to them.

Wishing he didn't have to talk to her about the "other thing."

The Skyline thing.

Because as soon as he did, this small moment of closeness would be broken.

CHAPTER 12

 adine stirred her soup, trying to adjust to her new feelings about Clint. Trying to figure out what to think of what he had just told her.

All her defenses against this man had suddenly melted away.

She glanced up at him, surprised yet again to see his eyes on her. Looking down, she busied herself with unwrapping her cracker from its cellophane wrapper. She felt she had to get the subject back to something more manageable.

All she wanted was to leave and be alone with him, not in this public place where everyone knew everyone else. Not with Anton and Carlos, the inn regulars sending her covert grins or Tess giving her a discreet thumbs up. Everyone knew too much here.

"When you left Sweet Creek you went to Europe, didn't you?" It was a much safer topic than thinking about the last time he had kissed her.

"My parents had a collective attack of guilt over their divorce, and sending me away on that trip was their way of making up for it." He spoke quietly, and she thought again of his comment about their divorce. How it had hurt him.

"You know, I lost my parents, but it sounds like you have too."

Clint gave her a gentle smile. "I lost my father years before. He spent so much time on his...on his business that he didn't have much time for me or my mother."

Nadine felt her cheeks warm, remembering all too well a snide comment she had made in this very place when sitting with Trace.

"That trip was one of the really good things that happened to me." Clint was quiet a moment, his finger tracing idle circles on the tablecloth, his supper forgotten. "I traveled through places of extreme wealth and extreme poverty. I learned that what had happened to me was small in the larger scheme of things. I stopped in churches that were older than any book I had read, visited castles and museums, and toured countrysides that had been home to generations of families. And in a busy square in Jerusalem, it was as if all the history I had seen in Europe, everything I had witnessed with your family, the myriad times I had sat in church with Uncle Dory and even my own parents, all coalesced. I realized that I had been given a precious gift of life and a promise of grace."

Clint looked up at her, his mouth quirked in a gentle smile. "I changed, and I accepted those promises. Then, I had to come home." He hesitated a moment, as if he wanted to say more and was unsure of how to proceed.

Nadine leaned forward, full of questions, yet unsure of where to go. Clint's confessions created space to get to know each other in new ways.

"That sounds amazing. I would love to do more traveling."

"I imagine taking care of your mother prevented any of that," he said.

"Yes. It did." But, she didn't want to dwell on the past. She was with a man she had dreamt of many times. She no longer had a boyfriend, and things were moving in a good direction. "Tell me more about Europe."

While they finished their supper, he did.

A gentle note permeated his deep voice as he talked of Rome, visiting the Vatican, trips through the Italian countryside, Paris and the famous landmarks, walking along the Seine, biking through Holland, and of hiking through England. Nadine felt a touch of envy as he spoke, but even after all that, he talked most animatedly about his uppermost desire to one day come back to Sweet Creek and take over his uncle's paper. It was a desire that had begun as a random thought and had changed into a real need as his own life changed.

Tess had taken their plates and bowls away and poured another round of coffee, thankfully keeping her comments to herself. Clint leaned his elbows on the table, sipping as he asked her questions and responded to hers.

She fiddled with her spoon, answering his own soft-spoken questions and telling him about the precious few things that had happened in her life since he had left Sweet Creek. A few times she caught his eyes on her.

At those moments, her heart quickened.

It wasn't until Tess had come around for the fifth or sixth time with coffee that she realized how long they had been sitting there. She snuck a quick glance at her watch.

"My goodness," she exclaimed aloud. "It's already ten o'clock."

Clint looked as if he didn't believe her. He glanced at his own wrist. "You're right." He looked at her and smiled. "I can't believe we've been sitting here so long."

Neither could Nadine. "I should get going."

"You were supposed to be out tonight anyway, weren't you?"

"Yes, but I never like to stay out too long. Grandma worries about me."

"Well, we had better leave." Clint pulled a few dollars out of his pocket for a tip and dropped them on the table. He also took the check before Nadine had a chance. "I'll get it," he said in reply to her protest. "I've never had a chance to take you out and often wanted to. Be back in a minute." Bemused at his parting comment, Nadine watched him stride across the deserted restaurant.

She gathered her discarded scarf, her purse, and her knapsack and got up herself, wondering what he meant and if she was reading more into the casual comment than he implied. By the time she came to the front desk, he was pocketing his wallet.

"I'd offer to drive you home, but I imagine you'll want to take your car?"

Nadine nodded, sorry now she had taken it and wondering what would have transpired if he had driven her home. "Thanks so much for dinner," she said.

Clint nodded, then, walking ahead, he opened the heavy glass door for her. They walked in silence along the deserted street to her car. The evening air held a faint chill coming off the mountains, as a hint of the winter that would soon fold them and the town.

Nadine fumbled through her purse for her keys, finally finding them.

"Here, let me," Clint said, taking the keys out of her hand. He paused then curled his fingers around hers.

"I'm glad you don't have orange streaks in your hair," he said. "And I'm glad you wore it loose."

Her heart stuttered at his touch. And for a moment, she couldn't speak—just a moment though. It wasn't like her to hold her tongue too long.

"I wanted to look nice."

"For Trace."

He said the words without rancor though his mouth tightened.

She nodded but then held his gaze, hoping he understood. "Trace was a mistake. A joke in many ways. A way to keep my grandma off my back."

"Not important to you then?"

"I don't think I would have kissed you if he was. I'm not like that."

"Your sister was."

"What?" The comment seemed to come from nowhere. "My sister was what?"

"I'm sorry. I...that slipped out. It's nothing."

Nadine caught his hand and held it tight, frowning at him. "It may be, but I sense there's something else you want to say. Are you talking about Leslie?"

Clint had a pained expression on his face, and Nadine closed the car door that she had just opened. A few weeks ago, she had accused him of breaking her sister's heart. Now, it seemed, there were other layers to the story.

"Tell me what you meant. Please."

"Let's walk and talk," he said, moving away from her.

Nadine wrapped her arms around her midsection, and together they headed down the street.

Clint shoved his hands in the pockets of his pants, looking ahead. In the dim light, his eyes were shadows accentuated by his dark eyebrows.

"What did you mean when you said that Leslie was...what was she?"

This netted her another sigh and another oblique glance.

"Please. Tell me."

"I promised her I wouldn't."

Nadine's heart shifted at his words, the serious tone of his voice.

"You know that I could just pick up the phone and call her myself. It's been a few years."

"I know it has, but I promised."

"What did you promise?"

Clint shot her a sardonic look. "You really are a reporter, aren't you?"

"Also an editor," she said with a grin.

Clint looked away, seeming to weigh his response.

"So what happened? Why did you break up with her? Was there something else going on?"

This was met with another beat of silence as they came to the end of the street, and turned and headed down to the path to the river. It was cooler amongst the trees, and Nadine shivered a moment.

"Are you okay?" he asked, a note of concern in his voice.

"I will be once you tell me what happened." She said, keeping her tone light. She didn't want to spook him and she was growing more apprehensive at his evasion.

Once they got to a bench that lay ahead around the curve, she sat and Clint joined her, resting his elbows on his knees as he watched the river flow past. They could hear only the gurgle of water slipping over the rocks.

Then Clint turned to look at Nadine, his expression serious. "You have to understand, this isn't easy for me to say." He bit his lip, and Nadine fought the urge to grab his shoulder and shake the words loose. Instead, she waited, knowing that silence was an interviewer's best friend.

"Your sister and I had been going out for a long time." Clint clasped his hands, tapping his thumbs together as he stared out over the river. "She seemed distracted, and I felt like she was putting me off. Trouble was, I was having my own doubts about the relationship from my side. There was someone else I was attracted to."

He stopped there and Nadine felt a prickling down her spine. When he looked at her, her breathing grew shallow. "I don't know if you realized it then, but that was you."

Nadine's heart thundered in her chest and she could only stare at him. "I...I...never knew. I thought you and Leslie were getting married. That was the plan."

"I don't think that was ever my plan, though for Leslie it might have been."

"So why was she putting you off?" Nadine felt confused, as if she was working her way through thick underbrush, unable to see where she was going, unable to know which was the right path.

"Because she was cheating on me."

Words failed Nadine.

"With who?" she squeaked out, shock stealing her voice.

Clint eased out a heavy sigh and waved off her comment. "It doesn't matter anymore."

There was something in his tone that bothered her.

"Why not?"

His heavy pause seemed ominous, and then he shook his head. "Sometimes it's better not to know."

Why would it matter who Leslie was with? Her sister had never had any secrets from her.

As Nadine held his gaze, she saw a flicker of sympathy in his eyes and then, as her thoughts flashed back, icy fingers slid down her spine. Memories of hastily ended phone calls between Leslie and someone. Dates that Paul cancelled.

"Was it Paul?"

Clint didn't need to say anything for her to know it was true. She could see it on his face.

She jumped to her feet, anger vying with grief. "How could Leslie do this?" she growled, her fingernails pressing into the palms of her hands and her shoulders rigid with fury and betrayal. "My own sister. And Paul. That useless—I didn't even like him that much. I just went out with him because he asked. Because my sisters both had boyfriends and I didn't. Because Leslie was dating —" she stopped herself before she finished that sentence.

Because Leslie was dating you, she had almost said.

Then Clint was at her side, his hand resting on her shoulder.

She held one hand up to keep him at arm's length. "Don't. Don't you dare feel sorry for me again."

He just looked at her, his expression unreadable, but he kept his hand where it was, his fingers curled around her shoulder. "I don't feel sorry for you. The last thing you need is my sympathy, and it's the last thing I want to give you. Paul, like Jack, was an idiot. He didn't appreciate what he had."

His words soothed some of her anger but didn't take it completely away.

How could her sister do this to her? She had Clint, why would she want Paul too?

She looked at him and realized that he too had been had. "I could say the same about Leslie," she said quietly.

"What do you mean?" His eyes held hers, unwavering, as if delving into her secrets and her soul.

But, she wasn't ready to go there.

"So, did you agree to break up?" she asked, feeling a need to get to the bottom of everything that happened all that time ago.

"She didn't want to. She told me Paul was over, that it was a mistake and she wanted another chance with me. I couldn't give that to her."

"Because..." Nadine prompted.

Clint turned and looked directly at her, his eyes glowing in the dusk. "Because, like I said, I was attracted to you. This whole thing with her and Paul became a good reason for me to break up with her."

His smile held a touch of melancholy, as if skipping back to that time. "Except my timing was as bad then as it is now. You had moved to the city and were still dating Paul. I was kind of messed up, and thought maybe you and Paul were trying to work things out. I figured you knew about Paul and Leslie by then."

Nadine sucked in a quick breath, fighting down another burst of anger at her sister.

Leslie never said anything. Her sister never let on. And neither did Paul. He just kept pretending everything was fine.

How could they?

"And you liked me?" she pressed, wanting to think about something else. Focus on the more positive things Clint was telling her.

"I've liked you for a long time, but you seemed determined to keep me at arm's length."

"I thought you liked my sisters. Like everyone else, including my boyfriend."

"I was attracted to your sisters, that's true enough. They were interesting and Leslie flirted with me. For a young guy who is in a new school, that's kind of heady stuff. But then I met you."

He brushed his fingers over her cheek, his eyes intent on her.

She swallowed, the old attraction weaving with the new emotions he was creating in her.

"You intrigued me. You challenged me, but you always talked to me like I was someone not worth your time."

"Defense mechanism," she said, swallowing as his fingers caressed her face, traced the outline of her lips.

"Against?"

"You. And how I felt about you. And the fact that you, like every guy I knew, were more attracted to my sisters than me—guys who pretended to like being with me in order to get to know them."

"Teenage boys can be shallow. You were probably way above them anyway."

He leaned closer, and Nadine wondered if he would kiss her again.

"I should have been smarter," he said, brushing a strand of hair back from her face, tangling his fingers in it and drawing her closer. "I should have spent more time with you. Pushed past that prickly exterior. I just never saw you as anything but a confident, smart girl who knew exactly who she was."

His words settled into the old wounds and soothed them. Filled the emptiness she had felt for so long. Resurrected old dreams, woven with new ones.

"And what is that?" she asked, knowing she was flirting with him. Just a little.

He chuckled, and she knew he realized it too.

"Gorgeous," he said, brushing a kiss over her forehead. "Stunning." Her eyes were next as his breath fanned her lips. "Amazing and smart." And with that, he claimed her mouth, pulling her close to him and wrapping his arms around her.

Nadine gave in, tangling her arms around his neck, feeling the warmth of his chest, the caress of his lips.

This, she thought, *this is what I've been missing. This is what I've needed.*

It felt like a slow, warm homecoming. A place she belonged, here in his arms.

After a while, he pulled back, looking intently down at her. "You mean a lot to me, Nadine. Always have."

She hardly dared believe this was happening; hardly dared to think they could be here. Together.

She stood in the warm circle of his arms, staring up at him, wondering what to think.

Clint pressed his index finger between her eyebrows. "You're frowning, which means you're thinking. What's going on behind those beautiful brown eyes?"

She smiled at the compliment, and angled her head to one side, as if to view him more objectively.

"I guess I'm just trying to be practical."

"As in, what's next?"

She nodded, thankful that he had been the one to bring it up.

"Well, why don't we let things go the way they should?" He brushed another kiss over her forehead. "Like we should have all those years ago."

151

"Okay. We can do that." Then she pulled away. "And...at the office? At work? How do we let things go there?"

A faint shadow crossed his face, and she wondered what caused it. Then decided she didn't want to know. She had waited so long for this moment, this time, she wanted to savor it.

"We let things go one day at a time," he said with a wry smile. "Which would be the best way to handle this."

Nadine returned his smile, thankful for his easy reply. His calm demeanor.

"You're probably right," she said.

"I usually am," he teased, tucking his arm into hers. "And right now, I think you should get home before your grandmother starts worrying about you."

"When Grandma finds out I was with you she won't care how long I stay out. She's your biggest fan," Nadine said as they walked back through the trees to the street.

"I kind of guessed that," Clint said. "That day she asked me over."

"I feel like I should apologize for being so snappy to you. About Leslie. Now that I know..." her voice trailed off, a glimmer of shame rising up.

"I understand," Clint said. "Though I'm glad it's all cleared up now."

They got back to her car, and Nadine reached in her purse for her keys, only to realize she hadn't gotten them back from Clint.

He remembered that at the same time, and as he handed them to her, a memory niggled at her.

"When you asked me out, you said you had a couple of things you wanted to talk to me about. Did we get them all?" She gave him a teasing smile, but he didn't return it.

"Doesn't matter," he said then gave her another quick kiss. "I'll see you tomorrow." He took a step back, and she sensed he was waiting until she got in the car. Watching out for her.

The thought gave her a surge of warmth. As she drove away,

she saw him standing in the street, watching her leave with his hands in his pockets.

Though the sight of him watching her should have made her feel protected, she couldn't help feeling uncertain.

Because she sensed that they hadn't covered what he wanted to talk about.

Worse than that, she sensed it had less to do with his and Leslie's relationship and more to do with Skyline.

CHAPTER 13

$\mathcal{T}$he next day was quieter than Nadine would have liked. Clint wasn't in his office when she arrived. A fire had come in over the police scanner, and because he was first in the office, he had gone to report on it. But, he had left a message for her that he wanted to see her as soon as he returned.

So, she headed to her office to get a few more things done. As soon as she clicked her mouse, the first document showing up on her computer was the Skyline story of the accident. Clint's fire would go above the fold in the next edition, but Nadine wanted this one below anyway. She had put off writing it, because she wasn't sure where it would end up. She rearranged the hastily scribbled notes on one side of the U-shaped computer desk, reviewing the information she had just about committed to memory.

As Nadine wrote up the story, weaving in the statistics, one part of her mind analyzed the flow while the other kept her emotions in check with difficulty. She had to prove to Clint that she could write this piece objectively.

She was immersed in her work when she heard a tap at the door behind her.

She closed the file she was working on, feeling guilty as she opened another file.

"Come in," she called out without looking up. She marked off one of the papers and turned back to the screen.

She kept her attention on the screen, her fingers flying over the keyboard. She was about to hit the backspace key to correct an error when she realized that whoever had come into the office still had said nothing. Glancing over her shoulder, she found her vision blocked by an expanse of white shirt, bisected by a brown tie.

Clint.

She swallowed down her anxious expectation, far too conscious of his hovering presence behind her. Her fingers stilled as she became all too aware of what had happened last night. Her breath came in shallow puffs and she struggled to concentrate. Surely he wasn't going to kiss her again? Not here in the office.

Then his hands came down beside her. She felt the faint warmth of his breath on her neck, his presence surrounding her.

"I see you're working on the subscription records?" His voice was a rumble behind her, raising her pulse and sucking her breath away.

Guilt suffused her. She tried to keep her eyes straight ahead and away from his hands bracketing her.

"You're distracting me," she said, her voice breathless.

"I'm sorry," he said.

He moved his hand, his weight shifted, and Nadine thought he would straighten. Instead, she felt his fingers brush her hair aside, sending shivers skittering down her spine. And then, impossibly, warm, soft lips touched her neck. They lingered a moment, their touch weakening her. She couldn't move, couldn't breathe, wished he would continue, prayed he would stop.

Then he straightened, and Nadine felt bereft.

He walked to one corner of her desk and perched on the edge, looking at her. "What's your plan for the subscription list?"

"I thought we could put out some ads, send out some newsletters." She stopped herself. She blamed her nervousness on a combination of his caress and the story she was hiding.

He gave her a smile, but she could see he wasn't fooled by her babbling.

"So, was that what you wanted to talk to me about?" she asked.

He frowned. "What do you mean?"

"Julie told me that you wanted to see me. I don't imagine it was for, well..." she let the sentence drift away, and he gave her a crooked smile.

"To try to kiss you?"

She shrugged. "Maybe."

He chuckled. "No. I'm trying to be professional and not succeeding. Though I had hoped the chance would come up."

She released a nervous laugh.

"I'm going out on a limb and guessing you were working on the accident story with Skyline," he said, picking up a piece of paper and scanning it.

On that paper were notes she had written up after the accident.

"Yes. I was." She leaned back in her chair, sorry for the switch in the mood, sensing this would not turn out well.

He pulled in a deep breath, then he set the paper down and crossed his arms. "I may as well jump right in. I was hoping you could give it to Wally or Allison."

She closed her eyes, their moment of closeness gone.

"Can I ask why?" She kept her voice low and controlled.

"Objectivity."

"Which you don't think I have."

Clint shook his head. "I think you're too close to it."

"Which you conveniently found out yesterday when I told you what happened to my father," she snapped, surprised at the sense of betrayal she felt. Was that the main reason he'd asked her out?

He told you about the kiss. The apology.

"I knew how that affected you before last night, Nadine."

"Yes. But you didn't know exactly how much it bothered me."

"I think I did."

"And you still want me to hand the story over."

"Yes. I do."

"You want to protect your paper from Skyline's lawyers."

"Believe it or not, it's not just about the paper. It's about you too."

She gave him a puzzled look. "What do you mean?"

He tapped his fingers on his arm, holding her gaze, as if delving deeper into her psyche. "I've seen firsthand how these vendettas can take over. I lived with it my whole life, watching my father's endless legal battles with his partner. The lawsuits, the visits with the lawyers."

"You don't want to go through it with the paper."

"No, I don't. I don't want to see you go through it either. I don't want it to take over your life, like it took over my father's. It won't satisfy you in the end."

"I've been a reporter long enough. I know how to be objective."

"Do you?"

Those two words seemed to strike at the very integrity she was always so proud of; they questioned her motives.

And? Could he be right?

Her emotions wavered.

"When it comes to Skyline, you seem to have blinders on," he pressed.

"Thanks to our date, you know exactly why."

"I do. And I sympathize for you, but I don't think you pushing this through to the end will make your father's death any easier."

"I loved my father and his name was dragged through the dirt. Skyline reneged on his benefits on his pension. They need to pay."

As she laid out her reasons, she heard the shrill tone in her voice. Saw the sorrow on Clint's face.

The pity.

The sharp ring of the phone broke the moment. Julie's voice came over the intercom. "Trace is on line one for you, Nadine." At exactly the same time, her office door opened and Elaine strode in carrying a pile of computer printouts that Nadine had requested.

Nadine pressed her hand against her face, confusion warring with a hysterical urge to laugh. She hit the button that connected her to Julie's speaker phone. "I prefer not to talk to him," she said sharply.

"Sure, hon." Julie broke off the connection.

"You're busy," he said as he pushed himself off the desk; then, without a backward glance, walked away.

Nadine followed Clint's exit with her eyes, still ignoring Elaine. Finally, she pulled herself together and took the documents from her.

"What did Clint want?" Elaine asked. "You look like you're in shock."

"It's fine," she said, waving Elaine's comment off. She felt as if she had come to a juncture in her life, as if everything she wanted stood in front of her—but she had to make a sacrifice to get it.

And she didn't know if she could.

"What happened?" Elaine asked, leaning on Nadine's desk, as if to get a closer look at her friend.

Nadine only shook her head. "Can we do this another time?"

"Sure." Elaine straightened. "I understand."

Nadine nodded and smiled her thanks. Elaine was a true friend, who knew when to ask questions and when to back off.

When the door closed, she looked back at the screen, trying to read the words she had typed just moments ago and trying to understand what she had meant.

She might as well have been reading Chinese. She let her eyes close with her hands idle on the keyboard. In the space of a day, she felt as if her entire world had rearranged. Yesterday at this time, she was contemplating a date with Trace.

Now...Trace was out of the picture and Clint had taken her out, and, today, had kissed her. Again.

Then he had told her, once again, to back off Skyline, choosing to protect his paper even after he found out exactly why Nadine needed to do this and how important it was to her.

Could she back off? After all these years, could she abandon this project?

CHAPTER 14

*T*hat night, Nadine prowled around the apartment, restless and uneasy, all the while berating herself for acting like a teenager in the throes of a crush.

At the same time, the words she'd thrown at Clint swirled and twisted through her mind.

Was she able to be objective when it came to Skyline?

Was she letting it take over her life as Clint accused her of?

She retreated to her bedroom-cum-office. Once there, she pulled up the Skyline file. She typed a few words, deleted them, and rearranged some of the copy, but it didn't help. Somehow the words sounded stilted and harsh. She didn't know if it was what Clint had said that haunted her, or the reality of what Clint said.

Frustrated, she fiddled with the words again. Nothing came. She decided to check some of the previous stories to see what she'd done with them.

A few clicks got her into her Skyline folder on Dropbox.

She highlighted them and opened them all at once. The first one came up on top and Nadine skimmed it, trying to read her reporting from a third-party point of view. It was easier to do now, this many years after the fact.

She wrote it five years ago, a year after her father died and she started working at the paper. She wrinkled her nose at the setup and the flow of the story. Obviously written shortly after taking too many journalism courses.

And obviously written from the perspective of a very angry and bitter young woman. Nadine sighed as she read through it, realizing how this must look to Clint and anyone else who read it. Long words, lots of rhetoric, and sprinkled with exclamation marks. With a click of her mouse button she closed it and skimmed through the next one, and then the next.

Clint was right. Her emotions had guided her writing. When she compared it to other stories she had written, the Skyline articles held a shrill tone.

On a hunch, she printed out the accident story she had written and some of the other Skyline articles and brought them to her grandmother, who sat on the couch knitting socks, humming along with a CD of hymns playing softly on the stereo.

"Can you do me a favor, Grandma?" Nadine asked, handing her the rough draft of her most recent article. "Can you read this and tell me what you think? I need another opinion."

"Okay." Barbara put her knitting down, took the paper, and slipped on the reading glasses hanging from a delicate chain around her neck. She took the paper from Nadine and started reading.

When she was finished, she looked at Nadine then back at the paper.

"Tell me the truth, Grandma," Nadine urged, sitting down on the couch beside her.

Barbara pursed her lips, glanced over it again, and then handed it back to Nadine. "It sounds very angry. You make it look like the accident is all Skyline's fault, without coming right out and saying that, of course."

Nadine bit back a rebuttal. She had asked for an objective statement and she had gotten it. That her grandmother's words mirrored so closely what Clint had said was not collusion or a conspiracy.

"Okay. What about these?" Nadine handed her a few of the other articles she had written. "These are some old articles I've written over the years about Skyline."

Barbara looked them over as well, her frown deepening with each one. "Funny that I don't remember reading them."

"You didn't always live here, you know."

Grandma gave her an oblique look that seemed to hold an edge of sorrow. "No. I didn't."

"Just read them please."

Barbara pushed her glasses up her nose again as she continued. The room was silent except for the rustling of papers as her grandmother laid each one down beside her. When she was done, she sighed. "Why did you give me these?"

"I wanted a second opinion." She looked away, choosing her words carefully. "Clint is having trouble with Skyline Contractors. In the past few years, each time I've written an article about them, they've threatened to sue us."

Barbara gasped. "What? There was nothing about it in the 'Court Docket.'"

Nadine resisted the urge to laugh. "It wouldn't end up in there, Grandma. That's for minor stuff. The major stuff gets handled neatly and tidily between lawyers who charge an arm and a leg to write threatening letters and file important documents back and forth." She picked up the articles, riffling through them absently. "They've always threatened, but never followed through. The trouble is that it costs the newspaper each time this happens."

"And this latest story..."

"Is newsworthy. I don't know if they'd sue over it."

"So why did you want me to read it?"

"Because I wanted to know if my boss was right." Nadine hesitated. It was difficult to admit that she might have been wrong. "I wanted to know if I've let my emotions rule my reason."

"I think where Skyline is concerned, you could never be completely objective." She stopped, tapping her forefinger on her lips.

"And..." prompted Nadine.

"I know there was more to the story of your father's death than what we were told. There was never a more careful and cautious boy than Sam Laidlaw. When that"—Grandma pursed her lips angrily—"slimy little man came to the door, trying to tell me that my son had done something unsafe and illegal..." Barbara glared at Nadine. "I was ready to go into battle. To prove them wrong. And I know you felt the same."

Nadine nodded, surprised at this side of her dear Grandma. Meddling, yes, but confrontational?

"But," Barbara continued, picking up her knitting again, "going into battle wouldn't bring your father back, trite as that may sound." Barbara knit a few more stitches, her needles flashing. "Your mother wasn't content to let things lie. She fought, battled, argued, spent hours on the telephone. When she got sick, she needed someone to continue, to be her hands and eyes, and the job fell to you."

Barbara paused, frowning at her needles. "I think your mother filled you with anger toward this company." Barbara looked at her granddaughter with a sad smile. "I think your mother took all the anger from her grief and poured it into you. I know you had your own anger, but you have never been one to mope and feel sorry for yourself." Barbara shook her head. "Your dear mother had a tendency to cling to righteous wrath. And when I read these pieces, I hear her anger, feel her pain."

Her grandmother reached over and squeezed Nadine's shoulder. "I want to know, too, the circumstances surrounding my son's death. But, it happened six years ago, Nadine. I've seen you spend a lot of time on the phone, writing letters to the government, talking to government officials, the police, and other Skyline workers. It was easing off just before your mother died, but I sense that you think you've failed her by not finding out after all this time."

Barbara slid over and slipped an arm around Nadine's waist. "Don't take on a burden that isn't yours to carry. You really have to let God take care of this one. Let Him comfort you, let Him carry that weight."

Nadine closed her eyes and let her grandmother hug her. At that moment, Nadine felt as if Barbara Laidlaw was taller and stronger than she could ever hope to be.

She straightened and picked up the papers. Shuffling them into a neat pile, she stared at them without really seeing them. "Was I wrong, Grandma? Was I wrong to write this? Was this a wrong thing to do?"

"I don't think so, dear." Barbara patted her on the shoulder. "You are a very good writer, very eloquent and very emotional. And someone needed to point out the mistakes. This company is not innocent by any means, but I think you are going about this the wrong way. Using the wrong tools."

Nadine laughed shortly, thinking of how Clint was trying to protect his paper and how she was creating a problem for him.

"I think it might be wrong to have kept your anger going so long." Barbara stroked Nadine's hair tenderly. "You are a wonderful, caring girl. I've never heard you complain, or grumble, even though you carry some heavy burdens." Barbara smiled at her granddaughter. "I've always been proud of what you have done in your life. Proud of the things you write, proud of the way your faith shines in your stories and articles. Maybe what you need to do is read over what you have written once again, for yourself, and see if what you know of God's love is shown in these articles."

Nadine nodded, realizing that no matter how much she thought she knew, she could always learn something from her dear grandmother.

Her grandmother stroked her hand. "More than that, I want to say that I love you, Nadine."

Nadine looked at her grandmother and caught her soft, wrinkled hand in hers, pressing it to her cheek. "I love you, too, Grandma."

Nadine gathered up her papers, stood and bent over to drop a kiss on her grandmother's head. "Thanks, Grandma," she said as she straightened. Her fingers feathered over her grandmother's gray head affectionately and, smiling, she turned and walked down the hallway.

Inside her bedroom, she stopped beside the computer, tapping the sheaf of papers against the top of her desk, chewing her lip. She still had all her notes at the office. Most of the groundwork had been done, and the story had to be told.

But not by me, she reasoned, looking down at the articles she had poured so much emotion into. Too much emotion. Her grandmother was right.

Allison could do it. It would be a good lesson in working under the pressure of a deadline.

Nadine dropped into her chair, pulled out the keyboard, and, with a few quick strokes, deleted the story she had just finished. For a moment, she stared at the white screen, wondering if she had done the right thing.

As the cursor blinked at her, she sat back, a sigh lifting her shoulders and dropping the weight she had been carrying since she had first heard of the accident. Her anger had been ignited, and all the stories of Skyline's misdeeds swirled around her head. She wanted to right what she saw as a wrong.

Now, it was as if the indignation had been swept away, the burning need to see justice done quenched under a blanket of peace. She bent her head, her fingers pressed against her face.

Thank you, Lord, she prayed, *thank you for my grandmother and what she teaches me; thank you for my job and what I can do in it. Help me to make wise decisions. In all my life.*

Then, as she lifted her eyes, a smile teased her lips. It was going to be all right. She didn't need to be the one to personally see that

Skyline was brought to justice as she remembered a poem that Grandma was fond of quoting: "Though the mills of God grind slowly, yet they grind exceeding small; / Though with patience He stands waiting, with exactness grinds He all."

She had to stop thinking she was the one to do the grinding. Things would happen on their own.

Clint was right.

~

Nadine got up and stood by the window, her hands in her pockets as she stared out at the darkened street, her revelation creating a surprising warmth and peace. The town looked exactly the same as it had a few minutes ago, but now it seemed to Nadine that she could look at it with more benevolent eyes.

A car's headlights swung around as it turned into their driveway. Puzzled, Nadine leaned closer, drawing aside the light curtain.

The car stopped, and the driver got out.

Trace.

What was he doing here? What did he want?

She dropped the curtain, and ran out of her room, determined to get to the door before Grandma. But, as she got to the kitchen, she realized she still wasn't as fast as her grandmother.

"Come in, Trace," Grandma was saying. "I'll tell Nadine you're here."

I should have told her, thought Nadine, *but now it's too late.*

She stepped into the kitchen as Grandma came in from the entrance. "Oh, there you are, Nadine. Trace is here." Grandma wasn't smiling, and neither was Nadine. *Nothing I can do about the situation,* she thought. She would have to do this with witnesses.

"Hi, Nadine." Trace stood framed by the kitchen door. He held out his hand as Nadine unconsciously stepped back. "You left this behind a couple of days ago," he said, holding out her sweater. "I thought I would return it."

"Thanks," Nadine said, reaching past her grandmother to take it from him. "I was wondering where it was."

Trace glanced over at Barbara, but when she made no move to leave, he squared his shoulders and faced Nadine. He hadn't shaved, his face looked haggard, heavy shadows circled his eyes. For a small moment she felt sorry for him. He looked worn and tired. "I'm really sorry about the other night."

Nadine shook her head. "Don't bother, Trace," she replied. "We have nothing to say to each other."

"We do. I need to talk to you. I have something to tell you that changes everything." Trace plunged his hand through his hair, his expression pleading. "Please come with me. Please hear me out," he continued.

Nadine didn't answer, but she suspected that if she didn't go with Trace, he wouldn't leave until she heard what he had to say. And she preferred not to cause a scene in front of her grandma. She turned to Barbara. "I'm going with Trace for a short drive." She put heavy emphasis on the word *short*. "I'll be back in a while."

Her grandmother scowled at her, as if questioning her wisdom, but Nadine shook her head.

As she walked past Trace, she caught a coat off a hook in the entrance and stepped out the door before he could open it for her. She shoved her cell phone in her pocket.

Trace started the car and drove down the street.

"Where are we going?" she asked as he turned left toward the highway instead of right toward downtown.

"I just want to get away from town, just go for a drive," he replied. "I have a lot to tell you."

"Can you start now?"

Trace glanced at her, biting his lip. "I don't know where to."

"What do you mean?"

Once he turned onto the highway, he sped up. The lights of town receded behind them, and Nadine felt a moment's apprehension. Trace seemed distraught, and she wondered at the wisdom of going with him in his car.

"I've had a lot on my mind lately," Trace said after a while. "I've had to make some hard decisions, and I haven't been able to tell you about them." He looked at her again, reaching out for her hand.

But Nadine kept her fingers wrapped around her jacket.

"What haven't you been able to tell me about, Trace?" she asked.

Trace hesitated, his hands wrapped tightly around the steering wheel. "When we met, there was an emptiness in my life I couldn't fill."

His words echoed thoughts that had tortured Nadine as well, and for the first time since he had started the car, she looked at him fully.

He glanced at her and smiled, and said, "I really care for you, Nadine. I do. I've never met anyone like you. Someone I could laugh with..." He paused and looked ahead again. "Someone I could admire and love."

"But..." she prompted, sensing he had much more to say.

Trace shook his head, as if to deny what he had to do. "The reason I've been so evasive with you is that, well, I'm married."

Married. Shock jolted her back into her seat.

Married. She had been dating a married man, spending time with him, laughing with him, and keeping him away from a wife, maybe even children.

"How..." she began, then stopped, unable to articulate her confusion and anger. "How could you do this?" she demanded, clenching her jacket. "Why didn't you tell me?"

"My wife and I have been living apart for almost eight months already, and I didn't think it mattered." Trace laughed shortly. "After I left Tina, I moved into a hotel in Sweet Creek. I bought the paper and would read your articles. I could tell that you had a strong faith, that you had a strength I was looking for. When I read the article about us going to the movie, I knew I had to come to the office. When I first saw you sitting there, I was stunned. You were, *are*," he corrected, "so beautiful."

"Why were you and your wife separated?" Nadine interrupted him.

"Tina and I are incompatible. She didn't want to go to church, and I did. She didn't want to raise our children to go, either."

"You have children?" Nadine asked weakly. She dropped her head against the back of the seat, nausea filling her stomach. How could he not tell her?

"That's why I haven't been able to keep our dates. 'Cause of my kids. But, it's not as bad as it sounds," he continued hastily. "I'm getting a divorce, I'm trying for custody of the children. Tina and I already live apart. I came to Sweet Creek to make a new start, and then I met you." He sped up. "Can't you see? It was meant to be."

"No, it wasn't," she said vehemently. "It was a terrible mistake. You have a wife and children." She couldn't get past that. "You went out with me when you should have been with them." Nadine couldn't continue, couldn't think. Were there no more faithful people in the world? Paul, Jack, her sister, now this fake boyfriend?

"Turn around," she said suddenly.

"Nadine, you don't understand. I visited them when I wanted to be with you. But once the divorce is final and we're together, with the kids—"

"Stop the car. I want you to turn around and take me back home. We have nothing more to talk about."

"I won't, Nadine, until you listen to me." Trace twisted his hands on the steering wheel, his jaw clenched. "My marriage to Tina was a mistake—"

"Don't even try to explain away what you have done. You

made vows and promises. You broke them each time we were together, and I helped..." Nadine couldn't help the catch in her voice as she thought of the time they had spent together. "You made me an unwitting part of that, and I can't forgive you. Not now." She bit her lip, unable to articulate the anger and frustration that flowed through her. "Bring me back home, Trace. Now."

He slowed down, and Nadine breathed a sigh of relief. But when he pulled in to a field and stopped, fear gripped her heart. Trace turned the car off and turned to her. Panic shot through her as she kept her eyes on him while fumbling for the door handle. "What are you doing?"

"You don't have to be afraid of me, Nadine." He reached out to touch her hair. "I would never hurt you. I wouldn't do that to you."

Her fingers continued to scrabble at the handle. *Please open, please open,* she prayed. With a quick jerk, she yanked on the handle. She jumped out of the car, and stumbled as her coat fell out of the car and tangled around her legs. The interior light of the car shone feebly on the freshly plowed field. She tried to run, tripped on a lump of dirt, and regained her balance.

Trace got out of the car, and she tried to increase her speed.

"Nadine, don't run. You'll hurt yourself," Trace warned.

She kept moving awkwardly, her feet unable to keep up to her head. *Hurry, hurry,* she urged, her ankle twisting as she hit another furrow, unable to find even ground.

"I'm not coming after you, Nadine. Just stop." His voice came from farther away and she spared a glance over her shoulder.

The car was well behind her, and she could see Trace's figure silhouetted against the open door of the car.

"Come back, Nadine. I'll drive you home."

Still she hesitated. She was too far from town to walk back, especially in the dark. But she knew she couldn't be with him one second longer. She shoved her hands in her pocket, thankful she had brought her cell phone. "Just go Trace. Just leave."

Then he banged his fists on the roof of the car, startling Nadine. "You have to change your mind, *you have to!*" he yelled. Nadine took another step back, ready to run again. Trace sounded out of control, and she was frightened.

"Trace, calm down. You don't know what you're saying." *Please, Lord, send him away,* she prayed.

He waited a moment as she poised, ready to run again.

Then, thankfully, he jumped into the car and slammed the door shut. He started it up and gunned the engine. Dirt flew as he backed out onto the road. Then he left.

Nadine watched the glow of his taillights as they receded in the distance, the roar of his engine growing fainter as the chill of the evening made itself known.

Her eyes adjusted to the dark. A pale crescent moon hung in the sky above her, shedding a faint illumination on the land.

For now, all she could see was that she was walking in an open, plowed field. Across the road was another open field; and to her left, a row of trees marking the quarter line; and beyond that, more bush.

"Don't panic and don't cry," she told herself as she picked her way along. "You did the right thing."

The furrows were deep and hard, and the lack of light made it doubly difficult to walk. She shivered in the chill wind, and then pulled her cell phone out of her coat pocket. One feeble little bar, barely enough reception to make a call, and the "Battery Low" sign was on.

She punched in the numbers to her house and lifted the phone, wincing as the static crackled in her ear. The phone at her home rang again and again. "Please answer it, Grandma, please," she pleaded. Finally, she heard, "Hello?"

Nadine sagged in relief. "Thank goodness you're still up, Grandma. It's Nadine."

"Nadine...are you..." Crackling static broke into the conversation.

"I'm close to the river." Nadine clutched the phone with one hand and her thin jacket with the other. The wind was picking up, and already, her ears were getting cold. "Trace dropped me off somewhere in the valley."

"Where?"

"I'm at least half an hour's drive out of town."

"Which—" her words were drowned by static "—direction?"

"West. We drove west out of town, then he turned north up the valley to Fort Henday." The static crackled louder. She turned to see if the reception got any better.

She was now walking into the chilly wind. Her fingers were numb, and her ears ached, but at least the static had died down.

"Is there anything you recognize?"

"I know where I am—up the Coal Creek road. Can you come and get me?"

"Yes. Of course. Just stay where you are." There was a moment's pause. "You are okay, aren't you?"

"Yes," Nadine replied, her voice unexpectedly shaky. "Yes, I am."

"Okay. I'll be...soon..." Grandma's voice faded away and Nadine lowered the now-dark handset. The battery was dead.

She dropped it into her pocket and turned her back to the wind. Nadine wrapped her coat closer around her, tucking her hands into the wide sleeves. It was her least practical coat, a thin corduroy barn jacket she had picked up at a garage sale a few days ago because it was red.

Trace said she looked good in red. Trace, who was married.

Nadine sniffed, swallowed, determined not to cry. She felt cheap, humiliated, and vulgar. She hadn't known he had a wife and children. He hadn't given an inkling during their many conversations.

Nadine looked up at the stars that spread away from her, feeling small, unimportant, disposable. She was walking along a dark, empty road—a tiny figure on a huge globe populated with many other tiny figures, each with their own sorrows and problems. What made her think her problems were so much worse than many others?

Even as she formed that thought, she knew that the same God who had created all this from nothing also heard her prayers, whether softly whispered or shouted aloud.

Now, walking along the road, she prayed. As she prayed, she felt God's peace wash over her, comfort, and strengthen her.

But her hands were still cold.

She shoved her hands farther up her sleeves and hurried, hoping the movement would get her blood flowing and warm her up. Behind her, the bitter wind pushed itself through the thin material of her jacket, whipped her hair around her face, and seeped into her bones.

She shivered and pulled one hand out of her sleeve and pressed its meager warmth against one aching ear. After a while, she traded hands. It helped a small amount, but her hands would not warm up.

Please, Lord. Let my grandmother come soon, before I can't move anymore.

Finally a faint light shone above a rise in the road ahead of her. It got brighter and brighter, and then headlights blinded her as a vehicle topped the rise and roared toward her.

Not Grandma, she thought with a sinking heart. Grandma's little car had only one headlight and about half the horsepower. She paused, clutching her coat, waving her arm. She didn't care who it was, she would ask if they could at least drive her somewhere warm.

But the vehicle drove past her, then slowed and turned around. She watched the SUV as it pulled up beside her, and her heart sank as she recognized the vehicle. The driver door opened and she took a step back as a tall figure stepped out.

Clint Fletcher.

Shock slammed through her. *How did he know? What had made him come at precisely that moment?*

Nadine hesitated, her heart beating in a staccato rhythm, her feet unresponsive. "How..."

"Doesn't matter, just get in." Clint moved around the vehicle and opened the door for her. She took a few shaky steps and climbed in, heart racing. Clint slammed the door shut behind her and walked around the front, momentarily illuminated by the headlights. He was frowning and his lips were pursed. Was he angry? As he closed his door, Nadine was surrounded by blissful warmth, blessed heat.

"Are you okay?" Clint asked, turning to her. He draped one arm over the steering wheel, while the other lay along the back of her seat.

She nodded, unable to look at him. "My grandmother is coming..." She could hardly speak, her lips were so numb.

"Actually, she called me and asked me to come and get you."

The thrum of the engine and the gentle hum of the heater were the only sounds in the dark intimacy of the SUV. Nadine bit her lip, trying to stop her erratic breathing.

"Are you sure you're okay?" There was concern in his deep voice.

Nadine nodded, shivering as she began to warm up. She laid her head back, felt Clint's hand, and sat up again. She swallowed, hardly knowing where to start.

His hand touched her head, curving around it, the warmth of his hand seeping through her hair, making him very real.

"He didn't hurt you, did he?" Clint's fingers tightened their hold.

"No. No, he didn't."

"Good."

Silence again.

"That's some kind of boyfriend you got there."

"I already told you, he's not my boyfriend. He just wanted to talk, and I thought, after the way I used him, I owed him at least that."

Silence followed her admission. Clint shifted his weight, and his hands engulfed hers, warming them. "You're freezing," he said quietly, rubbing her hands with vigor. "How long have you been out here?"

"About an hour, maybe more." She still couldn't look at him, because she still was absorbing what had happened, what was happening now.

"Trace just dropped you off?"

"I could have gotten a ride back to town with him, but I didn't think it was wise to stay around him anymore. He was quite...upset."

"Upset? Why?" Clint rubbed harder, then stopped when Nadine winced. "Sorry," he murmured, pressing her hands between his large warm ones.

"I got mad at him when I found out he—" Nadine's voice caught, and the words came tumbling out. "He's married, Clint. He has two kids and a wife named Tina. They've been separated for a while, and he wants to file for a divorce." Nadine turned to Clint, her fingers entangling with his. "I didn't know anything about it when I went out with him. Truly. I'm so, so ashamed."

Clint looked down, his thumbs caressing the backs of her hands.

"Of what?"

She released a harsh laugh. "Don't you see? I'm just like my sister. Going out with someone who belonged to someone else."

Clint raised his head, his eyes narrowed. "Did you know he was married?"

"No. I didn't."

"Then how do you see yourself as wrong here?" Clint's quiet question soothed her concerns, eased her shame.

"A couple of reasons."

"Like?"

Nadine eased out another sigh, realizing how foolish the whole situation was—she may as well tell him everything.

"It all started with trying to get Grandma off my back."

"What?"

"She'd been trying to set me up with all kinds of unsuitable and oddball guys—"

"Like me?" Clint said with a faint chuckle in his voice, which made her smile despite the situation.

"At the time, I didn't know the entire truth about Leslie, so in a way, yes."

"I hope you've changed your mind about that."

"You know I have," she said, sending him a gentle smile. Then she cleared her throat. "Anyway, Grandma. It was driving me crazy. I've been trying to get her to move out for months now, but she won't go until she thinks I've found someone and I'm engaged."

This was greeted with silence, and Nadine realized how that might sound.

But, she didn't know how to claw back from that so she plunged onward.

"I finally got tired of it and told her, in a fit of frustration, that I had a boyfriend and that I was fine. I was hoping she would get the hint and leave. When she asked me who it was, I pulled some name out of the ether."

"You made up his name?" Clint chuckled.

"Glad you can see the humor in this, but it wasn't completely made up. I had been doing a piece on the new equipment dealership in town, and Trace's name must have been in it, because his was the first name that came to mind. Then Elaine decided the 'romance,'" she made the ubiquitous bunny fingers, "needed some help. She knows Grandma always reads 'About Town,' so she wrote that piece about me and Trace going to the movie in East-bar. And then Trace showed up at the office and he was, well, attractive and fun and interested in me." At that moment, she was thankful for the darkness they sat in so Clint couldn't see her cheeks flush with embarrassment.

"He is kind of good looking, now that you mention it."

"You're laughing at me." She gave him a gentle swat.

"Well, it is rather funny."

"I guess."

"So, why did you break up with him?"

Nadine could see the soft glow of his eyes, remembered the kiss he had given her, their conversation in the restaurant. He had come for her. Grandma had asked him to, but he had come for her. She squeezed his hands as she took a deep breath and a chance.

"I like someone else better."

Clint's thumbs slowed, and he released her one hand, his coming up to touch her cheek. "That's good," he said. Their eyes met in understanding, and Nadine's breath left her body. His fingers stilled, and moved from her face to her neck.

"What are you doing?" she whispered.

"Kissing you again." He slid his fingers around her neck as his eyes held hers. Mesmerized, she drifted toward him. He drew her closer and then, finally, oh finally, their lips touched.

Hesitantly at first, as if the intimacy was too much to absorb at once. Then his hand tightened, pulled her nearer, and fitted his mouth closer, his other arm coming around to pull her against the solid warmth of his chest.

Nadine's eyes drifted shut, and her hand slipped across the breadth of his shoulder, around his neck. He was warm, solid, real.

She kissed him back, their lips moving carefully, exploring, discovering. This was where she should be. It was as if a mocking echo of her past had finally been stilled here, in Clint Fletcher's arms.

She drew back, her fingertips stroking his cheek.

CAROLYNE AARSEN

His features became serious, then, as his fingers explored her face: "So, here we are again."

She nodded, still trying to sort what had happened in the office with the articles she had shown her grandmother.

Trying to figure out what to do about Clint; what to do about Skyline.

She made the plunge. "I'm taking your advice," she said. "I'm letting Allison write up the accident story."

In the glow of the dashboard, she caught the glimmer of a smile.

"I figured that would make you happy," she said with a wistful tone. Though part of her still struggled with letting go, she knew allowing Allison to take the article was a first and very important step.

Clint reached across the console and caught her hand in his. "I hope it makes you happy."

"I don't know yet. Finding out the truth about my father has been such a large part of my life—too large it seems—so it won't be so easy to just walk away."

"No. I suppose not." He gave her hand a light squeeze.

"Anyway, I was going to tell you tomorrow, and then, well, this," she waved her hand around, as if encompassing everything that happened tonight.

"I'm glad you told me now. I'll be gone the next couple of days. I have a meeting in Cranbrook that I can't get out of."

She was surprised at the disappointment she felt.

"Well, I'm sorry to hear that."

"I'm sorry to tell you. I was looking forward to stealing a kiss in the break room again."

"You wouldn't," Nadine said, half laughing, half anticipating the idea.

"I'm the boss. I can do what I want," he said, lifting her hand to his and pressing a warm kiss to her palm. "Anyway, this one will have to hold you for now."

She smiled and curled her fingers around her palm. "I'll keep it in a safe place until I need it."

He laughed at that, then turned ahead, put the car in gear and headed down the road.

Back to town.

CHAPTER 15

"What do I do with this?" Allison stood in front of Nadine's desk the next day, her hands holding the sheaf of notes she took the previous week.

Nadine looked up at her, gathering her scattered thoughts.

"I'm supposed to get these into a coherent article by this afternoon?" Allison lifted her hand as if in surrender. "I thought you were writing it up. I don't have the background on this company you do."

"That's why I asked you to write it up." Nadine smiled at Allison as her intercom beeped. "You'll have a different perspective on everything."

"You've got a caller on line one." Julie's voice came in over the intercom.

"You'll do just fine, Allison," Nadine said, waving her away. "Now get to work. I'll vet it for you once you're done." She punched the button and picked up the phone, dismissing her new reporter.

Allison looked at the notes again and then left.

"Hello," Nadine said, with a grin at Allison's expression as she left. Nadine tucked the phone under one ear, putting the papers from the desk and into a folder.

"Miss Laidlaw?"

"Yes."

"I'm the lady who wants to meet you at the volleyball game Friday." The woman's voice was harsh and deep—the voice of a smoker.

Nadine flipped over the pages of her desk calendar, feeling confused. Nothing was written down. "Volleyball game?" She couldn't remember setting up an appointment.

"I sent you the letter. About Skyline."

Nadine clutched the handset, her heart fluttering as it all came back. How could she have forgotten?

"Five o'clock work out for you?" the harsh voice continued.

Nadine's thoughts immediately jumped to Clint. What would he think? Should she do this?

She pushed her questions aside. She wasn't doing anything with the information. It was only a meeting, a way to put an end to this once and for all, like he had encouraged her to.

"Yes," Nadine assured her, pulling a pen and a pad toward her. "I'll be there covering a volleyball game. How will I know you?"

"Like I said, I'll be wearing a green sweatshirt and gray pants. I know what you look like. Just stay in the main gymnasium and I'll find you."

"Okay. Five o'clock, main gym. Gotcha."

"No one else will know or be there?"

Nadine hesitated, wondering if she was getting set up. The lady sounded like a kook, but she didn't dare offend her. She had waited too long to find out what this informer knew. "No one else will know. Can I ask your name?"

"Chantelle."

"Okay Chantelle. I'll see you then."

Without saying goodbye, Nadine's mystery caller hung up.

Nadine laid the phone in the cradle and, blowing out her

breath, leaned back. There was altogether too much mystery surrounding this woman, and for a moment, Nadine was tempted to let it all go. She had promised Clint she would back off Skyline.

This is for me, she realized. *This is for my mother.*

While she had passed off the accident article to Allison, she knew she had to follow up on this.

~

Clint waited while Julie patched him into Nadine's office, feeling a moment's apprehension, wishing he was back in Sweet Creek and not stuck in a hotel in Cranbrook. But when a major advertiser calls to talk about an account, you go.

However, now he felt as nervous as a teenager and had to remind himself that he was Nadine's boss as well as...

He wasn't sure what, exactly. He knew only that he had no intention of letting Nadine slip from his hands again.

"Hello." Nadine's hesitant voice made him smile.

"Hi, this is your boss. I was wondering if you have some important school-board meeting to cover on Friday night."

"Wally's doing that." She sounded reserved.

"No volleyball games?"

"I've got Allison on them."

She sounded distant, and it bothered him. Was she regretting their times together? Was she thinking of Trace again?

Clint leaned his forehead against the cool window of his hotel room. He wished he were back in his office just down from Nadine's. He wanted to hold her and remind himself that she had come willingly into his arms. He didn't know where to begin with this girl who had him tied up in knots for so many years. "Then you can spare some time for me?"

"Friday night? This Friday night? I thought you weren't coming back until Saturday."

I'm coming earlier because I missed you.

No way he was telling her that.

"I thought I could pick you up at about six from your apartment."

She was silent a moment, then said, almost breathlessly, "Can we make it later?"

She sounded like she was putting him off, and Clint didn't know if it was his overactive imagination or if she was avoiding him.

He really had to let this go. Remind himself of the good times, of the moments of closeness, of the things they shared. She was probably busy.

"Okay. How about six thirty? I'll call you once more, just to confirm." *Goodness,* he thought, *sounds as if you're making hotel reservations.*

And he said his final farewells, feeling distinctly unloverlike.

He wished he could go back to Sweet Creek right now, before Nadine changed her mind about him.

Just as he was trying to figure out how to duck out of his meetings early, his cell phone rang.

He glanced at the screen. His lawyer.

"Hey, how's it going?" he asked, hoping and praying Matthew wasn't calling to talk to him about Skyline.

"Not bad. Been busy. My dad has me running. He asked me to talk to you about Nadine and Skyline again. She's been ruffling a few too many feathers and they've been calling. As your lawyer, I thought I should let you know the firm doesn't want to get in Skyline's crosshairs. We've got too many things going on right now and can't afford the exposure."

"I think things are in check. There was an accident last week with a Skyline employee, but Nadine passed the article off to the new hire so I think it will be more balanced."

"She going to leave them alone?"

Clint stood by the hotel room window, looking out over the lights of the city spangled below, wishing he were home instead of here. "She said she would, and I trust her."

"I hope so for her sake, yours, and the paper's," Matthew said, his voice holding an ominous tone. "Skyline is getting a rather itchy trigger finger."

"Enough with the shooting analogy. I get it."

"Like I said, I hope so."

Clint said goodbye then held his phone in his hand, feeling a sudden need to call Nadine again. To make sure she was doing what he asked.

Would that make me look needy?

He tossed his phone aside then returned to his desk.

But as he opened his laptop, he couldn't help but wonder why Nadine sounded so evasive about Friday night.

CHAPTER 16

*B*y Friday afternoon, Nadine was in such a dither, she couldn't concentrate. She didn't know what to attribute which emotion to—Clint was taking her out that night, and she was meeting with Chantelle. In a few hours she would, hopefully, discover the truth about her father. And after that...

She had committed herself to meeting this lady yet felt that she was betraying Clint.

You're not doing anything with it, she reminded herself. *It's just for information. Just to bring this full circle.*

She tried to keep herself busy and her eyes off the clock, but it didn't work. At about four thirty, she gave up. She didn't have to feel guilty about not working until five; goodness knows she had enough overtime hours at the office.

She drove home then showered and changed, her mind bouncing between a loyalty to Clint and a need to find out what this lady knew.

Thankfully Grandma was gone, which meant she didn't need to explain her actions. She hadn't told Grandma about the mystery lady, just in case it turned out to be a hoax. Nadine didn't want to disappoint her, nor did she want to listen to a lecture about leaving things alone, especially after their little chat the other night. So, she wrote a quick note, letting Grandma know she was at the school.

Teams were warming up by the time Nadine entered the foyer, and the shrill sounds of whistles echoed through the gym. She stood in the doorway of one of the gyms, checking the bleachers. Spectators lined the walls, but Nadine didn't spot a green sweatshirt. She went to the other one, but nothing. Thankfully Allison hadn't seen her. She wandered restlessly around the hallways, returning every few minutes to check.

Half an hour later, Nadine's stomach was in knots. It was five thirty. Clint was coming at six-thirty.

At ten to six, she was pacing the hallway. She had maybe fifteen more minutes before she absolutely had to leave.

What if this was all a hoax, she wondered as she glanced at her watch. *What if Skyline planted this lady just to sabotage my life?*

Don't be ridiculous. You're getting paranoid because you're feeling guilty. You told Clint you would back off.

She wondered if she should leave a note. Where? How? Did she dare walk away?

Did she dare risk her relationship with Clint?

Nadine almost laughed aloud. It was as if she had to choose between silencing the echoes of the past or grasping a hope for the future.

Nadine glanced once more at her watch. Her stomach tightened as the hands moved steadily on to six fifteen.

Was she sabotaging her chance with Clint? She reminded herself that he had said six thirty at her house; she had a few minutes before she had to leave.

She stepped back into the gym to make one more circle before leaving.

A movement in the bleachers caught her eye, and Nadine saw a green, hooded sweatshirt and gray pants. Her shoulders sagging in relief, she ran around the edge of the court and caught up to the slight female figure exiting the stairs.

"Excuse me," Nadine said, tapping her on the shoulder. "Were you looking for me? Nadine Laidlaw."

The woman spun around. Slight, fair-haired, streaks of gray glinting at her temples. Her eyes seemed weary and her smile forced as she looked at Nadine. "I thought that was you." She shoved her hands into the front pocket of her hoodie and indicated with her head that she wanted to talk outside.

Nadine followed her, trying to get her pounding heart to slow down. *She's just going to answer a few questions, nothing major,* she thought. *Don't expect too much.* Nadine had to wipe her sweaty palms on her pants as they stepped from the noisy foyer into the relative quiet of outside.

The woman lit a cigarette, and Nadine was surprised to see the flame of the lighter tremble. She pulled in a deep drag, blew it out, and looked at Nadine. "You know who I am. Chantelle. My brother, Gordon, used to work for Skyline. He worked with your father."

This is it, Nadine thought. *What my family has been waiting for, all this time.*

"My brother was hired by Skyline almost seven years ago, a month before your father died." Chantelle left the cigarette in her mouth as she dug into the pocket of her jeans. She pulled out an envelope and handed it to Nadine. "Six months ago, he tried to commit suicide and failed. Before he tried, he wrote a suicide note."

Nadine glanced at Chantelle's face and back at the envelope.

"Go on," urged Chantelle, shoving the envelope into Nadine's hands. "Take it. It's a photocopy. I read it already, know what it says. He worked for that company for two months after the accident, and he hadn't been the same since. I wanted to know what caused it. What made him want to kill himself?" She released a bitter laugh. "I almost wish I hadn't."

"What happened?" Nadine asked, her voice breaking. "That he tried to commit suicide, I mean."

Chantelle shrugged. "Gordon wasn't what you'd call scholarship material, so we were really glad when he got the job." She took another drag from her cigarette. "He was there when your father died. He'd been threatened by unknown people telling him to keep his mouth shut. I know you write articles about Skyline and are not afraid to call them what they are. Cheats, liars." Chantelle waved the burning cigarette at the letter, the smoke wreathing between them. "Your father didn't die because he was careless. He died because of my brother but also because of Skyline." Chantelle dropped her unfinished cigarette and ground it out with the toe of her running shoe. "The letter explains everything." She looked up at Nadine, her eyes almost glowing in the gathering dusk.

Nadine held up the envelope and looked at it once again. "I'll read it. For sure I'll read it. Thanks." She was fully aware of the passing time, and now that she had fulfilled one obligation, she was anxious to get home.

"I want to see those guys pulled down for what they did to Gordon and to your family." Chantelle took a step forward, her eyes burning with intensity. For a moment, Nadine feared what she saw in Chantelle's eyes. "You can show everyone what they are. Now you have proof."

Nadine swallowed. "I'll do what I can, Chantelle."

Chantelle stared hard at her. "I hate them, Laidlaw. I really hate them." She pulled out her cigarette package and withdrew another cigarette. "I hate what they do to the community, I hate what they did to my family. They're a pack of lying, cheating..."

As she listened to her rant gain momentum Nadine thought of her own anger, her own sorrow. Yes, she wanted to see justice done. Yes, she wanted to see Skyline brought down just as Chantelle did. But surely, she didn't have the same deep, intense hatred as Chantelle?

"What are you going to do?" Chantelle asked, inhaling on her cigarette.

Nadine pocketed the letter. "First I'll read the letter and find out exactly what your brother knew then take it from there."

"You're not wussing out on me, now, are you?" Chantelle waved her glowing cigarette at her. "It's all in there. In that letter. You read it." Chantelle walked backward toward the gym, still talking. "I'll call you in a couple of days and you can tell me then. Now I gotta watch my kid play." She pulled open the door, a flood of noise spilling out. When it slammed shut, it cut off the sounds of the tournament. Nadine leaned back against the wall, her insides trembling in reaction and with a touch of fear. Chantelle had seemed almost fanatical, and Nadine wondered what in the world was in the letter.

She glanced at her watch. Six-fifteen! She turned and ran. It would take her ten minutes to get home. The thought that Clint might be waiting hurried her steps and lightened her heart in spite of her meeting.

She and Clint were going on a real date. A planned date.

Her feet pounded out a steady rhythm as her breathing became more labored. *Only a little farther*, she reassured herself. *Just a few more blocks. Let him be there, Lord. Let him be waiting.* She didn't dare stop—could hardly keep going—and almost skidded around the corner to her street. When she saw only her grandmother's car and her old car in front of the house, she slowed her pace and clutched her side, her chest heaving, wishing she had driven to the school instead of walking.

By the time she got to the apartment, her breathing was slowing, but her legs were trembling with a combination of the extra exertion and anticipation. She walked into the entrance, her heart still pounding.

"Hey, Grandma," she called out, kicking off her shoes and setting them neatly in the porch. "I'm home."

"Nadine." Grandma's voice chided her from the end of the

hallway just as Nadine hung up her coat. "I got your note. You're late."

Nadine stepped into the kitchen, her heartbeat finally slowing. "Sorry. I had to meet someone for an interview at the school."

Grandma stood in the kitchen, her arms folded across her chest and her head pitched to one side. "Clint has been here waiting for you. He just left."

Nadine's heart stopped, beat once, and began racing again, this time in fear. "What—what did you say?"

"I said Clint just left."

"I tried to phone you."

Barbara Laidlaw looked sheepish. "When I came back, I wanted to have a nap, so I turned off the ringer. I remembered at six to turn it back on."

Nadine took a slow breath, willing her heart to still. "How long was he waiting here?"

"He came here at six, said he was way early. Then someone named Allison phoned here at a quarter past six asking for you. I asked if she wanted to talk to Clint. She did, and then after he talked to her, he left." Grandma walked over to Nadine. "What is happening? Were you and Clint supposed to have a date tonight, and who is this Allison?"

"She's a new reporter at the paper." Nadine chewed her lip, remembering how she had told Clint that Allison was covering the volleyball games at the gym, not her. Now it looked for sure as if she was hiding something. What should she do now? "Did Clint say where he was going?"

"He just thanked me for the tea and left."

"I gotta go, Grandma." She turned and ran into the entrance. "I don't know when I'll be back. Don't wait up for me." As she grabbed her car keys off the hook, she flashed a nervous smile at her hovering grandmother. "I'll tell you all about it later."

Her stomach was churning by the time she pulled into a parking spot at the school.

As she strode down the sidewalk, she glanced at the vehicles. No sign of Clint's silver SUV. She took a shortcut across the lawn, and just as she came to the corner of the gym, she heard a vehicle drive out of the parking lot.

With a sinking heart, she watched Clint Fletcher's vehicle slow and then spin around the corner and down the road.

CHAPTER 17

*N*adine leaned against the brick wall of the gym as she watched Clint's SUV leave. What was going on? Was he going back in the direction of her apartment?

"You still here? I thought you were gone."

Nadine's heart stopped at Chantelle's all-too-familiar voice. She turned. "I was, but I was hoping to meet someone."

"That new guy at the paper?" Chantelle rubbed one hand along the side of her pants, jerking her chin in the direction Clint's car went. "You just missed him."

A coldness gripped Nadine's chest. "How do you know?"

Chantelle snapped her gum. "I recognized him and talked to him. Told him some of what I told you. Figured it wouldn't hurt if two people knew the story."

Nadine's hands felt like ice, and her heart, a heavy weight. Clint knew why she had come here, why she had missed him.

"He didn't seem real interested at first," warned Chantelle. "But when I told him it was about Skyline, he looked as mad as I felt."

Each word she spoke added to the heaviness in her chest. Nadine nodded in acknowledgment then ran to her car. Her head ached, and her side still hurt by the time she pulled in her driveway. No silver SUV was parked in front of the apartment.

Nadine laid her head against the steering wheel and allowed herself a few moments of tears. Was the letter worth it? Even if it proved that her father was innocent, would it change anything? She wasn't doing anything with the letter. But would Clint know that?

Nadine remembered Chantelle's bitterness and knew she also had the same burning need for revenge. But, she had learned that it wasn't up to her to bring justice into the world; she had done what she could, and she had to let go.

But Clint. What was he thinking right now?

Her stomach plunged again as she thought of him talking to Chantelle, hearing what she had to say.

Can we back up and do this again, Lord? I'd like another try. I'll make the right choice this time.

As she looked up at the lights of her apartment, extra bright through her tears, she knew she'd had her chance and had made her choices. The letter in her pocket wasn't worth the opportunity with Clint Fletcher she was throwing away.

She bit her lip and indulged in a few more minutes of tears. Then, palming away the moisture from her cheeks, she opened the door and trudged back to the apartment.

Nadine slipped into the apartment and, with a tired sigh, kicked off her shoes for the second time in fifteen minutes.

"Is that you, Nadine?" called her grandmother from the living room.

"Yes," she called out, suddenly bone-weary. She wanted to go to her bedroom, shove her head under a pillow, and stay there until she felt moved to leave. Which, in her present state of mind, might be never.

"Come sit with me a minute and tell me what is going on."

Nadine stopped at the doorway to the living room. "Nothing is going on, Grandma. I missed Clint. I didn't know when he was coming, that's all."

Barbara turned to her granddaughter, her mouth drawn tight. "You leave the poor man sitting here for almost an hour, and you say 'That's all'?"

"What else am I supposed to say?" grumped Nadine. She didn't need her grandmother's censure—she had enough self-disgust to spare. "I don't want to talk about it, Grandma."

"Well, I do. Clint Fletcher is a fine young man. He's handsome, smart, and a sincere Christian. Quite a potent combination, I'd say."

I'd say, too, thought Nadine as she dropped into a nearby chair.

"Where were you, Nadine?"

"In the first place, I didn't think Clint would come here early. We were supposed to meet at six thirty," she answered, ignoring her grandmother's question.

"He said he phoned the office. Where were you?" Barbara repeated.

Nadine hesitated, wondering what to say.

In answer, Nadine slid her hand into her pocket and tugged on the envelope Chantelle had given her. "I went to meet with a lady who had some more information on how Dad died."

Barbara had opened her mouth to shoot another question at Nadine, but obediently closed it.

Nadine stared at the envelope, wondering what it said, and yet, somehow, not caring. It couldn't begin to make up for what she had passed up. Would she be able to explain? How would it sound?

You asked me to lay off Skyline, and then I keep you waiting while I go digging for more stuff to use against them?

"Is the information in that?"

Nadine nodded, bone-weary and exhausted.

"Aren't you going to read it?"

Nadine sat up, holding the envelope between her fingers. "I

guess I may as well. So that standing Clint up wasn't for nothing."
She ripped open one end and pulled out the photocopy of the
letter. Pursing her lips, she unfolded it to read the tight, crabbed
writing.

It felt eerie reading what was supposed to have been read only
after the writer had taken his own life.

She skimmed over the references to personal events that
would matter only to Chantelle. And then, halfway down, there it
was: Her father's name. Sam Laidlaw. Nadine slowed her reading.
As if to help, she traced the words with her finger. Her heart
pounded as she read, and her hands were clammy.

"What does it say, Naddy? You look stunned."

Nadine finished reading, staring at the letter. She slouched
back in the easy chair. "It wasn't Dad's fault, Grandma," she whispered, letting the letter drop into her lap. "It wasn't his fault, just
like we figured. That poor boy."

Barbara got up and pulled the piece of paper out of Nadine's
limp hands. She held the letter at arm's length, squinting irritably
at it. She slipped on the reading glasses hanging around her neck.
Her mouth moved slowly as she read the words, and when she
finished, she looked at Nadine.

"Who is this from?"

Nadine blew her breath out, her bangs fluffing up as she did
so. "Believe it or not, it's a suicide note from a young man who
worked with Dad the day he died."

"Suicide?" Grandma pressed one hand to her chest, the other
reaching out blindly for some support. Nadine jumped to her feet
and caught her arm.

"It's okay, Grandma. He didn't kill himself. And this is just a
photocopy." Still holding the letter, Nadine led her back to the
couch. She helped her grandmother sit down and then smoothed
the now-crumpled piece of paper. She glanced over it once more,
rereading about her father's death.

Gordon Hayward had been training as a hand-faller. He had

been sent out into the bush totally green. He made a mess of the trees, and a few days later Sam Laidlaw had been sent in to help. Sam told Gordon to wait in the truck where it was safe while he cleaned up. Then a Skyline foreman came by and sent Gordon, over his protests, back to falling. Gordon got too close to Sam, and a tree he was cutting went the wrong way and fell on Sam. When the foreman came by again to check on Gordon, he found him crouched in front of the pickup, crying. The foreman told Gordon that he was liable and could end up paying a fine. His family counted on his paycheck, and other jobs were scarce, so Gordon signed a written statement made by Skyline saying that he'd heard the foreman warn Sam about his work. They were going to say he was careless.

Gordon worked for them until he found another job. But Sam's dying cries haunted him. The knowledge that he had implicated and killed an innocent man stayed with him, and he couldn't bear the burden any longer.

"How did you get it?"

Grandma's quiet question jolted Nadine back to the present. She pulled her scattered thoughts together. "His sister, Chantelle. I met her at the gym tonight." Nadine folded up the letter and laid it on the coffee table. "I got a letter from her a while ago, telling me that she had something I should see. We finally connected a few days ago and had made arrangements to meet tonight at the gym."

"I wish I could say I was glad," whispered Barbara, her fingers resting on her lips. "But to think of Sam lying there..." Her words were choked off, and she began to cry.

Nadine pulled her close, hugging her fiercely, her own emotions unstable.

Six years of speculation, finally answered. Her father, killed by the carelessness of an inexperienced logger, covered up by an irresponsible company. Nadine clenched her teeth thinking of Gordon listening to the dying cries of her father.

Her father, dying alone.

She choked down a sob, struggling for self-control.

Barbara straightened and brushed her tears off her wrinkled cheeks. She turned to Nadine and touched her cheek lovingly, her eyes still bright with tears. "I'm sorry you had to be the one to find this out, Nadine. You've worked so hard on this, done so much."

Nadine shook her head. "I didn't do anything. Nothing has changed. Dad is still dead."

"Yes, but it is good to know he wasn't at fault." Barbara sniffed and got up to get some tissues.

Nadine slouched against the couch, her hands clasped over her stomach. Her mind drifted back over the years. She easily imagined her father sitting in his leather recliner in their old house, a wreath of aromatic pipe smoke surrounding his head as he worked his way through the *Sweet Creek Chronicle*. Her mother would be bustling in the kitchen, putting the final touches on dinner, and she and her sisters would be sprawled over furniture and floor, books spread around them as they pretended to do homework. Home was a comfortable haven then. What would have happened if he lived?

"I have to write something up on this." Nadine snatched the letter off the table and strode past her grandmother. She had to do something, *anything*, instead of dwelling on might-have-beens, thinking about her father left to die. She hadn't intended to write a story, but now she realized she had nothing to lose that she hadn't already lost.

Clint had talked to Chantelle. He knew what Nadine knew. Knew that she would be angry at Skyline.

She switched on her computer, found the Skyline file, started a new document, and began typing. Her fingers flew over the keyboard, the keys clacking her anger and determination, a pinnacle of years of seeking the truth. Words flowed across the screen, angry and frustrated and demanding justice.

An hour later she looked up from the screen and rubbed her

neck, now tight with tension. She saved the article, e-mailed it to her computer at the office, and pulled in a long, slow breath.

She leaned back in her chair with her eyes closed, wondering how she would work the article into the paper. Editorial? Tie-in with the accident of last week?

Nadine dragged her hands over her face and sighed deeply.

Why do it at all?

She leaned over and clicked the mouse on the print command. She needed to hold it in her hand and to read it as words on a piece of paper.

She read the pages as they printed, the editor in her pleased with what she had written. The article had bite and punch and flowed smoothly, a perfect culmination of all her articles and editorials on Skyline.

She lowered the papers with a sigh. She had a wonderful article written with emotion and good cause. After six years her own instincts about her father's death were proven correct. Tonight all the questions were answered and all the i's dotted.

Then she read it again, thinking of Chantelle's anger—the way her eyes glowed, the fierceness in her voice—wondering if she had spoken to Clint the same way. Wondering what Clint thought of her now, after she had promised she would lay off Skyline.

She opened the e-mail again, and horror dropped on her shoulders as she read the top.

She had mistakenly sent it to everyone in the office.

Clint included.

What have I done, Lord, she prayed, dropping the papers on her desk and falling into her chair. *I gave up something precious just to prove myself right.* She spun her chair back and forth with recriminations filling her head and fighting with memories of Clint smiling at her across a table, holding and comforting her.

All she had wanted as a young girl had been given to her as a gift, and she had just thrown it all away.

CHAPTER 18

*C*lint wearily rubbed his eyes. This day had been one of the longer days of his life. All the way back from Cranbrook, he'd been happy and eager and looking forward to seeing Nadine. When he got to her apartment and she wasn't there, he chit-chatted with Grandma. Until Allison called Nadine's apartment, wondering why Nadine was at the gym. He wondered too, but figured he would just meet her there.

And then some woman named Chantelle waylaid him and he discovered exactly what Nadine was up to.

With a sigh, he reread the e-mail he'd received from his lawyer. Skyline had filed nothing yet, but their lawyers were still threatening.

He didn't know whether to ignore the threat or worry about it. The accountant's report and Matthew's letter dealt with different aspects of the business, but they both said the same thing: A prolonged battle with Skyline would put the newspaper so far into the red that Clint stood to lose everything.

Clint dropped his head against the back of the chair. From the sound of the e-mail he'd just seen, Nadine was bound and determined to bring Skyline to justice, regardless of his wishes and needs. He thought he had laid out the consequences for the news-paper, thought he had given her enough reason to back off. Obviously it wasn't enough.

Did you think she was so in love with you that she would give up a six-year battle just because you asked her to?

What could he possibly think he meant to her after spending a few evenings together? Nadine had made it clear what she thought of him from the first time he met her.

Surely he hadn't imagined the way she'd looked at him when they'd shared a meal, the way she seemed to drift back against him when he came to her office? Too vividly, he remembered how she had willingly gone into his arms that evening in the car. Surely her reaction was more than gratitude?

The timing of this week's meetings was terrible. How badly he had wanted to stay and reinforce the fragile bond begun the evening before. He and Nadine had had no chance to solidify their relationship, if indeed they had a relationship.

Clint got up and pulled his tie off, threw it into a corner, and rolled up the sleeves of his shirt. Hands in his pockets, he walked to the window, staring past his blurred reflection to the meager light of the streetlights. Was it only a few months ago he stood here with a sense of eager expectation, a realization that his life had come, if not full circle, then at least to a point that he knew it should be? It was as if God had been pushing him here by cutting off some opportunities and opening others. His job at the city newspaper had become unsatisfying. Uncle Dory, out of the blue, had offered him his share of the business.

He had found out that Nadine was still single.

Clint leaned his forehead against the glass, the coolness soothing his tired head.

For a few days, he'd thought his life was coming together and was finally getting some kind of cohesion: He had a business he loved and the affection of a woman who had been on his mind for years. It was as if all the things he had been seeking were there in one neat package.

Now it looked as if he would lose it all.

Skyline was at fault for Nadine's father's death, at least according to the scanned letter Nadine had attached to the e-mail. Clint guessed this was the letter Chantelle was referring to when she cornered him at the school gym.

Could he blame Nadine for wanting to bring this company to justice? When he read the letter, it bothered him as well.

Skyline is getting an itchy trigger finger.

Matthew's warning rang through his head.

Surely it wasn't wrong to want to run a healthy business and take all necessary steps to make sure that his employees kept their jobs? He tried to keep the newspaper in perspective and to keep a balance with his faith and his work.

Yet could he blame Nadine for wanting to run this?

He straightened, shoving his hand through his hair, thinking of his father, and how his lawsuit had taken over his life.

He had warned Nadine not to fall into the same trap, but was he protecting her? Or his paper?

Clint shook his head and rubbed the back of his neck. He didn't want to judge Nadine. He wanted to love and take care of her. He wanted to show her that love yet didn't know how to do it.

Yes, you do.

Clint paused, the voice pulling him up short. It had come from his own conscience. On a hunch, he walked over to his briefcase and opened it. He hadn't unpacked it after his meeting and brought it in after his aborted date with Nadine tonight.

In one corner of it lay his Bible. Clint took it out, closed the briefcase, and straightened.

Still standing, he thumbed through the New Testament until he came to Corinthians. With one hand in the pocket of his suit pants and the other holding the Bible as it lay open, he read the words that had struck him so many years ago.

"Love is patient, love is kind, it does not envy, it does not boast, it is not proud. It is not rude, it is not self-seeking..." Clint paused at that one. Was it self-seeking to want to see his newspaper post a profit? John, his previous lawyer, and now Matthew warned him against a battle with Skyline because of the cost, not because of its morality.

Was it right of him to deny Nadine this chance to expose Skyline via her article?

It's your paper. She shouldn't use it as a vehicle for her vendetta.

Yet, he said he loved her. If this Chantelle was right, if her brother had truly been coerced...

What? Another lawsuit that dragged on and on?

Clint dragged his hand over his face, wishing he could figure out what to put first and trying to find a neat solution that would satisfy everyone.

Skyline would sue him if Nadine ran the piece, and then what?

Sure, you're running a small-town newspaper, but you still have a responsibility to expose the truth.

He sat down and leaned back in his chair, his thoughts and emotions warring with each other.

Nadine sighed and rolled over. Six o'clock: The sun was barely up, and she was wide awake, had been since five o'clock. Since five, she'd been trying to find a way out of going to the office today. It would be so much easier to stay home and avoid Clint.

Again and again she relived yesterday, imagining different scenarios: cutting Chantelle Hayward off, coming home on time, and sharing the letter with Clint. Or not going to the gym at all and spending a delightful evening with Clint.

Even more, not sending the article she wrote in the heat of angry passion to everyone in the office. Especially Clint.

Finally she threw the blankets back in frustration and stalked to the bathroom. She had to do something instead of lying in bed castigating herself for being so narrow-minded.

Her anger at herself simmered through her shower and continued to simmer as she got dressed. She took extra care, pulling out an outfit that Sabrina and Leslie had chivied her into buying last spring—narrow, gray corduroy pants and a snug T-shirt, also in gray and topped with a collarless tunic in an unusual shade of apricot that complemented her brown hair. Nadine finished toweling off her hair and blew it dry, deciding to let it hang loose.

The way Clint liked it.

The kitchen was still dark when she tiptoed into it. She pulled out an apple, poured herself a glass of milk, and ate her breakfast leaning against the counter behind her. Nadine was thankful that Grandma still slept; the last thing she wanted right now was a postmortem on last night. It was bad enough that she would see Clint in a few hours.

She drove to the office, and as she parked her car in her stall in the back of the building, she noticed with a thump of her heart that Clint was already in. With apprehension, she unlocked the back door and walked down the darkened hallway past the cubicles of the copy editors. One of the computers was on, the screen saver bouncing around on the monitor. Frowning, Nadine walked over to it and hit one of the keys. The e-mail program was on, and the article she had written last night was on the screen.

She looked around, wondering where Clint was now. She walked to her office. Pausing at the door, she glanced up the hallway toward the front entrance and Clint's office. His door was open, but the room was dark. Puzzled, Nadine stepped closer.

A figure was slouched over the desk, one arm flung out.

In the early morning light filtering in through the window she could see it was Clint. His head moved, disturbing the papers underneath him.

He was asleep.

Had he been here all night?

Clint shifted and Nadine turned to leave, but he only sighed and settled again. Feeling like an intruder, she stepped into the office, closer to his desk. She watched him a moment, his hair falling across his forehead, his soft lips slightly parted. His jaw was stubbled, the collar of his shirt open. His one arm was flung across the desk, and his other hung inches away from her. He looked vulnerable and utterly appealing. Nadine felt a gentle ache in her heart as she thought of all that she could have had, and then, without thinking, reached over and brushed his hair back. Her hand lingered on his cheek.

She didn't expect his eyes to open, and she froze as the hand that hung down caught hers.

"Hey, Nadine," he murmured as he blinked and sat up, still holding her hand. He smiled blearily. "Come here," he said, his voice husky from sleep as he rose from his seat and tugged her toward him.

Surprise and shock threw her off balance as he pulled her into his embrace. His arms surrounded her, his chin rested on her head, and she felt his chest rise and fall in a protracted sigh.

She thought he would be angry, but he didn't seem upset.

"Don't say anything," he murmured, holding her close, rubbing his chin on her hair. "I like this dream better."

You have to go, Nadine told herself, cherishing the feel of his arms holding her, being surrounded by his warmth. *You can't stay here, this isn't right,* she thought. He's still dreaming.

Instead, she closed her eyes, allowing herself this one moment of wish fulfillment, this brief taste of might-have-beens. She let her hand slip around his neck, allowed her fingers to touch his hair as she finally relaxed in his embrace. She felt so secure, so accepted, and so cherished simply being herself.

She loved him.

The words began as a small thought, but then as she closed her eyes, they grew until they were so close to her lips, she had to say them. "I love you," she whispered in a voice so soft, she wasn't even sure she had spoken them aloud.

She swallowed the lump in her throat and then, turning her head away from him, slipped out of his embrace and stood in front of him.

His hand still held hers. Puzzled, she turned, only to see him staring at her with alert eyes, no sign of sleep clouding their piercing gaze.

Unnerved, she pulled on her hand again, but Clint held fast.

"What's happening, Nadine?" he asked.

She could only stare at him, aware of what she had just done. "I'm sorry," she whispered finally.

"For what?"

His quiet question hung, echoing in the silence of the office.

"Everything," she said, looking down at their intertwined hands, unwilling to pull hers free as she realized he had been fully awake when he'd held her so close a few moments ago. "Standing you up last night, not being honest with you, writing the article about Skyline..." She stopped, unable to say more.

His hand lifted her chin, cupping it. His eyes met hers, his mouth curved in a half smile. "You've done nothing to be sorry for." He stepped closer, then, with no warning, he bent down and touched his lips to hers.

Nadine swayed toward him, and her hand came up and rested against his wrinkled shirt, as if to support herself. Then his arms were around her again, his mouth on hers.

It made no sense.

It made perfect sense.

Nadine let herself slip away to a place she had never imagined would be hers. A place where mind, heart, and spirit were one with another, a place of surrender and strength, of peace and tumult; Clint's arms surrounded her, his body warming hers and his mouth caressing hers. She returned his kisses, clinging to him.

When he ended the kiss then tucked her head once again under his chin, she did not dare think what it could all mean.

They were silent, as if each needed to absorb the moment.

Finally Nadine pulled away, looking up at him. "I know you saw what I wrote last night. You need to know I'm not running the article."

Clint frowned, as if puzzled by what she said.

"I wrote it after I got the note from Chantelle." Nadine looked down, fingering the cuff of her tunic top. "I was upset. All those questions we've had about my father were finally answered." She looked at Clint, praying he would understand. "I discovered how he died, what happened..." A wave of sorrow welled up as she remembered what Gordon had written about her father's cries. Her words were choked off, and once again she was in Clint's arms. Hot tears slid past her eyelids and flowed down her cheeks.

"It's okay, Nadine. It's okay to cry," he murmured as he held her. "I read the letter that you attached to the e-mail. It was awful."

Nadine nodded. She drew in a steadying breath as the tears subsided. "I'm sorry. All I do lately around you is cry," she said with a shaky laugh.

"I don't mind," he said softly, his hand on her shoulder. He angled his head, his hand squeezing her shoulder. "I want you to know, Nadine, that I think you should run the article on your father."

"What are you talking about? I thought Matthew said Skyline was threatening the paper with a lawsuit?"

"So far it's just the usual threats." Clint traced the track of a tear down Nadine's cheek, his eyes following the path of his finger. "I would be lying if I said I wasn't concerned, but your battle with Skyline has shown me something important, reminded me of the reason I went into this business: to print the truth, to expose wickedness and collusion." He smiled a wry smile, stroking her hair away from her face, tucking it behind her ear. "I learned from you in all of this. You have shown me how a child should love their parent, and how strong love can be. I never cared for my parents that way."

"Please," she begged, shaking her head. "Don't look to me as an example of filial love. My mother and I had a totally different relationship."

"Probably, but you did the same for her that you did for your father. You sacrificed for her. A career, a marriage—"

"Breaking my engagement to Jack wasn't a huge sacrifice," she interrupted.

"That's good to hear." He fiddled with a strand of her hair, sending delicate shivers down her spine at his casual touch. "You have always been someone who holds fast to her beliefs. Your faith in God and your strength has always been an example to me. I've often wished for the same strength, the same ability to face problems head-on."

Nadine felt ashamed as he spoke. He was making her out to be so much better than she was. "Please, Clint. I'm not like that. I battled many times with God over my mother's illness. When she died, I was relieved and had to ask God to forgive me for that, as well."

"It doesn't matter, Nadine," he said. "You have a beauty, a strength of character, a faith that has depth," he continued, his eyes on the hands that still played with her hair. "You're not the kind of person someone can get to know in one night, or one week, or even a month. You always intrigued me and scared me at the same time."

What he said began a faint stirring in the depths of her being.

"I think I've always cared for you. I *know* I have," he amended. "I don't know exactly how to say this, except to be very honest." His hand stopped, resting on her shoulder, his finger caressing her neck. "I love you, too, Nadine."

She saw his lips move, heard the words as they settled into the empty, lonely part of her heart that she had kept blocked off for so long. As if in a daze, she slowly shook her head. "What did you just say?"

"I said I love you."

Nadine closed her eyes as if to hold the words in her mind. The words echoed and resounded, drowning out so many other tiny voices she had stored away—voices of friends of her sisters, old boyfriends. Voices that had humiliated and hurt, sometimes unintentionally. She opened her eyes again, and then, surprising herself at her audacity, reached over and pulled Clint's head down to hers.

Their lips met, seeking at first then moving more slowly as pain was eased and loneliness filled. Finally, Nadine pulled away, her heart as full as when she had first fully experienced God's love for her.

"I love you, too, Clint. I have loved you for years," she said simply, her hands resting on his shoulders, and his clasped behind her waist.

He drew in a deep breath, as if he had been holding it since he first declared himself to her. "So that means if I ask you to marry me, you'll say yes?"

"More than likely," she returned.

He pulled her close once again, and as she rested against his heart, she let her arms slip around him, enjoying the solidity of him.

"It worked, you know," she said softly, rubbing her cheek against his shirt.

"What do you mean?"

"My life." Nadine lifted her head so she could look up at him. "It seemed so unorganized, like anything I started would end up going in a different direction. Yet God took all those scattered pieces and made them work."

Clint smiled down at her. "And now I hope that your life can become a part of mine. I know we can't expect a life without trouble, but I still choose the kind of marriage your parents had, with their faith and their love. They built on a strong foundation, and I pray that we will, too."

As Nadine returned his smile, she sent up a prayer of thanks.

And then she stood on tiptoe and kissed her man. She pulled back, smiling at him.

"There's just one more thing I need to do," Nadine said. "I hate to ask you, but I'm really going to need your help."

Clint nodded. "Okay. Sounds interesting, but I'm willing to go along."

"It's just to my apartment. I need to talk to Grandma."

CHAPTER 19

"So, Grandma, Clint and I need to tell you something."

Clint held Nadine's hand, wishing he had a ring on it to show Grandma and everyone else that he and Nadine were, indeed, getting married.

They sat across from her at the dining room table. Barbara was finishing her breakfast and drinking a cup of tea when they came in, the newspaper open on the table beside her.

She now looked from Nadine to Clint, a smile hovering at one edge of her mouth.

"And, what is that?"

"Nadine and I are getting married," Clint put in before Nadine could.

Barbara sat back in her chair, looking rather smug. "Well. I'm not surprised. You two were meant for each other, that's for sure." She got up and gave Nadine a tight hug. "Congratulations, my dear." She turned to Clint, shooting him a self-satisfied grin. "And to you too. I'm sure you'll make my granddaughter very happy. She deserves it, you know."

"I do. And I will try my best," Clint promised.

"But, I have a problem." Nadine tightened her grip on Clint's hand as if seeking support and strength from him. "I'm going to be making wedding preparations and buying things and, well, I'll need the room. For the wedding things."

"You want me to move out?" Barbara sounded shocked, her eyes wide, with her one hand on her chest, her teacup wobbling in her other hand. "I...can't...I could help you...I can't believe you would want me gone when I can really help you."

Thank goodness Nadine had warned him about her grandmother and how she could manipulate. But this was Nadine's grandmother and he didn't want to interfere.

"I know you can help, Grandma, but I really, really need to be on my own."

Barbara's hand moved to her mouth, covering it as if she were crying.

"Grandma, please don't do this," Nadine said, her voice wavering. "I'm sorry—"

She's going to cave, Clint thought. *She's going to let her dear, sweet, disingenuous grandmother wrap her around her little finger.* He needed to help.

"But we think it's best for you if you have your own place," Clint said, interrupting when he sensed Nadine's wavering. "I understand you have a home in Fort Henday? I'm sure you'd love to get back to it? Work in your flower gardens, be on the yard?"

Barbara blinked then zeroed in on him. "But Naddy will need me now more than ever."

"Not really; she has me," Clint said. "I know you're very happy about that."

He held Barbara's gaze, surprised to see a faint challenge in her eyes. But, he held her gaze look for look and, to his surprise, he caught a glimmer of admiration in their blue, guileless depths.

Nadine squeezed his hand as if thankful for the support.

"Well, I see that but—"

"And Nadine will be helping me at the house from time to time—"

"She will be moving in with you after the wedding?"

"Yes. I have a lovely home that I inherited from Dory."

Barbara nodded slowly. "And your uncle, when is he returning and where will he live?"

"He bought a condo. In that new development that went up along the tracks."

Barbara nodded slowly. "Wonderful. Well, I suppose I could go back; though, I hope I'll be allowed to visit from time to time."

"Of course you can visit—"

"For an afternoon," Clint put in, interrupting his future fiancée and adding a smile for Grandma's sake. "I'm sure Nadine would love to see you once in a while. For an afternoon," he repeated.

This netted him another shrewd look from Grandma, as if she sensed that she had come up against someone who could negotiate like her.

"Of course. That would be nice."

Nadine shot Clint a look of gratitude.

"So. I guess I better start packing up." Grandma got up but waited by her chair as if hoping Nadine would stop her.

"Do you need a hand?" Clint asked, taking a step backward, toward her room, as if ready to help her out.

"No. I can manage. It's just my suitcase and some of my personal items." Barbara sighed then gave Nadine a smile and moved in for another hug. "I'm happy for you, my dear." She bracketed Nadine's face, shaking her head slowly. "I wish your mother could be here to see this."

Nadine nodded, pressing her hand to her mouth, and Clint slipped his arm around her shoulders for support. "I do too," she whispered.

"Well...I should get going," Barbara said, patting Clint on the arm. "Next time I see you two, I hope to see a ring on my granddaughter's finger."

"That's the next thing we need to take care of."

"I'm so glad. I'll say goodbye now." She looked at Clint. "So, when is your uncle moving in?"

"A couple of weeks."

"Excellent." She gave Nadine another hug then walked away.

Nadine watched her go, regret flashing over her face, but Clint pulled her close and brushed a kiss over her forehead. "She'll be fine," he assured her.

"I know. It's just, I feel a bit bad. Like I'm kicking her out."

"I have a feeling we'll be seeing more of her," Clint said. "And I'm thinking we might not be the only one she'll be visiting."

"Your Uncle Dory," Nadine said with a sigh.

"You caught that, didn't you?"

"Oh yeah. I know when Grandma is on the hunt."

"Then you know she'll be okay," Clint said.

"I know she will be." Nadine flashed him a grateful smile. "And thanks for the support."

"My pleasure. I want you to know that I'll always be here for you. Always."

Nadine's lips quivered a moment, and then she turned her head into his chest, slipping her arms around him.

Clint held her close, looking around the apartment and thinking of the house Nadine and her family used to live in. He was thankful to be able to give that to her again. A home.

She pulled away and drew in a shaky breath.

"I guess we should get back to work," she said, her tone reluctant.

"We've got time," he said. "Personally, I'd like to go downtown. Make a purchase."

Nadine grinned. "I like where this is going."

Clint slid his knuckle over her face, smiling back at her and still trying to absorb the fact that he and Nadine were finally together.

"I do too. It's been a long haul with some missteps along the way, but I think we're both where we should be."

Nadine's expression clouded, and a faint frown marred her features.

"What are you thinking of?"

"My sister. Leslie."

"You'll have to talk to her sometime, I'm sure," Clint said.

"I will. But not for a while." The frown left her face, replaced by a broad smile. "Because right now I've got bigger and better things to think about."

"I agree," Clint said. "Do you want to wait to say goodbye to Grandma or should we just leave?"

"I kind of want to make sure she goes," Nadine said, chewing her lip. Then she shook her head. "If you've got my back, I'm sure you'll make sure it happens."

"I do," he said. "I do have your back."

"And I have yours."

"Then we'll both be in good shape." Clint kissed her again, then catching her by the hand, led her into the bright sunshine. He looked up at the blue sky then at Nadine. "What do you think of a winter wedding up in the mountains?"

"I think you're reading my mind," she said.

"Let's go pick out a ring. I want to make this official," Clint said. "I want everyone to know that we're together."

"Finally," she said.

"Finally." He kissed her again, and the two of them went off on the first step of their future together.

DEAR READER

Dear Reader,

Whenever I tell a story, I start with my characters. What are their dreams, hopes, and wishes? All of us have things that we want from life, yet prayerfully wonder if our motives are right.

Nadine wanted a number of things, but she had to learn to reevaluate her motives and her reasons for wanting them.

As we live our lives, our own wishes and dreams change with our situation. Sometimes we get what we want and then wish we hadn't. Sometimes we don't and are glad we didn't. I think the important thing is to remember that God uses all the good and bad things in our lives to shape and mold us, if we are willing.

Yours truly,
Carolyne

COMING SOON

PRE-ORDER the next book in the Sweethearts of Sweet Creek Series by clicking on the title:

#3 - CLOSE TO HIS HEART

Other books coming up in the Sweethearts of Sweet Creek -
1. Homecoming
4 - Divided Hearts
5 - A Hero at Heart
6 - A Mother's Heart
In this series you'll get to know the residents of this town set in the Kootenay mountains and surrounded by ranch land and populated with interesting characters.

Nadine Laidlaw, a newspaper reporter, who can't seem to get rid of her meddling, matchmaking Grandmother and Clint Fletcher, her new boss, who is a reminder of all she wants to forget.

Tess Kraus whose pain has sent her back to her hometown of

Sweet Creek trying to find redemption. When her ex-fiancee, Jace Scholte shows up and she's forced to work with him on a fundraiser, she struggles with her old feelings for him and the secret she can never tell him.

Cory Luciuk is working her way through life, waitressing at the Riverside Inn. And then the man who broke her heart and tainted her past shows up again.

Kelsey Swain, a widow with a small boy has seen her share of sorrow when her husband died. She now runs the Riverside Cafe, struggling to get it off the ground. Then his ex-partner comes back to Sweet Creek and with him a reminder of what she lost.

I hope you have a chance to read them.

CHAPTER ONE

The door of the coffee shop opened with a cheerful jingle of bells, and when Tess looked at who had come in, her breath sucked out of her.

He had returned...dragging along the darkness of the past.

It had been a week and a half since she heard that Jace Scholte came back to Sweet Creek. In those ten days, Tess jumped at the sight of any man with dark hair wearing a suit. The sound of any deep, rough voice sent her heart into overdrive.

But each jolt had been a false alarm; she hadn't seen him face to face. Until now.

Jace's suit sat easily on his broad shoulders. His tie was cinched and his collar enhanced his sculpted cheekbones. He was tanned, but it didn't hide the scar down one side of his face, which added a sense of mystique to his strong features.

Then his icy blue eyes latched onto hers and narrowed.

She didn't want to know what he was thinking or feel this trembling deep in her soul.

She forced her gaze back to the espresso machine, failing to contain her chaotic thoughts as she tamped down the ground coffee for her current order. Why did Claire have to choose this time to do inventory at the back of the store? Tess could use her sister's support right now. She swallowed her apprehension and wiped her hands on her apron then steamed the milk, disappointed to see her hand trembling.

"So, Tess, is that coffee coming anytime soon?"

Tess fought for self-control and turned to Nate Krickson, who was watching her with curiosity in his expression. The thirty-something man wore a cowboy hat and plaid shirt rolled up at the sleeves. "Sorry. Still learning," she said.

Nate shrugged. "Well, I'm sure it's quite a switch from working at the Inn. I would have gone there for my coffee, but Mark said I had to try this place. Not sure I want to pay this much for coffee, but hey. Happy to support your sister; though it seems to be a thing, these single moms and their restaurants."

Tess nodded, forcing herself to not look past him to Jace. She didn't correct Nate. Coffee Creek wasn't technically a restaurant. When Claire started the coffee shop, she hoped to be around for her daughter when school was out. She also didn't want to create too much competition with Kelsey Swain, who ran the Riverside Inn. So, Coffee Creek was open early in the morning and closed by four. Claire's menu was quick and easy: coffee, sandwiches, and pastries.

Tess attended the espresso, pouring milk into the stainless steel container and turning on the steamer. She mentally counted as the coffee dripped into the mug, and she hoped it was done right. Though she had made hundreds of lattes, just knowing Jace was watching made her self-conscious.

Though she told herself she didn't care what Jace thought, she still wanted to show she was good at what she did. That she had chosen this job—on purpose.

She took extra care pouring the milk in, creating a pretty flower in the foam, then handed it to Nate.

He chuckled. "Well, that flower makes it a whole lot easier to part with four dollars and fifty cents," he said, handing her some cash. She gave him his change and he dropped it into the tip jar. "There. Go crazy," he said.

She tried to think of something witty to say, something that would forestall having to say something to Jace.

The bells jangled again and her mother bustled into the shop, moving directly to the counter. She always said that as mother of the owner and chief barista, she should have priority over the other customers

Claire had tried to explain nepotism to their mother, but Deborah was oblivious. This was one time, however, that Tess was thankful for her mother's brash boldness.

"My dear Theresa, I'll have the usual." Her mother was the only person who called Tess by her full name and always insisted other family members do the same.

Then her mother saw who she had butted in front of and 'dear Theresa' was roundly ignored.

"Well, hello Jace," she said, her smile growing extra bright. "We finally meet face to face." She turned to Tess. "We've been chatting on the phone up to now."

This didn't sound good. Her mom had always liked Jace. In fact, while her mother had been upset that Tess had quit university, she was even more upset that 'dear Theresa' had broken up with the very eligible and attractive Jace Scholte. Her mother had been "chatting on the phone" with Jace? That frightened her almost as much as seeing Jace did.

"Hey, Mrs. Kraus," Jace said. He gave her one of his signature smiles, and Tess felt a tremor of attraction.

"Jace, you are as good-looking as ever, though I'm thinking you've lost weight," her mother said, lightly touching Jace's arm.

"Maybe. I've been busy the past year," Jace said with a shrug.

"And now you're here in Sweet Creek. That's just lovely, isn't it Theresa?"

This had to stop.

"Mom. What can I get for you?" Tess pasted on her brightest smile and zeroed in on her mother, who was easier to face than Jace.

"I'll have my usual, Theresa," her mother said, glancing from Jace to Tess. "You must excuse me butting in line," Deborah said, "but I get specialty treatment. Claire and Theresa being my daughters and all."

"Of course. I understand," Jace said sounding way more reasonable than some of the customers could be.

"Cappuccino it is," Tess said cheerfully, steeling herself as she faced Jace to take his order.

He was a potent reminder of what could have been. A reminder of happier times when they had dated through high school and college, and that first year of working together at MacGregor Holdings for Carson MacGregor.

Tess clenched her fists and willed the memories away. She could deal with this. It had been six years and a lot of sadness. Their life together was over.

She took another breath, relieved that the shaking in her hands subsided, that the thudding in her chest had settled to a steady beat.

"What would you like, Jace?" she asked, keeping her tone light. "Your usual as well?" She flashed him what she hoped was a casual smile to offset her lame attempt at a joke.

"Just a coffee to stay." He held her gaze as if trying to figure her out. Tess was the first to break the connection. "I'll get Jace's first," she told her mother.

She filled a paper cup, snapped a lid on it, and handed it to Jace.

"Is this a hint?" Jace asked wryly, as he took the cup.

"I believe he wanted his coffee to stay," Deborah reminded her daughter.

A flush crept up Tess's neck as she reminded herself to get a grip.

"Sorry. I'll give you a mug."

"No. This is fine." Jace took the cup as he glanced around the coffee shop. "So this is where you're working today?" Did she imagine his sarcastic emphasis on his last word?

"Yeah. Saturday is the farmer's market. Monday afternoon I'm back to the thrift store. I keep busy." His question made her defensive. She knew her work schedule differed vastly from the one she would have led with Jace. They had once mapped out their lives when they were college sweethearts.

The plan had been to finish business school, work for Carson MacGregor, and, after a suitable length of time, start their own business and get married.

Tess pushed down a wave of old, too-familiar grief. Jace's unwelcome presence resurrected the agonizing memories. She should have followed her first instinct and stayed away from town until he returned to Vancouver. Except that would have meant running away again—and she was tired of doing that.

"Is there a day you don't work?" Jace asked.

"Sunday."

"Day of rest, like you used to tell me," he said. "Day to attend church."

Don't read more into the comment than necessary, Tess reminded herself as she nodded and turned away from him. *You don't have to make excuses for your choices or that you don't go to church as much as you used to.*

She started her mother's cappuccino, the bean grinder drowning the conversation her mother struck up with Jace. She made quick work of her mother's drink and handed it to her in a mug, like she preferred.

"I imagine I'll be seeing you at the meeting tonight, Theresa?" Deborah asked, as she took the mug from her daughter.

Tess's mind skipped frantically backward, mining for a hint of which meeting her mother was referring to.

"You've forgotten, Theresa. Haven't you?" Deborah's disappointed sigh cleaved the air. "After promising me you would come? If you'd come regularly to church, you would have read the notice on the bulletin." She turned to Jace. "I swear this girl would lose her head if I knew she wasn't so stiff-necked and stubborn."

Her mother's teasing smile almost negated the reprimand in her mother's voice. But not quite.

"Tonight is the second meeting for the fundraiser for the Crisis Counseling Center. You said you were coming to the first one, and you missed it." Deborah cupped her hands around the mug, angling her head to one side in question. Not a hair on her perfectly coiffed head moved. "You do owe me." Her arched brow underlined the simple statement, reminding Tess of how grateful she'd been when her parents helped her move to her new apartment. When she told her mother that if she ever needed anything, just ask. That was six months ago, and she assumed her mother had taken her promise as another way of saying thank you.

Apparently she'd been wrong.

"I'm sorry. I forgot." Tess reached up to push a stray strand of hair back behind her ear, then stopped, trying not to fidget. Thankfully, Jace had moved to a table, so she and her mother spoke privately.

"You can make up for lost time. I asked Dale Andrews, the chairman of the fundraiser, if you could still come, and he said yes." Deborah glanced past Tess and smiled again as Claire showed up behind Tess. "There you are, Claire. I had wondered where you'd gone. Maybe you can help me convince Theresa to live up to her obligations and help out with the fundraiser?"

"Is that the one for the Crisis Center?" Claire asked, tossing a towel over her shoulder, then adjusting the bandanna holding back her dark hair.

"That's the one."

Claire frowned, then shook her head. "Sorry, Tess. You can't go to that fundraiser, anyway."

Thank goodness. Her dear sister was getting her off the hook. She knew she could count on Claire to have her back around her mother.

"Why not?"

"That's Tess's birthday," Claire explained.

Deborah lifted one perfectly plucked brow. "And?"

Claire sighed. "I was going to have a party. It's her thirtieth, remember?"

Right. Tess preferred not to remember that inevitable milestone. While it was lovely that her sister had come up with an excuse to get out of the fundraiser, Tess would have preferred the reason to be anything but this—it was a reminder of where she was in her life.

Many years ago, she hadn't imagined that on her thirtieth birthday, she would be a single woman flitting from job to job, still unable to settle down with either a man or a career.

Her vision, at that time, included a promising career as a real estate developer.

That same vision included being married to the man now sitting in her sister's cafe drinking coffee as he glanced over some papers spread over his table.

"But I'll be attending the fundraiser, as will your father," her mother protested. "Surely you can have her party on another day?"

"We always have the thirtieth birthday parties right on the day. Tradition," Claire said, angling her sister a triumphant look.

Tess glanced from her sister to her mother, dread settling into the pit of her stomach.

Caught between a rock and a hard place. Commit to the fundraiser and end up working with her mother, or commit to the birthday party and spend the night being confronted with the stark reality of her life.

"I think we can make an exception to this tradition," Deborah said. "This is for a superb cause. The meeting will be at six-thirty. Tonight," she said, turning to Tess, her voice rife with expectation.

Tess caught her mother's implacable look, wondering if it was worth the battle.

"You know how important it is to live up to your commitments. We talked about this." This was a gentle dig at other times

Tess had missed or forgotten things, even though in the past few years, she'd gotten better. She wanted to tell her mother that she wasn't flaky, wasn't forgetful and irresponsible. She had simply been...distracted.

"Okay. I'll be there." Not willingly, but she had no other choice.

"That's wonderful. Even better, Jace will be on the committee, as well."

Jace? On the committee? No. No way. She couldn't do this.

* * * *

To order Close to His Heart, click on the link below:

CLOSE TO HIS HEART

FREE STUFF

FREE BOOK

If you enjoyed this book, you might enjoy my free book, Toward Home.

click on the link below to find out more:

Get me my Free Book!

Do you want to be the first to get free books from Carolyne? To be the first to read the books before they come out? To, maybe, have input on what you liked or didn't like?

Then join my Reader Team by clicking on the link here:

READER TEAM

I'll be giving away other freebies from time to time to members of my Reader Team. Freebies you won't get anywhere else.

All I ask in return is that you agree to write a review for the books you are getting the day they are released.

If you like free, like being the first in line, being on the 'in' and have a chance for some fun freebies, then please sign up!

Thanks so much.

ALSO BY CAROLYNE AARSEN

The Only Best Place is the first book in the Holmes Crossing Series.

The Only Best Place

All In One Place

This Place

A Silence in the Heart

Any Man of Mine

ABOUT THE AUTHOR

Carolyne Aarsen was a city girl until a tall, blonde and handsome man entered her life and she convinced him to marry her and he did. Then he brought her to live on a farm where her resume garnered some interesting entries. Growing a garden, sewing blue jeans, baking, pickling and preserving. She learned how to handle cows, ride a horse, drive tractors, snow machines and a John Deere loader. Together they raised four amazing children and took in foster children. Somewhere in all this she learned to write. Her first book sold in 1997 and since then has sold over fifty books to three different publishers with 1.5 million copies of her books in print. Her stories show a love of open spaces, the fellowship of her Christian community and the gift God has given us in Christ.

To find out more about Carolyne
www.carolyneaarsen.com
carolynewriter@xplornet.ca

EXCERPT - THE ONLY BEST PLACE

Smile. Think happy thoughts. Take a deep breath and...

"Hello. I'm Leslie VandeKeere, and I'm a farmer's wife."

No. No. All wrong. That sounds like I'm addressing a self-help group for stressed-out urban dwellers.

I angled the rearview mirror of my car to do a sincerity check on my expression and pulled a face at my reflection. Brown eyes. Brown hair. Both the polar opposite of the VandeKeere signature blonde hair and blue eyes repeated throughout the Dutch-based community of Holmes Crossing.

During the past hour of the long drive from Vancouver to here, I'd been practicing my introduction to varied and sundry members of the vast community of which I knew about four and a half people. I'd been trying out various intros. That last one was a bust. I'd never been a farmer's wife. Would never be a farmer's wife. I'm a nurse, even though my focus the next year was supposed to be on our marriage. Not my career.

I cleared my throat and tried again. "Our year here will be interesting."

Worse yet. Most women could break that code faster than you could say "fifteen percent off." *Interesting* was a twilight word that either veered toward the good or the dark side.

Right now my delivery was a quiet and subdued Darth Vader.

I had to keep my voice down so I wouldn't wake my two kids. After four *Veggie Tales* and a couple of off-key renditions of "The Itsy Bitsy Spider," they had finally drifted off to sleep, and I didn't want to risk waking them. The eighteen hour trip had been hard on us. They needed the rest. *I* needed the rest, but I had to drive.

I stretched out hands stiff from clutching the steering wheel of my trusty, rusty Honda, the caboose in our little convoy. My husband, Dan, headed the procession, pulling the stock trailer holding stage one of our earthly goods. Next came his brother-in-law Gerrit, pulling his own stock trailer loaded with our earthly goods stage two.

I had each bar, each bolt, each spot of rust on Gerrit's trailer indelibly imprinted on my brain. Counting the bolt heads distracted me from the dread that clawed at me whenever I saw the empty road stretching endlessly ahead of me.

A road that wound crazily through pine-covered mountains, then wide open, almost barren, plains. Now, on the last leg of our journey, we were driving through ploughed and open fields broken only by arrow-straight fence lines and meandering cottonwoods. Tender green leaves misted the bare branches of the poplars edging the road, creating a promise of spring that I hadn't counted on spending here.

I hadn't gone silently down this road. I had balked, kicked, and pleaded. I had even dared to pray that a God I didn't talk to often would intervene.

Of course I was bucking some pretty powerful intercessors. I'm sure the entire VandeKeere family was united in their prayers for their beloved brother, son, cousin, nephew, and grandchild to be enfolded once again in the bosom of the family and the farm where they thought he belonged. So it was a safe bet my flimsy request lay buried in the avalanche of petitions flowing from Holmes Crossing.

The one person I had on my side was my sister, Terra. But she only talked to God when she'd had too much to drink. Of course, in that state, she chatted up anyone who would listen.

The friends I left behind in Vancouver were sympathetic, but they all thought this trip would be an adventure. *Interesting* adventure, my friend Josie had said when I told her.

I glanced in the rearview mirror at my sleeping children. Nicholas shifted in his car seat, his sticky hands clutching a soggy Popsicle stick. The Popsicle had been a blatant bribe, and the oblong purple stain running over his coat from chin to belly would probably not wash out. A constant reminder of my giving in.

Since Edmonton, I'd been tweaking my introduction, and now that we had turned off the highway, time and miles ate up what time I had left. I had only ten minutes to convince myself that I'd sooner be heading toward the intersection of "no" and "where," otherwise known as Holmes Crossing, Alberta, than back to Vancouver.

We would still be there if it weren't for Lonnie Dansworth-- snake, scumbag, and crooked building contractor. The $90,000's worth of unpaid bills he left in the "VandeKeere Motors" inbox tipped Dan's fledgling mechanic business from barely getting by to going under. The Dansworth Debacle, in turn, wiped out the finely drawn pictures I'd created in my head of the dream life and home Dan and I had been saving for. The home that represented stability for a marriage that had wobbled on shaky ground the past year.

The second push to Holmes Crossing came when Dan's stepfather, Keith Cook, booked a midlife crisis that resulted in him doing a boot-scootin' boogie out of hearth, home, Holmes Crossing, and the family farm, leaving a vacuum in the VandeKeere family's life that Dan decided we would temporarily fill.

Temporary had been a recurring refrain in our life so far. The first two years of our marriage, Dan had worked for a small garage in Markham while I worked in the ER at the Scarborough Hospital. When an oil company needed a maintenance mechanic, we moved to Fort McMurray, and I got a job as a camp nurse. Two years later, an opportunity to be his own boss came up in Vancouver. When we packed up and moved, Dan promised me this was our final destination. Until now.

"It's only a year," Dan assured me when he laid off the employees, pulled out of the lease on the shop, and filed away the blueprints we had been drawing up for our dream home. We could have lived off my salary while Dan got his feet under him and worked on our relationship away from the outside influences of a mother Dan still called twice a week. But Dan's restless heart wasn't in it. Being a mechanic had never been his dream. Though I'd heard plenty of negative stories about his stepfather, Keith, a wistful yearning for the farm of his youth wove through his complaints. We were torn just like the adage said: "Men mourn for what they lost, women for what they haven't got."

The final push came when a seemingly insignificant matter caught my attention. The garage's bilingual secretary, Keely. She could talk "mechanic" and "Dan," and the few times I stopped at the garage, she would chat me up in a falsely bright voice while her eyes followed Dan's movements around the shop.

When her name showed up too often on our call display, I confronted Dan. He admitted he'd been spending time with her. Told me he was lonely. He also told me that he had made a mistake. That he was trying to break things off with her. He was adamant that they'd never been physically intimate. Never even kissed her, he claimed. She was just someone he spent time with.

I tried not to take on the fault for our slow drift away from each other or the casual treatment of our relationship as kids and work and trying to put money aside for our future slowly sunk its demanding claws into our lives, slowly pulling us in separate directions.

I also reminded him that I had remained faithful, taking the righteous high road. Dan was chastened, Keely quit, and her name never came up again. But her shadowy presence still hovered between us, making Dan contrite, and me wary.

Now, with each stop that brought us closer to the farm and Holmes Crossing and the possibility of repairing our broken relationship, I'd seen Dan's smile grow deeper, softer. The lines edging his mouth smoothed away, the nervous tic in the corner of one eye disappeared.

Mine grew worse.

A soft sigh pulled my eyes toward the back seat. Anneke still lay slack jawed, her blanket curled around her fist. Nicholas stirred again, a deep V digging into his brow, his bottom lip pushed out in a glistening pout. Nicholas was a pretty child, but his transition from sleep to waking was an ugly battle he fought with intense tenacity.

I had only minutes before the troops were fully engaged.

My previous reluctance to arrive at the farm now morphed into desperation for survival. I stomped on the gas pedal, swung around the two horse trailers, and bulleted down the hill into the valley toward my home for the next year.

My cell phone trilled. I grabbed it off the dashboard, glancing sidelong at Nicholas as I did.

"What's up?" Dan's tinny voice demanded. "What's your rush?"

"The boy is waking up," I whispered, gauging how long I had before his angry wails filled the car.

"Just let him cry."

I didn't mean to sigh. Truly I didn't. But it zipped past my pressed-together lips. In that too-deep-for-words escape of my breath, Dan heard an entire conversation.

"Honestly, Leslie, you've got to learn to ignore--"

Dear Lord, forgive me. I hung up. And then I turned my phone off.

GET THE ONLY BEST PLACE

EXCERPT - ALL IN ONE PLACE

Chapter One

By the time I left British Columbia, I'd stopped looking over my shoulder. When I started heading up the QUE2, my heart quit jumping every time I heard a diesel pickup snarling up the highway behind me.

I was no detective, but near as I could tell, Eric didn't know where I was.

Four days ago, I'd waited until I knew without a doubt that he was at work before packing the new cell phone I had bought and the cash I had slowly accumulated. I slipped out of the condo we shared, withdrew the maximum amount I could out of our joint account, rode the city bus as far as it would take me, and started hitchhiking. Phase one of my master plan could be summed up in three words: Get outta town.

Okay, four words if you want to be precise about it.

Now, as I stood on the crest of a hill overlooking a large, open valley, I was on the cusp of phase two. Again, three words: Connect with Leslie.

I let the backpack slip off my shoulders onto the brown grass in the ditch and sank down beside it in an effort to rest my aching feet and still my fluttering nerves. I was leery of the reception I would get from my sister and not looking forward to what she might have to say. Since August, nine months ago, I'd tapped out two long, rambling e-mails telling her what was happening in my life and laying out endless lists of reasons and excuses. But each time I read the mess of my life laid out in black and white on a backlit screen, guilt and shame kept me from hitting the Send button.

I knew she had a cell phone, and I knew the number, but a text message couldn't begin to cover either apologies or explanations.

So I was showing up after nine months of nothing hoping for a positive reception.

But at the same time my heart felt like a block of ice under my sternum, the chill that radiated out of it competing with the heat pouring down from above.

The click of grasshoppers laid a gentle counterpoint to the sigh that I sucked deep into my chest. I slowly released my breath, searching for calm, reaching into a quiet place as my yoga instructor had been yammering at me to do.

I reached down, tried to picture myself mentally going deeper, deeper.

C'mon. C'mon. Find the quiet place. Anytime now.

The screech of a bird distracted me. Above, in the endless, cloudless sky, a hawk circled lazily, tucked its wings in, and swooped down across the field. With a few heavy beats, it lifted off again, a mouse hanging from its talons.

So much for inner peace. I guess there was a reason I dropped out of yoga class. That and the fact that my friend Amy and I kept chuckling over the intensity of the instructor as she droned on about kleshas and finding the state of non-ego.

The clothes were fun though.

I dug into my backpack and pulled out my "visiting boots," remembering too well how I got them. Eric's remorse over yet another fight that got out of control. On his part, that is. He had come along, urging me to pick out whatever I wanted. I had thought spending over a thousand dollars could erase the pain in my arm, the throbbing in my cheek. But those few hours of shopping had only given me a brief taste of power over him. His abject apologies made me feel, for a few moments, superior. Like I was in charge of the situation and in charge of the emotions that swirled around our apartment. That feeling usually lasted about two months.

Until he hit me again.

I sighed as I stroked the leather of the boot. For now, the boots would give me that all important self-esteem edge I desperately needed to face Leslie.

As I toed off my worn Skechers and slipped on the boots, I did some reconnoitering before my final leg of the journey.

Beyond the bend and in the valley below me, the town of Holmes Crossing waited, secure in the bowl cut by the Athabasca River. For the past three days, I'd been hitching rides from Vancouver, headed toward this place, the place my sister now called home. In a few miles, I'd be there.

I lifted my hair off the back of my neck. Surely it was too hot for May. I didn't expect Alberta, home of mountains and rivers, to be this warm in spring.

In spite of the chill in my chest, my head felt like someone had been drizzling hot oil on it, basting the second thoughts scurrying through my brain.

I should have at least phoned. Texted.

But I'd gone quiet, diving down into my life, staying low. I wasn't sure she'd want to see me after such a long radio silence. I knew Dan wouldn't be thrilled to see me come striding to his door, designer boots or not. Dan, who in his better moments laughed at my lame jokes, and in his worse ones fretted like a father with a teenage daughter about the negative influence he thought I exerted on my little sister. His wife.

Leslie had sent me e-mails about my little nephew Nicholas's stay in ICU and subsequent fight for his life, pleading with me to call to connect. I knew I had messed up royally as an aunt and a sister by not being there. Not being available.

And I'd wanted to be there more than anything in the world. But at the time, I'd been holding onto my life by my raw fingertips and had no strength for anyone else.

You had your own problems. You didn't have time.

But I should have been there for my only sister. I could have tried harder.

The second thoughts were overrun by third thoughts, the mental traffic jam bruising my ego.

I pulled a hairbrush out of my knapsack. Bad enough I was showing up unannounced. I didn't need to look like a hobo. As I worked the brush through the snarl of sweat-dampened curls, I promised myself that someday I was getting my hair cut. I stuffed my brush back into my backpack and brushed the grass off my artfully faded blue jeans, thankful they were still clean. Zipping up my knapsack, I let out one more sigh before I heard the sound of a car coming up over the hill. My low spirits lifted as I turned to see who might rescue me from walking on these stilettos all the way to town.

They did a swan dive all the way down to the heels of my designer boots.

A cop car, bristling with antennas and boasting a no-nonsense light bar across the top, was slowing down as it came alongside me.

Did Eric sic the Mounties on me?

I teetered a bit, wishing I were a praying person. Because if I believed that God cared even one iota about my personal well-being, I'd be reciting the Lord's Prayer, Hail Mary--anything to get His ear right now.

My nerves settled somewhat when I saw two young girls huddled in the backseat of the cruiser. They didn't look older than seven or eight. What could they have possibly done to warrant the heavy artillery of a police car and two officers?

And what would the cops want with me?

....

You can find out more by ordering

ALL IN ONE PLACE

by clicking on the title

EXCERPT - THIS PLACE

My life had come full circle.

Abandoned child. Check.

Uncertain guardianship of said child. Check.

Only this time I wasn't the one crying upstairs, cast off yet again by my biological mother, rejecting hugs offered by a loving foster parent.

The time it was my niece who lay prostrate, staring sightlessly at her bedroom wall, so quiet it seemed she was afraid to draw even the smallest bit of attention to herself.

Earlier in the evening, I had sat beside her until she fell into a troubled sleep, my hand curled around hers, my heart breaking for so many reasons. I wanted to stay at her side all night. To drink in features I had imagined so many times. To be there for her if she woke up, crying.

But I had other issues I couldn't put off. So I reluctantly drew myself from her side, and returned downstairs to find a small blaze crackling in the corner fireplace of the living room. The heat warmed the house but did little to melt the chill in my bones. It had settled there, deep and aching, as I watched her parents' coffins being lowered into the icy ground.

Duncan Tiemstra, Celia's uncle, hovered by the fire as if attempting to absorb all of its warmth, one arm resting on the mantle, looking at a picture he held in his other hand. He had aged since that first time I met him at Jer and Francine's wedding. Then he looked young. Fresh. Ready to face life. And very interested in me.

Now he looked like a grieving Visigoth, with his blond hair brushing the collar of his shirt and framing a square-jawed face. The hint of stubble shadowing his jaw made him look harder and unapproachable. When we met at the funeral all I received was a taciturn hello. No memory of the feelings we had shared eight years ago.

My heart folded at the contrast from then to now.

Then we were dancing on the edges of attraction, flirting with possibilities. I was twenty-two, my life ahead of me. He was twenty-seven, looking to settle down. We laughed together. Even went on a couple of dates.

Now, we were separated by years and events that had pushed us apart, yet connected by the little girl that lay upstairs.

You can find out more by buying
THIS PLACE
By clicking on the title

EXCERPT - A SILENCE THE HEART - COMING SOON

HOLMES CROSSING #4

She thought she heard the cry of a child.

The haunting sound slid through the early-morning quiet just as Tracy stepped out of her car. Still holding the door, she canted her head to one side, listening.

There it was again. Softer this time.

Tracy strode around the concrete-block building trying to pinpoint the origin. But when she came around the side, the street in front of the clinic was empty as well.

The tension in her shoulders loosened and she shivered, pulling her thin sweater closer around herself. Ever the optimist, she had left her warmer jacket hanging in the hallway closet of her apartment this morning, counting on the early-September sun to melt away the coolness of the fall morning.

Then a movement caught her eye.

She stopped and turned to face whatever might come.

Then a small boy shuffled cautiously around the corner of the clinic, his head angled down, his thin arms cradling something. He looked to be about six or seven.

Tracy relaxed as she recognized him. For the past two weeks

she had seen him walking past the clinic in the early morning on his way to school. The last few days he had stopped to look in the window. It had taken a few encouraging waves and smiles from her to finally tease one from his wary face.

She always felt bad for him, going to school on his own, remembering too well her own early morning treks as a young child.

Tracy might have been inadequately dressed for the weather, but this little boy was even more so. He wore a short- sleeved T-shirt, faded blue jeans and in spite of the gathering chill, sandals on bare feet. As she watched, he shivered lightly.

"Hey, there," Tracy said quietly, sensing he might startle easily.

"I want to see the doctor," he said, sniffing lightly as Tracy came nearer. "This kitten got hurt." He angled her a suspicious glance through the tangle of dark hair hanging in his brown eyes.

"The veterinarian isn't in yet." Tracy crouched down to see what he was holding. The tiny ball of mangled fur tucked in his arms looked in rough shape. One eye was completely closed, the fur around it matted with blood. A leg hung at an awkward angle. Probably broken.

"What happened to it?" she asked quietly.

"I dunno. I just found him laying here." The little boy stood stiffly, his body language defensive. "Can you fix him?"

Tracy's heart sank. She knew the little boy couldn't pay the vet fees, and from the looks of his clothes, doubted his parents could.

"Where's your mommy?" she asked, touching the kitten lightly.

"I dunno."

Those two words dove into her soul. Too familiar.

"Is she at your home?"

He kept his eyes down, looking at his kitten. Tracy looked over his worn clothes and the dried smear of tomato sauce on his face and stained shirt and filled in the blanks. She guessed he had gone to bed looking like this and that there was no one at his home right now.

"I wanna keep him," the little boy wiped his nose on the shoulder of his T-shirt, a hitch in his voice. "He can be my friend when I'm by myself."

Tracy's thoughts jumped back in time. She saw herself a young girl of eight, standing in the kitchen of her apartment she and her mother shared, saying the same words, also holding a kitten, hope lingering.

"Not enough money," her mother had said, though Velma managed to use those same limited funds for lottery tickets and liquor. How Tracy had longed for that kitten. A friend. Someone to hold when there was no one around.

Tracy pushed herself to her feet. "Let's go inside."

The boy slanted her a narrow-eyed, wary look, holding back as she unlocked the door and opened it.

"It's okay," Tracy said quietly. "We have to go inside to look at your kitten."

He nodded and slowly stepped inside, his head swiveling around, checking out the reception area of the clinic.

"What's your name?" she asked as the door fell shut behind them.

"Are you a stranger?" he asked, suspicion edging his voice. "My mom says I'm not s'posed to talk to strangers."

"I'm a vet technician," she answered, sidestepping the guarded question. "And my name is Tracy Harris."

He stood in the center of the room, a tightly wound bundle of vigilance, clinging to the kitten like a lifeline. His eyes darted around—assessing, watchful. They met Tracy's as he straightened, as if making a decision. "My name is Kent," he said with a quick lift of his chin. "Kent Cordell."

She had been given a small gift of trust and in spite of the kitten that might be dying in his arms, she gave Kent a smile. She skimmed his shoulder with her fingers. "Good to meet you, Kent."

The back door slammed and a loud singing broke the quiet. Crystal, the other vet technician burst into the room with her usual dramatic flair, bright orange sweater swirling behind her. "And a good morning to you, my dear," she called out snatching a knitted hat off her deep red hair, then stopped when she saw Kent.

Kent tucked his head over the kitten, his shoulders hunched in defense. Like a turtle he had withdrawn again.

Crystal angled her chin at Kent as she tossed her hat on the desk. "Who's the kid?"

"This is Kent, and I'm bringing him and his kitten to an examining room. As soon as Dr. Harvey comes in, can you send him my way?"

"Not Dr. Braun?" Crystal asked, her voice holding a teasing tone.

Tracy was disappointed at the faint blush warming her neck. From the first day that David Braun had started at the clinic four months ago, Crystal had been avidly watching the two of them, as if it was only a matter of time before they started dating. Because, you know, two single people were always on the lookout for a mate.

Negatory.

There was no way Tracy was putting herself there again. Her old relationship with Art was the textbook version of 'bad relationship'. And she wasn't putting herself there again.

But that didn't stop her from feeling extra self-conscious around David—which in turn annoyed her.

"Just send Dr. Harvey in when he comes," she said.

Crystal pouted. "Okay, okay. I'll just be in the supply room." She swung around, her lab coat flaring out behind her as she strode down the hall. But from the glance she tossed over her shoulder and the wink she gave, Tracy guessed Crystal hadn't gotten the hint.

At all.

Find out more by clicking on the title to purchase:
A SILENCE IN THE HEART

EXCERPT - ANY MAN OF MINE

"If I have to drop a quarter off one more set of abs," I hefted two four-liter jugs of milk onto the conveyor belt of the grocery store with a grunt "--punch one more stomach--," I followed it with two jumbo sized boxes of breakfast cereal "--trip... over...one...more...saddle--." I punctuated each word with the toss of a bag of chips, peanuts and sunflower seeds. "--I am throwing an old-fashioned, fully feminine hissy fit." I glared at Tracy, who stood behind me in the line at the cash register, daring her to deny me my well-earned pique.

"Just stay away from the high C on the scream," was all Tracy said. "You're more of an alto than a soprano."

As my best friend, Tracy would feign sympathy with my rants against my brothers, but I knew she was never fully on my side. From the first day she stayed overnight at my parents' ranch and had been bombarded with my brothers' spitballs as she came into the kitchen, my dad's booming voice yelling at her to come on in and join us for dinner and my mom's yelling at my dad to stop yelling, Tracy had fallen head over heels in love with my family.

"I still can't figure out why each of my 33, 32 and 29-year-old brothers still want to live at home," I continued.

"You're really venting this morning," Tracy commented with a wry tone.

"Just getting started," I returned. It was Tuesday, the second day in a week that had begun badly, the first day was yesterday. Today wasn't looking so good, either.

The flat tire I'd had on the way to work didn't help, nor did the fact that I'd had to change it wearing high heels and a narrow skirt on the side of a quiet gravel road.

"You still live at home and you're 27," Tracy pointed out.

"At least I, at one time, had plans to move out." I allowed a flicker of self-pity to creep into my voice. "Then Dad had his heart attack."

"How is your dad doing?"

"It will still be a few weeks before he's back to normal. The doctor also said often people suffer deep depression after a heart attack. So I'm still hoping and praying he'll perk up and get more involved in the ranch."

Four weeks ago, my dad, Arnold Hemstead, had collapsed at the auction mart and had been rushed to emergency. He was diagnosed with a cardiac infarction, spent ten days in the hospital and came home to three anxious sons. And me.

Neil, Chip and Carter hovered, helped and catered to my dad for a thoughtful 36 minutes then they went back to their welding, fixing and farming, knowing I'd take over.

"I caught a glimmer of my old dad the other day," I continued. "He's getting more interested in what's happening. He asked me if I was unloading bales for Carter next week."

"Are you?"

I dismissed her comment with an exasperated eye-roll. I learned long ago to keep my nose in my business and in the house, away from anything to do with machinery, tractors and animals. The few times I offered my help and didn't understand what needed to be done, my brothers' method of informing me of my mistakes was to repeat the instructions verbatim and increase the decibels.

Such cozy bonding time that was, working with the guys.

"Okay, I'm guessing that's no." Tracy picked up one of the magazines lined up by the counter. "Sounds like you should take this quiz--'Is the male in your life a man or a guy?'"

"Guy, guy, guy and absolutely guy." The only not-guy in my life had been a few assorted boyfriends, the last one being Anthony.

However, I broke up with him in the fall and had found no one who appealed to me since.

And Wyatt? Where did he fit?

In the past, I told myself. Even after all this time memories of him could still create a twist in my heart.

"Okay, I sense we're not done with the sisterly pique yet." Tracy straightened the magazine and tilted me a grin. "Are you going to tell me which one of the guys in your life triggered this latest outburst?"

I pulled from the painful past into the annoying present. "Chip. Hands down or in his case up in the air so he can flex his lateral deltoids." I sighed. "And don't I sound like I know too much about that."

"So what did Chip do to earn this attack?"

Where to start, where to start?

"Let me set the stage," I said, watching the cashier bag the trans fat-loaded food. "It's Monday at 6:30, and Monday usually means a cranky supervisor, cranky foster parents and cranky foster kids who've had two more days worth of complaints to pile on me. One deranged biological father threatening me with a lawsuit if I didn't return his children to him the minute he steps out of jail, two runaways over the weekend and another case worker who won't return my calls. I come home tired and ready for a cup of tea and a smidgen of sympathy. I step onto the porch and stumble over Chip's roping saddle parked square in front of the door. As I try to gain my balance, I end up tangled up in a set of reins and fall in a most ungraceful heap on Chip's greasy coveralls. End result-- a cleaning bill, bruised hip and a broken heel on the new boots you and I spent an hour and a half looking for in West Edmonton Mall. So you have a stake in my misery, considering all the grumbling you did on the two-hour drive back from said mall."

I could see from the faint twitch of Tracy's lips that, while as a friend and fellow woman she felt sorry for me, as a normal human being with a dose of guy genes herself she could picture my ungainly fall and see the humour in it.

Growing up with three brothers who revelled in their "guyness" had provided me with me lots of ranting fodder, but Tracy often took their side. Other than a frequently absent mother, Tracy had grown up on her own. The noise and busyness in our house was a welcome change for her and she enjoyed it.

And she enjoyed Holmes Crossing. So when she graduated from her vet tech course she had returned to Holmes Crossing out of choice. I came back because it was one of the few places I could get a job in my chosen field of social work. There had been government cutbacks, and while I would have preferred to work in Edmonton, Calgary, Red Deer or any of the larger Albertan cities, Holmes Crosssing had been a temporary option. Besides, I could live at home cheaply, which helped me pay off my student loans and get a decent savings account, AKA "escape" account, started.

And then I met Wyatt.

I sucked in a deep breath. Seriously. Why was I going back to that? Four years now and I still felt like he was hovering on the edges of my mind. Unwelcome hovering, but showing up none-the-less. Maybe it was because of Anthony. Breaking up with him had been necessary, but hard. He was a nice person. Just not my person.

I handed the cashier my debit card and gave the groceries a

once-over, making sure I didn't miss any vital items such as chocolate-covered peanuts, pop or something equally nutritious.

"So...moving on to the more mundane things in your life. What are you doing the rest of this afternoon?" Tracy asked as she put her own groceries on the conveyor belt. I glanced at the fresh lettuce, cucumbers, green peppers and fruit, and suffered a moment of grocery envy. Tracy's husband, a "man" in my estimation, didn't think eating salad would diminish his manhood and gladly ate the occasional meatless meal without thinking he would faint when he left the table.

"After bringing you to the clinic, picking up my dry cleaning, getting my shoe repaired and dropping my flat tire off at my brother's mechanic shop?" I asked, trying for one last bid of sympathy.

"Yeah." She seemed distracted so no joy there.

"I have to head back to the office to give the other 'guy' in my life, my beloved supervisor, Casey Braeshears, a few moments of my time." I gathered up the Super-Size-Me groceries and swung the last bag into the cart, taking my frustrations out on Neil's nacho chips.

"Forget to paper clip your invoices again?" Tracy asked, in mock horror.

"I'm thinking it's something worse, like letting that teenager I had to drag home from a party borrow a government-issued pen without making him return it." I gave her a resigned look. "The budget, you know, doesn't cover these major, unforeseen expenses."

"He still talk about leaving?" Tracy asked.

"Unfortunately, no." It was the tantalizing thought of my annoying boss quitting like he had promised for the past six months that had kept me parked at my current job. Thinking I could take over from him. That and the fact I still had a boyfriend.

But I broke up with Anthony, Casey back-pedalled on the quitting thing and just as I was making plans to go, my father had his heart attack. "Life is what happens when you are making other plans," the old saying goes.

"But he's sticking around until he retires," I continued. "Which means I need to cast my professional eye further afield."

"Not for a while, though, right?" Tracy asked, a concerned frown on her face as she waited for her groceries to get bagged.

"I don't know how much longer I can last with Casey," I said, slowly edging toward a conversation I knew she wouldn't like. "And I think the boys are getting better at managing on their own." While not exactly a nose-growing whopper, it wasn't exactly true. But I figured I was just enabling them by staying as long as I had.

"I can't believe you would do that. Besides me, what is in the big city that isn't in Holmes Crossing?" Tracy asked pretending innocence.

"Men?"

"C'mon. I think you could find a few 'men' scattered through Holmes Crossing if you looked hard enough."

My eye was drawn to the neon yellow of a reflector strip glinting back at me from a hard hat worn by a man behind Tracy.

His grease-stained plaid jacket, torn blue jeans and work boots showed that this was a working man. He wore sunglasses that hid his eyes, and in spite of his full beard and moustache, I caught the smirk on his mouth, the arrogant tilt of his head that showed he was also a full-fledged guy.

That and the rolled up motorcycle magazine he tapped against his thigh.

Then he lowered his sunglasses enough so I could glimpse his bloodshot eyes, and then, incredibly, he gave me a slow wink.

I gave him my best so-not-interested look, then turned my attention back to Tracy. My case was rested.

"Holmes Crossing is guy-haven," I grumbled, raising my voice for the benefit of the guy dropping his magazine in front of the cashier. "There's not a decent single man to be found anywhere in this town. I've lost faith in the whole 'seek and ye shall find' concept," I said as Tracy loaded her groceries into my cart.

"You haven't had much of a chance to exercise that faith with the hours you've been working the past year," Tracy protested as she pushed the cart toward the exit.

In spite of my momentary pique with the guy now at the till, I couldn't help a glance his way, surprised to see him looking directly at me. Or so it seemed from the direction of his sunglasses.

What was worse, he was smirking, as if he had expected me to give him a second look.

Which I stupidly had.

I turned away, flustered, then angry at myself.

The electric doors of the supermarket swooshed open ahead of us. "When was the last time you were on a date?" Tracy was asking.

I pulled my attention back to her. "Does sitting beside Dr. Harvey in church count?"

Tracy ran her fingers through her dark hair and angled me an exasperated look. "Danielle, the man is 60."

"He's widowed and he's a gentleman," I offered. "Of course, I don't know why I'm fussing about not having a man in my life. I wouldn't have the time for the proper care and maintenance of a relationship if I did."

"You need to let Casey know you're not a machine," Tracy continued, ignoring my feeble attempt at humour. "That you can't keep working these obscene hours. None of the other social workers in the department do."

"It's not just Casey. My dad and brothers seem to think supper appears out of thin air every day. The boys are even childish enough to believe in the laundry fairy, who comes and does their clothes every day."

"You should get them to help more."

"I should also try to bring about world peace and reconcile every broken home."

"You are working on the last part."

"I might have a better chance at a city job if I can show how invaluable I am here." I grabbed the handle of the cart and traversed the parking lot.

"Why not tell Casey to hire another social worker?"

"Like that's happening. He's got to submit his budget for the next fiscal year and he's squeezing water out of coins to maintain his cheapskate status. I wonder if he gets frequent flier miles for every penny he saves the department." We rattled our way to my waiting car, the sun shining benevolently down on us. It was spring in the country and usually the lengthening days and the increasing warmth brought out joy and happiness in me. But work had kept me too busy to take time to appreciate the freshness of the air and the unfurling of new green leaves.

Tracy's car was getting an oil change and she had needed a ride from work to the grocery store, so I had quit work a half hour early to help her out. Casey must have received wind of my defection, and this little meeting was his way of wringing out every possible minute of work from me.

But now I paused, wondering when and how I should tell her.

Like pulling a bandaid off, I told myself. Make it painful but quick.

"You may as well know I'm already looking at another job." I rattled out the words faster than the wobble on my grocery cart. "It's regular hours, and I'll be reporting to a normal boss."

"Good for you. It's about time. Who is this for?"

"It's for a private adoption agency." I waited a moment, gathering my strength to drop the next bomb. "It's in the city. In Edmonton."

I didn't want to see Tracy's face. So I pushed on, keeping my eyes on my trusty Honda Civic, fifteen years old and still going strong, thanks to Chip's mechanical abilities and body filler, courtesy of Neil. My brothers had their good points.

"But that's a two-hour drive away," she wailed

"Depends on who's driving," I offered. "Chip's done it in one hour ten minutes."

"Chip is also about half a demerit point from having his license taken away," Tracy retorted, put out with my breaking news. "You can't go. I need you. Your foster kids need you. Your family needs...your father needs you," she hastily amended.

I sighed. And that was the crux of the matter. Six weeks ago I had looked around for another job and my own place to live. I was tired of spinning my wheels in Holmes Crossing. Then Dad had his heart attack and my plans were put on hold.

All my life, Dad had been the epitome of strong faith and good humour. Even after my mother, Alice, died five years ago, Dad had grieved hard, then told us all he put his trust in God and went back to being the fun-loving, encouraging man I knew him to be. In the following years, I wondered how he had stayed so positive. How he had pulled out of his grief.

It took me a lot longer than that.

After the heart attack, Dad had become weak and frail and given to bouts of deep depression. These days he didn't even have the strength or the will to get up from his recliner or to crack open the Bible that he used to read every day. My brothers, who stopped going to church when my mom died, didn't share my concerns. Reading the Bible did not seem to be on the "approved" list of activities for guys.

I couldn't leave my father this way, but I had stayed as long as I could. It didn't look like things were changing on the work front so I was the one who needed to do the changing.

"I'm not moving to New Zealand." I pulled open the back door of my car.

"I don't drive like Chip so it would be a four-hour round trip for me." Tracy set her bags in the back and slammed the door shut.

"That's a lot of time to spend in a vehicle just for the pleasure of your company."

"I would come home most weekends," I said, still loading up my own groceries. A week's supply of healthy food obviously took less time to load than three days' worth of junk food. "I have enough reasons to come back to Holmes Crossing."

Tracy didn't reply as we got into the car. She said nothing as I reversed out of my spot and turned onto the street. She said nothing when we headed toward the garage where they were working on her car. She said nothing as I pulled into the customer parking stall.

It was her turn to talk, but as I put my car into park I gave in. "Tracy, you said yourself that I needed to get another job. I heard you. I'm simply following your advice."

"I said you needed to talk to your boss about your job. Not...not..." She spun her hand in a circle, wiping away what I had told her. "This moving thing you want to do. That you didn't even talk about with me. That you couldn't even bother to ask me questions about even though you knew I would be as upset as I am now." Tracy complained in a voice that conveyed to me her utter disbelief that I would seriously want to leave our home and community and head to the big, bad city.

I tried to find the words that would make her understand as I wrapped my hands around the steering wheel staring through the window of Wierenga's garage.

"So there's Cor DeWindt, regular at Terra's Cafe," I said lifting my pinky finger to point at the older gentleman leaning against the counter, frowning at Blane Wierenga behind the counter, his canvas coat covering his usual plaid shirt and crazy suspenders. "He pulled me out of Frieson's pond when my brothers dared me to skate across it. He told me to be quiet in church when I was a crazy teenager sitting with her friends. He loves to tease me about an especially touching moment of the Christmas program when I, as an innocent girl of five, lifted up the skirt of my best Sunday dress, displaying my underwear to my horrified family members and an amused public. And that's only him. There are at least a dozen other people who have some memory of me that is either unflattering or embarrassing. There are no secrets in this town for me. There is no mystery. No surprises."

And a few bad memories.

Find out more by clicking on the title to purchase:
ANY MAN OF MINE

DISCLAIMER

All characters in this book have no existence outside the imagination of the author and have no relation whatsoever to anyone bearing the same name or names. They are not even distantly inspired by any individual known or unknown to the author, and all incidents are pure invention.

Made in the USA
Monee, IL
15 January 2023

25342444R20163